THE AGE OF HOPE

ALSO BY DAVID BERGEN

The Matter with Morris
The Retreat
The Time in Between
The Case of Lena S.
See the Child
A Year of Lesser
Sitting Opposite My Brother

David Bergen

The Age of Hope

A NOVEL

A PHYLLIS BRUCE BOOK

HARPERCOLLINS PUBLISHERS LTD

A Phyllis Bruce Book, published by HarperCollins Publishers Ltd.

First published in a hardcover edition by HarperCollins Publishers Ltd: 2012
This trade paperback edition: 2012

The author acknowledges the assistance of the Manitoba Arts Council.

HarperCollins books may be purchased for educational, business, or sales
promotional use through our Special Markets Department.

HarperCollins Publishers Ltd
2 Bloor Street East, 20th Floor
Toronto, Ontario, Canada
M4W 1A8

www.harpercollins.ca

Library and Archives Canada Cataloguing in Publication
information is available upon request

ISBN 978-1-44341-136-3

Printed and bound in the United States
RRD 9 8 7 6 5 4 3 2 1

To Doris

THE AGE OF HOPE

1

Age of Innocence

Hope Plett would certainly have married her first love if he hadn't died in a plane crash minutes after flying at a low altitude over her house. As the small plane passed overhead, a hand appeared out of the cockpit window and she shouted, "Hello, Jimmy." Though Jimmy Kaas could not hear her and she knew this was so, she felt that she should say something, as he had gone to all that trouble of creating a drama. The plane made a steep climb and then disappeared in the direction of the golf course. She learned that he had crashed while attempting a "touch-and-go" on the grass landing strip. His family, a small Norwegian island in a sea of Anabaptists, left town shortly after his death.

She sometimes thought of Jimmy, though not with any great emotion. She had cried for a day after his death, and she had cried at his funeral, and for a month she had felt that her heart was broken, but then her emotions settled down and

1

she began to understand his death as something that had happened to him, not to her. Years later, after she had children, the death of her first boyfriend became an interesting story, one of romance cut short. She liked to play up the tragic aspect of the moment: a young life snuffed out, her broken heart, Jimmy's strong jaw and debonair clothes, the scarves he wore. And always, in the telling, she arrived at the point where she became cavalier, almost indifferent. "Jimmy was too arrogant, in any case. He came from money and he felt entitled. The relationship wouldn't have worked." There was an undertone of dismissal in her voice, as if she were implying that he had not been good enough for her. The simple fact was that hers was a plain life, full of both poverty and pride.

The year was 1948. She lived in a small town called Eden, Manitoba, in the middle of Canada, fifty miles above the American border. She was the only child of Grace and Ernie Plett. Grace was a slightly built Scottish woman from Kenora, Ontario, who had got a job teaching elementary school in Eden, a predominantly Mennonite town, in 1929. Grace met Ernie at the Saturday night dances that were held in a hall three miles out of town. Though Ernie came from a strict Mennonite background, he took wholehearted joy in things of the flesh, a drinker in a town of teetotallers. He paid close attention to Grace, wooed her with his panache and wit, and she married him.

Hope was born in 1930 and was raised not as her friends were, with German spoken in the home and the Bible as an anchor, but in a looser fashion. Her parents continued to attend the Saturday dances and when Hope was young they took her along. Only occasionally, perhaps once a month, did she attend church with her mother. Her father was typically sleeping off the night before, and at any rate, he had no use for religion. Eden had many churches and the reasoning in town went thus: the closer you were to God, the more you were blessed. Blessed, Hope discovered, had a monetary value. The wealthiest people in town were usually perceived as the most pious. Misfortune and bad luck tumbled down around the heads of the poor. Her parents' heads. Her own. And yet, even at a young and tender age, she thought the reasoning must be faulty. God, she thought, could not be as simple as that. Her own father, a baker for a local businessman, was a hard worker. Yes, he also drank and he spent time with the English townspeople and he did not go to church, but he worked ten hours a day, six days a week, baking bread and rolls and buns, which the wealthy then happily purchased. And if his rewards were few, it might be that Mr. Buhler, his boss, did not pay him enough. Her mother said, "Mennonites have a hard time having fun, except for your father, who's having too much fun."

Hope understood early on, then, that she was different, not only in the matter of faith and background, but also in the matter of property and status. So she learned to observe and blend in. She picked up her German from the children she played with on the block. Her mother did not speak German: in fact, she refused to learn. During the war years, she was asked to patrol the school playground and deter the students from speaking the language of the enemy. Hope, when she heard of this, was ashamed for herself and for her mother and for the children who didn't know better. Though perhaps shame was too strong a word. Indignity?

She could not have been certain, but her young life hovered at the edges of indignity, as if she might never be good enough, though as she grew older she discovered that a smidgen of arrogance could carry her a long way.

As an only child, Hope received much attention from her parents, though she wasn't exactly spoiled. Her family rented a small house on Reimer Avenue, they did not own a car, and new clothes were rare. Most of her finer clothes were handed down to her by Frida, a second cousin who lived in Altona, west of the Red River, fifty miles away. Frida was slightly taller than Hope, and bigger across the chest, and so Hope's mother had to shorten the dresses and cuff the slacks and take in the tops. Still, for all the lack of finer things, Hope was a bit of a knockout, and sometimes, at extended family gatherings, Frida would look at Hope's outfit and marvel, saying in Low German, "Now but that dress never looked so sharp on me when I had it once. Very Sunday." Any onlooker would have said that beauty had fallen down on her. Her dark hair was an anomaly in a town of blond Russian Germans, and by the age of eighteen she had begun to pull it back loosely so that it framed her face and exposed her eyebrows and her slightly crooked though very open smile.

She wasn't vain, though she knew what vanity looked like, and knowing this, she avoided it. Nor was she falsely humble. She could be stubborn and dismissive of foolishness in others, but for the most part she was level-headed and had already begun to use the phrase that invariably popped up when hardship or misfortune presented itself: "This too shall pass."

So when Arnold Dick sat beside her at a bonfire party held by the Mennonite Brethren young people and said that he intended to go to Africa, possibly the Congo, as a missionary, and that God had indicated to him that Hope should be his wife, she knew what to say. She felt the heat of the fire on her knees and ankles. The smoke drifted upwards and made her eyes burn and water. Arnold, noticing this, thought that she was moved to tears over his proposal, and he was reaching out to take her hand when she said, "That's ridiculous, Arnold. God hasn't talked to me about this and until he does, I'll be making other plans. I'm sorry. But thank you for thinking of me."

Hope's mother felt that it was important to expose her to the wider world. They went to the city to watch movies and to take in the occasional ballet. She put an emphasis on rigorous intellectual pursuits and believed that books, imagination, and clear thinking were necessary for a flourishing life. She explained that a satisfying life was made up of two essentials. Hope was struck by the force of that word, "essentials," as if life were a machine made up of nuts and bolts. The essentials were: find something that you love doing, and find someone whom you enjoy spending time with because you're going to be with him till you die. "Some of us find only one of those things. A lucky few find both," her mother said. Hope wondered if she would be one of the lucky few.

At the age of nineteen, she decided to pursue nursing as a career and began a two-year intensive training at St. Boniface Hospital in Winnipeg, where she lived in residence. Her roommate was an Italian girl, Petra, who had a boyfriend even though dating and marriage were not allowed during the two-year program. Petra often broke curfew, returning in the middle of the night smelling of alcohol and cigarette smoke. Hope always woke when Petra entered the room, and Petra knew this, because immediately, as she leaned in to the mirror to remove her makeup, she started up a soft intimate monologue. Hope was shocked to hear her talk of having sex. None of her school friends had ever admitted to this. One night Petra said, matter-of-factly, "Jesus. The trouble with sex. I told Aldo he had to pull out but I'm not sure if he was quick enough. It's really exhausting, all this bobbing and weaving. I'd like to make love in a proper bed, in my own house, without the fear of the head nurse, or God, or the priest. Christ." She was a short girl, with a full chest that Hope coveted, and she was standing now in the middle of the room, in her underwear, her weak mouth turned down. Hope envied her freedom, or at least the appearance of freedom.

She studied Hope in the dim light. "If the boys could see *you* in your uniform, Hope, they'd go crazy." She removed her bra, turning away, and Hope turned her head away as well. She knew it wasn't only the boys. The older men on C Ward, the ones with quick hands and dirty mouths, they too liked Hope in her uniform. She shushed them, lightly slapped their arms, and pretended not to hear. The head nurse, Sister Andrea, an older nun with the kind of cruel tongue that arrives with dashed hopes, told Hope one day that she would have to be careful with her looks. "Who do you think you are? We must strike the snake before it rears its ugly head." After that admonishment, Hope began to pull her hair back more severely. She smiled less frequently. She tried to bark at the patients. To no avail. She was still admired.

At Petra's family cottage one fall day, she met a young man named Anthony who wooed her for a month or so, pushed his nose against her neck in the darkness of his car. She felt not a hint of passion. Anthony was a large indistinct boulder on the road of life and she gently shouldered him aside. It was difficult to breathe around certain men and she began to think it might be best if she never married.

When she returned home for the weekends the first year, she attended one of the smaller Mennonite churches and found herself in a Sunday school class for adults her age taught by a man named Roy Koop. Roy was four years older and had spent two years in Flint, Michigan, at the General Motors School. He now worked in his father's GM dealership. He was a tall thin young man with sharp elbows and a strong jaw. His hair was blond and cut short and this made his small ears appear even smaller. He often wore suits. He sold cars after all and needed to make a good impression. The suits he wore were sometimes dark blue, sometimes charcoal, and she wondered if her own clothes were noticeably inferior, though she had a knack for accessories such as scarves and paste jewellery and belts that she pulled tight at her thin waist. She was aware that her body was appealing and that her face was striking. She had skin like the cream that rises to the top of the milk pail before it is skimmed. She wondered sometimes if her beauty made her seem superficial, though she didn't believe she was shallow, and in fact saw herself as a thinking woman.

She discovered that she could breathe around Roy. He wasn't silly like the younger men she had known. He was thoughtful and took notice of her and always smiled in a shy manner whenever he greeted her with "Hello, Hope." Here was a man who could pay attention. He had an intimate knowledge of automobiles and could recognize the make and model of a car simply by the taillight. Over a period of Sundays, she approached him after church, and together they would stand beside his 1949 Chevy and she talked. At first about herself, keeping it brief and self-deprecating.

She had spilled a bedpan over her shoes one day. Sister Andrea, "a dried-up prune," had upbraided her for ten minutes. "She wants to make me into a smaller version of her. I'm afraid she might be succeeding."

"A prune? I don't think so."

She did a slight pirouette. She was wearing a knock-off Dior that her mother had sewn for her. Floral-print cotton, bright greens and pinks. A cinched-in waist and a wide black belt like a strip of fallow earth, and below the earth her legs, in real stockings and high heels. He certainly noticed. She touched the flank of his car. "Chevrolet," she said.

"The only car worth driving."

"It's yours?"

"Every salesman gets a car. It's easier to sell them if you're seen driving them. So, it's not mine."

"It's beautiful."

"You want a ride? Do you have a way home?"

A Chevy Fleetline fastback, two-door, with an immaculate interior. Over the next month, when Hope returned home for the weekends, she and Roy took long drives in the country, the late fall sky the colour of pewter, Crosby on the radio, the dust floating out behind them like a tail, and sometimes, when their windows were rolled down, the dust found its way inside, leaving a light coat on the interior of the car. One time Roy pulled to the shoulder and got out and walked around and opened the door for her. "Your turn," he said, and she found herself behind the wheel as he instructed her on how to let out the clutch slowly while pushing down on the gas pedal. The car was big and cumbersome and it jerked and stalled and she started it again, determined not to make a fool of herself. Three on the tree. This was the term he used for the gearshift, which was on the column of the steering wheel. He placed his hand over hers and gently showed her the movements. And then they were moving, picking up speed, and she squealed softly, the same noise she would make several months later when he first kissed her, one of pleasure and surprise, as if there were an engine deep inside of her that had been switched on. Sometimes they ended up in the city, where they went to a movie or out for a meal, but it was in the cocoon of the car, in that enclosed space where she could observe his fine hands on the wheel and where he talked to her about his dreams of one day owning his own dealership, that she felt at home with him.

One Saturday afternoon, on a surprisingly warm weekend in late November when she was home for a visit, he dropped by her house on Reimer Avenue, where he found her drinking tea with her mother in the kitchen. She was wearing a dark blue dress that hugged her hips and legs and fell just below the knee, and this accented her calves, though Roy took only one glance at her legs and then looked away. She placed him at the table next to her mother, aware of the meagreness of the house and the furnishings. She wondered briefly if she was ashamed of where she came from, and then her stubbornness set in and she thought that Roy should know and comprehend who he was dealing with. She said, "We were just talking about you, about your fondness for cars. I said that you speak of them as if they were breathing human beings. We don't even have a car, you know." She smiled and narrowed her eyes, just to let him know she was having some fun.

"Perhaps I love them too much?" he asked. He thought he should pay attention to her mother, it was only polite, and he had engaged her at first and made small talk, but the time had come now to look at Hope. Her eyes were a distraction, a dusty blue, verging on green, and her nose too was something he tried not to focus on: it was delicate yet forceful, but not too forceful, nor was it too aquiline, though it was aquiline enough. In other words, to Roy's mind, her nose was perfect. As for the rest of her body, all one hundred pounds of it, he was too respectful to imagine the possibilities, and so he shook his head as if to indicate his own sense of folly and he held his hat in his lap. This was the age when men still wore hats and Roy had a collection of them, at least five, and he would switch them up, the grey for the brown, the wider brimmed fedora for the snappy-looking black one with the band of charcoal ribbon. She liked his hats, though she wasn't sure if she liked them because they were striking or because she anticipated the removal of the hat and the revelation of the blond hair on Roy's head, as if this were an invitation to touch his hair, though she did this with complete freedom only after they were engaged to be married.

On this Saturday, Roy said that he was driving out to a farm near Giroux to repossess a vehicle and he wondered if she didn't want to join him.

"I would," she said, and asked if she should change her clothes. "Is this a dangerous mission?"

"No, what you are wearing is just fine, and it isn't dangerous."

"But you're taking back a car from a man who won't want to give it up."

"It's a half-ton, actually, and the wife called me to come get it."

He was driving the tow truck from the dealership and he laid down a blanket on the passenger's seat for Hope, telling her to watch for grease and dirt, and then he helped her climb in. There was a stick shift between them and Roy rested his right hand on the knob of the stick shift as he drove. His fingers were shapely and his nails appeared to be manicured. They were very clean for a man who worked in a garage, though she knew that he sold cars and did not spend his time in coveralls sliding beneath the vehicles. The tendons in his hand moved every time he shifted. She thought he might catch her ogling him and so she turned away to look out the window.

He said that the half-ton they were repossessing belonged to a farmer who hadn't made payments for a year. "We tried to pick it up last month and he ran us off his land. He actually had a rifle and was pointing it and waving it around. No shots were fired."

"And today? It'll be different?" She hadn't imagined that Roy's life could in any way be touched by violence. She felt oddly thrilled.

"His wife dropped by the garage and told us he would be gone today. We could come and get it. That's what she said. 'Come and get it.' She has some kind of grudge against him."

The farmyard was derelict, there was nothing better to be said for it. The house was ramshackle and the wife, when she appeared in the yard with a brood of children who swarmed around her along with several chickens, a dog, and three cats, seemed to match the abandonment of the buildings in the yard. She might have been thirty years old, though she looked over forty. Hope was shocked by how worn out and tired she was, a testament to a marriage that can produce both children and poverty, and the confusion as to which came first. Much to-do was made of the backing up of the tow truck to the half-ton. Hope stood off to the side in her high heels, wearing a dark pea coat, with sleeves that had been lengthened so that the original crease of the cuff still showed. The trees in the yard were nearly bare and the wind blew in gusts and lifted the leaves and swirled them about. One of the cats ran beneath the chassis of the pickup and crouched there as if in protest. The eldest son, not yet a teen and wearing pants that were too short, stood with clenched fists. He called out, "You'll pay for this."

The mother hit him with an open hand across the face. "Shut your mouth," she said.

The boy looked at Hope, his face full of shame and hatred, so much so that Hope could not hold his eyes. Roy had seen the slap and heard the words but he said nothing. He beckoned, indicating that she should climb into the tow truck, and then they were off, wending their way up the narrow drive, past sway-backed granaries. Hope turned to look back and she saw the mother leaning forward and holding the older son by the shoulders and she was talking and then her hands were in the air. Roy said, "Acch. I never should have sold them the truck."

"That's right. Why did you? Did you see that boy?"

"I saw him. He's growing up way too fast."

It was an odd thing to hear and she wondered if Roy's heart wasn't bigger than he let on. Not that he was full of bravado and male bluster. He wasn't. He could be surprisingly soft.

The thing was—she would realize this only much later, after she had spent numerous weekends with Roy, him picking her up when she was free from her training so that they would spend the day together driving about, sharing thoughtful intimacies, talking about what they wanted in life, driving out to Lockport for a hot dog—the thing was he never smelled of alcohol. She knew the smell from her father. A sweetish bitter scent, sometimes minty, often sour, caught not so much when the subject breathed but more so as he passed by, as if the pores emitted the secrets of a closet drinker. Not Roy. Ever. When she asked him about it, he said that he wasn't against drinking, he just didn't have the taste for it.

She started to yearn for his company. Her thoughts turned constantly to him and she began to make mistakes on the ward, errors that were not life-threatening to the patients, but little mistakes that accumulated. Sister Andrea cornered her one afternoon and, wagging her finger, asked, "Is it a man, Hope Plett? Every year one or two girls think they are extremely special, the only ones to have ever experienced love, and so they blindly run off following their animal instincts. You are a nurse, not a trollop. What do you want?"

Indeed, what did she want? She told Roy that she would not see him for a while. She needed to focus on her studies.

"You're breaking up with me?" Roy asked.

"Oh, no. No." She paused. "If you could wait. Give me some time."

"How much time?"

She was almost halfway through the first year of a two-year program and she couldn't imagine that he would wait eighteen months.

"Till Christmas. I'll have a two-week break then. I'll be home. Sister Andrea hates me. I have to make her at least respect me." She imagined that if he loved her, he would say yes. She did not know yet if she loved him.

"Sister Andrea, the prune?"

"Yes."

"Okay. But at Christmas, I want you to meet my family."

She went up on tiptoe and kissed his cheek. They were standing outside the residence in St. Boniface. The wind was cold, the sky promised snow, and even so, his face was warm. "I'll write you a letter every day."

Over the coming weeks, she ached to see him, to talk to him in person, but she ignored her feelings and focused on being a good nurse, studying late into the night and then pouring her thoughts into the letters she wrote him, aware that the written word allowed her to be more audacious. The first time she wrote the words "I love you, Roy," she stared at them and for a time considered ripping up the letter and starting again, but then she added "I do" to the end of the sentence and she folded the letter and sealed it. Mailed it the next day. Roy did not write as eloquently as she did and she waited for his own declaration back. He did not write those words, however. Instead, in the rare letter she received, he spoke of his work and the cars he had sold and the new models that would be arriving in the showroom in spring. The Styleline Deluxe convertible had leather seats and Powerglide transmission. The top opened and closed automatically. "It's a beauty," he wrote. "At Christmas I'll give you a ride. Top up, of course." She was disappointed that he couldn't come out and say that he loved her, or even that he missed her.

And then one morning Petra announced that she had got married over the weekend. She reached into her purse and took out a ring, put it on, and showed it off.

"But how?" Hope said.

"Oh, Hope, you're hopeless. It's so easy." Petra's black eyes appeared to hold a vision of the future that was limitless. "I'm quitting. At Christmas. Aldo has a good job as a plumber's apprentice, he just bought a house, and I'm thinking there's no way he'll wait for me. He's too good a catch."

"But if he loves you, why wouldn't he wait?"

"Now he doesn't have to wait, does he?"

"Aren't you worried? That you might be throwing something away? Or about what people will say?"

Petra wasn't at all worried, and Hope wished that she had some of her roommate's nerve, her devil-may-care attitude.

Hope wrote Roy to tell him that her roommate had suddenly got married. "She was worried that he wouldn't wait for her. Impetuous, wouldn't you say? And not very trusting." Still, she wondered if there might be girls in Eden who were making Roy all knock-kneed and weak. She wanted to say, "Please tell me that this isn't so," but she didn't, because that would appear to be desperate. Instead, she wrote that on Sunday mornings, at 6 a.m., when she woke, she stood by her window, which looked out onto the street, and had happy memories of seeing his car idling at the curb. "I wonder if what I want and what I expect from life are the same thing. Sometimes at night I wake from a deep sleep and all is dark. And I am aware of being alone. I mean this in the strongest way. Even when we are surrounded by others and there is laughter and food and conversation, do we let others know who we are? Oh my, you will probably find my thoughts alarming. I am fine. I am working hard. I look forward to Christmas."

Sometimes, on Saturday afternoons, after washing a few clothes by hand and ironing her uniform, she would walk across the river from St. Boniface into downtown Winnipeg to Eaton's and the Bay, where she would wander through the women's clothing departments and admire the clothes and the shoes on display. She loved to touch the expensive cloth of a certain dress, holding it up in front of her as she gazed into a mirror. There were times when she imagined that she might have enough money to buy this dress or those shoes, black with tan piping. She had her eye on a coral silk taffeta dress. The price was impractical but she kept coming back to stare at and touch it, and one day, just because, she tried it on. The sleeves were short and flouncy and the neckline plunged slightly, but not too much. A small bow centred the navel. The hem came just below the knee and set off her bared calves. She stepped out of the change room and studied herself. The shopgirl was behind her.

"It's perfect," the shopgirl said.

Hope, turning sideways to observe her profile, said, "I look flat."

"No, no. You can carry it off, no problem. I have just the thing." And she hurried off and returned with a Maidenform bra and told Hope to try it on. "You'll be amazed at the difference."

Hope loved the effect, but wondered if she might not be fooling herself, and especially Roy. She blew up her cheeks and tossed her head. She truly didn't recognize herself, and for some reason this pleased her.

The following Saturday her cousin Frida drove in from Altona and met her at the Bay. Hope tried on the dress for her.

"Fine, very fine," Frida said in Low German. She whistled. "Your breasts are bigger."

Hope giggled. "I know."

Hope had told Frida about Roy, and that she was going to meet his family at Christmas.

Frida said now, "If I had your looks? Man alive, I'd marry you."

"Oh, stop it." Hope showed Frida the price tag. She shrugged and returned to the dressing room.

A week later a box was delivered to her room at the residence. In it was the dress and the bra. A note in the package read, "Merry Christmas, Hope. Knock him out."

She called Frida immediately. "You can't afford this, Frida," she said. "I'm going to return it."

"You'll do no such thing. Anyway, you can't return a gift."

"But, Frida, it's far too generous. What will I buy for you?"

"When you marry Roy, get me a deal on a car." She laughed in her way, with a little snort.

"It's amazing, Frida. You're amazing."

"Yeah, amazing Frida."

On Boxing Day, she went for turkey dinner at Roy's house. She wore the dress and pulled her hair up, allowing several tendrils to tumble as if at random. She clipped on a pair of her mother's pearl earrings and painted her lips a soft rose, to blend in with the dress. Her gloves, off-white, extended to her elbows. When Roy saw her he tilted his head and said, "Wow." As he helped her into her well-worn car coat, his hands brushed her arms and shoulders. He whispered, "You're beautiful."

"Thank you," she said. She carried with her a box of chocolate mints that had cost a fair bit. When she handed them to Mrs. Koop, there seemed to be little recognition of the gift. The box was placed on a side table in the hallway and forgotten. Mrs. Koop was pleasantly cool until Hope, at the dinner table, spoke a few words of Low German, and Roy's mother lifted her head in surprise. Roy's father, Ernest Koop, bald and garrulous, sat at the head of the table. She had heard about him. He came from a family of six brothers who were constantly in competition. They all owned businesses of some sort. They were rowdy, aggressive, and growing up there had been fisticuffs and general mayhem in the house. Their mother, now dead, had suffered her six sons mostly in silence, with the occasional futile outburst.

Harold, Roy's older brother, was present at the table. He had, during the war, going against the beliefs of most of the young Mennonite men in Eden who were conscientious objectors, been based in India for three years as a tail gunner, and then he had come home and begun to work in the parts department at the dealership. He never talked about himself and certainly didn't mention the war years. He didn't have the quiet confident salesmanship that Roy had. There was a sister as well, Berta. She was a year younger than Roy, but she seemed older. Dour and matronly, dressed in a dull grey dress that hid her femininity, she resembled her mother. They were two fierce women standing guard at the doorway to Roy's heart.

Mr. Koop, helping himself to more turkey and *bubbat*, a raisin-filled heavy dressing, mentioned Hope's mother. "Harold had her as a teacher. Didn't you, Harold?"

Harold nodded.

Mr. Koop said, "Very sophisticated, your mother. Every time I talk to her, I imagine that we will suddenly be speaking the King's English, or that I will be tested on Shakespeare. She wears hats, always a different shape and colour."

Berta looked at her father, sharply, as if surprised by something.

"Do you think the same of me? That I will test you?" Hope realized that the question was quite forward, and that in asking it, she was setting herself apart from Berta and Mrs. Koop, but she didn't care. She had caught on quickly that Roy was the favourite child, and that this gave her leverage, especially with Mr. Koop, who laughed and said, "Please don't. I dropped out of school at the age of eleven."

Berta said, "An education can puff people up. Like peacocks."

"Berta. Get the bread." This was Mrs. Koop, who was busy fetching food and replenishing the punch and generally huffing about, her dreary dress passing from here to there.

Hope wondered how often Mr. and Mrs. Koop were intimate. She pushed the thought away.

"Still, there's nothing like college, is there?" Mr. Koop continued. "Roy went to Flint for two years."

"That's not the same," Roy said.

"Yes it is," Hope said. She touched his arm. She had been aware, throughout the meal, that he was beside her and yet quite far from her, and she wanted to claim him now. She left her hand on the sleeve of his shirt. "You studied physics and chemistry eleven hours a day. And accounting."

"He got all A's," Berta said, back at the table, letting Hope know that her big brother was brainy.

"I know." Hope smiled at Berta. "He's a smart one."

"Well, I'm happy that my boy's marrying a nurse." Roy's father held a hand to his chest. "The Koop ticker is a weak one. Genetically unsound. We need you."

She dipped her head and waited for Roy to clarify. But it was Mrs. Koop who said, "What are you going on about, Ernie? She's just Roy's *friend*. They have loads of time anyhow. Marriage tastes good, but it costs too."

Later that night, when Roy dropped her off at home, she said, "Your mother doesn't like chocolate."

"Sure she does. She has a sweet tooth. So does Berta. They're probably digging in right now."

"They didn't like me. They said almost nothing to me, and when they did, I was a peacock."

"Oh, ignore Berta. She's protective, like my mother."

"And when we're married, they'll still want to protect you?" Having blurted this out, she could not take it back, though she wanted to immediately. This was so forward, so contrary to her careful behaviour, that she was mortified. "Oh my," she said.

But Roy was neither surprised nor upset. "I like it when you talk like that."

"It doesn't frighten you?"

"Hah. Takes more than that."

"It's just not terribly romantic. I feel like everything is backwards. Like I'm the man."

"Well. Would you?" he said. "Marry me?"

"Yes. I would. I will. Yes."

And when we are married. Such a simple statement that opened up all sorts of doors and shut others. She must have wanted to say those words, must have wanted to hear them, to feel them in her mouth. As she explained to her mother the following day, Roy was established and she knew that she wanted to have children, and what would be the use in completing school, never to work at a nursing job?

"Well," her mother said, "he could die, or he could leave you for someone else, and then what? You'd be poor once again."

"He won't leave me. He's too good a man."

"He's good now, so you think. And you may be right." She wasn't given to directing her daughter's life. "If this is what you want."

Hope told Roy that she wanted to finish out the year, as if this would prove something both to herself and to him. "It wouldn't feel right to run away. We can marry in the summer."

He agreed, though not happily. This meant that they wouldn't have sex until summer, and he was so looking forward to sex with Hope. She was a great kisser. They had first kissed that night after the dinner at his parents', and with each kiss he wanted to burrow deeper, to tear the wrapping from her. But he knew that sex was for marriage, and so they would wait.

She worked that summer, before the wedding, as an operator at the telephone office in Eden, taking care of the switchboard. She wore earphones and overheard conversations she should not have been privy to, was in fact expected to turn off the connection, but there were times when a certain inflection in the voice or the sultry response of a woman made her hang on to the conversation a little longer than required. She discovered that Mrs. Cornie Dueck was an incredible gossip. And that Ed Wiens, who owned a chain of grocery stores throughout southern Manitoba, was probably having an affair with his secretary, Leona. Ed would often call her long distance when he was out of town. Hope would patch him through and hear Leona's voice answer, and once, before she could turn him off, Ed said, "Sweetheart." It quickened her breath and made her queasy as well. She didn't like the power of that knowledge. Roy liked to call her as well. He'd dial "0" and when she answered, "Hello, operator," he'd say, "I just wanted to hear your voice." And they'd talk, sometimes at length, though she would have to keep cutting him off and then come back to him, and so their conversations were elliptical and disjointed. One night he phoned her and said that he was driving up to Fort Frances the following morning, just for the day. He had to deliver some parts. Would she like to come along?

She said she might. She had the day off, and she'd never been to Fort Frances before.

"We'll take the American route, though it's not much different. But at least you can say you visited Minnesota."

Later, after the trip, she would realize that she had taken quite a risk in going along with Roy. What turned out to be a romantic two days might just as easily have dissolved their relationship if Roy had been a different man. But he wasn't a different man—he was Roy. It was a hot day, late July, and certain crops had already ripened and so farmers were swathing the fields. As they drove she pointed out the farmyards, horses grazing, and the white clouds high in the sky. "They look like sheep," she said. Roy took pleasure in her curiosity and in the attention she paid to little things and in the attention she paid to him. She held his hand. Touched his cheek. Adjusted his hat, took it off and placed it on her own head in a jaunty manner. They stopped for a chicken sandwich and mushroom soup in Baudette, on the American side. When the waitress, a very pretty girl who looked like Marilyn Monroe, delivered their food, she laid it out before them and then stood back and said, "You two wouldn't be newlyweds, would you? It's just you *look* like it."

"Oh, no," Roy said, and he laughed.

After the waitress had gone, Hope said, "Are you embarrassed by me, Roy?"

"What do you mean? Of course I'm not."

"She's a very pretty girl, that waitress."

"She is."

"You didn't want her to think we were married."

"But we aren't married."

"We're almost married. In a month. You could have at least told her we were engaged."

"You could have told her that, Hope."

"She was talking to you. She didn't even look at me."

"Are you jealous?" He was grinning.

"Should I be? If I hadn't been here, sitting across from you, would you have had a longer conversation with Norma Jean?"

"Who?"

"The waitress. She looks just like Marilyn Monroe."

"She does?"

"Oh, Roy, you're impossible. You should be careful, playing innocent like that. Something really good-looking will come along one day and slap you on your backside and you won't know what hit you. You have to be prepared for the world. Girls *like* you."

"I'm not interested in girls. I have you."

"Even so."

Later, back on the road, Roy grew tired and asked if Hope wanted to drive. She said that she didn't, he should pull over and have a nap. He stopped on the shoulder and turned off the engine. He fell asleep immediately and she watched him, his head angled towards her slightly. She had rolled her window down halfway. A fly entered the car and landed on Roy's hat brim. She waved her hand. The fly took off and came back and landed on his cheek, crawling down to his slack mouth. She spent the next fifteen minutes shooing the fly, keeping it off Roy's head as he snored lightly. When he woke, he did so with a start, as if embarrassed by his vulnerability. "Was I snoring?" he asked.

"Not a bit," she said, and she folded her hands in her lap.

She had imagined that he would deliver the parts to the garage in Fort Frances and they would head back to Eden immediately. This was not to be. He said that he wanted to pay a visit to a doctor.

"What, are you sick, Roy?"

"Naww. You'll see."

He drove to the hospital and parked in the visitors' lot and said he would be right back. She sat and waited, and then got out of the car and walked about. She was glad that she had worn a sleeveless dress, what with the heat, though she wished she could remove her nylons and let her legs feel the breeze. She sat on a bench in a nearby park and waited some more. The sour smell of the paper mill floated in the air. An hour passed and she wondered if Roy had abandoned her. She thought she might be feeling resentful, but she counselled herself to be patient. She wished that he were more thoughtful, that he wouldn't just take her for granted. "Oh," she said to herself, "if I go away, no matter how long, I'll come back and Hope will still be here, prepared to shoo flies from my face."

When he finally reappeared he was walking with a shorter man with a square face, older than Roy. They stood beside the car and they talked. They walked around the car. It was a Styleline Deluxe, a hardtop. Brand new, except for the few miles Roy had put on. The two men shook hands, and taking this as a sign, she rose and ambled over and stood off to the side. Finally, she was noticed. Not by Roy but by the other man, who stepped towards her and held out his hand and said, "Doctor Challis."

"Hi, I'm Hope Koop. Roy's wife."

"Your husband here just sold me his car."

"He did?" She looked at Roy, who was studying her, shaking his head.

"Yes, he did. He's quite the salesman. In any case, you're coming to our place for dinner tonight. You'll have to spend the night as well, as Roy here has sold out your transportation from underneath you. Nice to meet you, Mrs. Koop. We'll meet again at our house. You go on ahead. I'll let Florence know."

Driving over to the doctor's house, Roy was silent. She didn't care. Just before they arrived, she said, "If you're going to treat me like a submissive wife, I might as well *be* your wife, Roy. You walk away and leave me for an hour. I wait, and I wait. And then it turns out that we don't have a car to drive home. I work tomorrow. In the evening. Will we be home by then? And do I want to spend the night at some stranger's house? You might have consulted me. I don't like to be in the dark."

"I was doing my job, Hope. He bought the car. I made three hundred dollars in one hour. Just like that. And now you've jeopardized the sale."

"How? What have I done? Because I said we're married?"

"What if he finds out? In any case, I don't like to lie. I'm not a liar."

"Oh, Roy. Goodness. He won't care. And you didn't lie. I did."

"You're so stubborn, Hope." His voice was disappointed.

They had arrived. The house obviously belonged to a doctor. It was large and made of brick and a second car was parked in the driveway. Three children were playing in the front yard.

"What was his wife's name?" she asked.

"Florence. Her name is Florence."

———————

They were given a bedroom together, because of course they were married. She had not anticipated that this would be the result of her little white lie, and she was amused by Roy's mute acceptance of the fact that they would be sleeping together. Not in the same bed, but in the same room, lying in close proximity—him fully dressed, Hope wearing a nightgown that the doctor's wife had given her. "Oh, Roy, we can sleep here, side by side," Hope whispered, pointing at the bed. "I promise not to touch you." He shook his head, and lay on the floor beside her bed, a small blanket covering him. She giggled, besotted by his rectitude. What a wonderful man. And this allowed her more leeway, more freedom.

She held his hand before they slept, talking to him, her arm falling down to touch his chest. "What a handful those children are. Especially that boy Adrian," she said. "Florence must be exhausted." They had eaten late, much later than was typical for them, and the meal, with three courses that included a leg of lamb, had gone on and on, with much conversation that eventually turned to politics and then religion, which had been quite interesting because it turned out that the doctor was an atheist. Hope was especially curious about his lack of belief.

"Not a lack of belief," he had clarified. "I believe in humanity, in caring for one another, in the continuation of the species. I just don't believe in God."

"But how is that possible?" Hope asked. "Where did you come from? Where are you going?"

The doctor's wife tried to temper the conversation, though she was quite occupied with the food and the children, but by then the talk had turned elsewhere, back to cars, perhaps, or to hunting and fishing, activities the doctor was especially fond of.

In the middle of the night, when Roy thought Hope was sleeping, he rose and left the room and went down the hallway to the doctor's bedroom and knocked on the door. She heard a single knock, and then another, louder this time, and then she heard voices talking, and then it was quiet, and finally Roy returned. He lay down and covered himself.

In the darkness, she spoke. "What were you doing?"

Silence, and then, "I was talking to the doctor."

"Now? What time is it?"

"Three o'clock."

"You woke him?"

"Yes."

"What were you talking about?"

"I told him that you and I aren't married. We are engaged though. I thought he should know."

"Oh. The deal is off then? He doesn't want the car?"

"He didn't care. He laughed. He said that I worry too much."

"What else?"

"He called me terrifyingly honest. And then he said, 'Go back to your wife.'"

"You feel better?"

"Yes. I do." And he whispered as he held her hand, "I love you, Hope. You can be stubborn, but I wouldn't have anyone else."

And they both fell asleep.

When she woke to sunlight falling onto her bed, Roy was up and gone, downstairs with the doctor eating breakfast. She heard the muffled voices, the children calling out, and she lay there for a long while, holding on to the enchantment of the night.

It rained the day of the wedding. The men sat on one side of the church and the women on the other, and the music was unaccompanied and there were no harmonies. All of this was typical of the conservative Mennonite Church that Hope's father had been raised in and then rejected. Cousin Frida, from across the river, was Hope's attendant. She wore a pale blue dress and matching satin shoes, and a hat to which were pinned white flowers. Hope wore a white gown with long sleeves made of lace that revealed subtly the whiteness of her arms. A veil fell over her face. She carried a bouquet of carnations. Roy wore a charcoal suit that he had bought in Winnipeg for the occasion. The cut of the suit was narrow but still practical. He intended to wear it again at work. The tie was paisley. The wedding was a simple event, with a reception held in the church basement where the guests sat on wooden chairs around collapsible tables covered with swaths of paper and ate the fare prepared by the local ladies: bean soup, white buns, farmer sausage, cheddar cheese, and dainties that consisted of cherry tarts and matrimonial cake. Hope hadn't wanted a wedding cake. She thought it was ostentatious.

Petra attended with her husband. She was eight months pregnant and proudly waddled about introducing herself to Roy's mother and Roy's sister, Berta, asking anyone and everyone where the alcohol was. Hope knew that she had the capacity to be slightly scandalous, and she worried that Mrs. Koop might be insulted. She wasn't. She said later that Petra was a treasure, certainly a good friend, and *terribly interesting.* This was how things worked in Eden. The outsider's behaviour was easily excused.

In the evening there was a smaller gathering at the home of her parents, and it was there, in the living room, that Hope's father took out his whisky and his fiddle, and Hope and her mother, along with several guests who didn't care what people thought, danced in the space that had been cleared in the centre of the room. Roy's brother Harold was the only one of his family who was present, and he drank a little too much and danced with Petra, showing off moves that he must have learned overseas, during the war. Hope thought then that for several years he had had a secret life, and only now were they catching a glimpse of it. Hope slipped out of her shoes and lifted her wedding dress so that it didn't drag across the hardwood, and she moved dreamily around the room to the tune of "Hey, Ho, My Honey." She had removed her veil and now everyone could see her eyes, which *sparkled.* The guests thought that she was beautiful and happy.

They spent their first night in the small house that Roy had bought three months earlier in preparation for their life together. During the night she woke and wandered through the house, touching the things she now owned: the new fridge, the Kenmore stove, the matching couch and chairs, the dining room set made of oak, the flatware, a sixteen-place setting of silver given to them by Frida's parents, teacups, the Mixmaster, the brand new towels and napkins stacked on the kitchen table, and more teacups. She felt guilty and imagined offering her mother the gift of the Mixmaster, though she knew she would refuse. While Hope was making love to Roy for the first time several hours earlier, her mind kept slipping away to the trove of treasures that surrounded her in this new place, and in this too she had felt guilty, aware that she should be enjoying the moment. Not that she hadn't found pleasure in Roy. She had. Though perhaps his pleasure had been greater. He had been in awe, struck by the gift before him, which was Hope. She had assuaged his nervousness with lighthearted humour and comforting words, and had been surprised by her own lack of nervousness and by the sense that she was in control. When she had completed the tour of the house and touched all of her things, she went back to bed and Roy woke and reached for her again. This time the lovemaking was less anxious, and slower.

In the morning she and Roy drove up to Lake of the Woods, where Roy had rented a cottage for the week. Because Roy was just starting out in his father's business and didn't have a lot of money, he expected that Hope would use the small kitchen in the cottage to cook the meals during their stay. She made toast for breakfast the first day and warmed up tomato soup from a can for lunch. She had no plans for dinner. She imagined that if she were Mennonite, or if she had grown up Mennonite like Roy's mother, and had some training in the ways of the kitchen, then she would have created a lovely roast beef dinner and baked *zwieback* and perhaps even made a soup from scratch. As it was, she stood in the kitchen, surveyed the mismatched cups and plates, and sighed and asked, "How about toast again?" The next day, she announced that she was ready to eat a restaurant meal. Enough was enough. This was their honeymoon. She said that she had to save her energy for other things. She smiled at her husband, who looked away in sheepish agreement.

That evening, she wore her taffeta dress and high heels and she put on makeup. Roy wore his wedding suit. They found a restaurant that served chicken and mashed potatoes and salad and a brownie for dessert. It pleased her to watch her husband eat, just as it pleased her to catch him unawares in the bathroom brushing his teeth or shaving, leaning into the mirror as he ran his free hand over his jaw, his shoulder blades moving beneath his undershirt. He finished a second brownie and then talked about his twenty-year plan: children, a bigger house, buying his father's business. She listened and smiled and nodded. She said she wanted at least three children. "Children should outnumber their parents, don't you think?"

It rained most of the week and they spent their time inside the little cottage, playing board games and reading magazines and falling into bed in the middle of the afternoon. On the second-last day the sun finally appeared and Roy rented a boat from the marina, a sixteen-footer with a thirty-horse Evinrude. Hope wore a yellow slicker and green rubber boots and she made a little lunch of leftover chicken and canned fruit cocktail and water in a sealer jar. Roy had borrowed two fishing rods and a tackle box, and so they trolled the edge of the lake and Roy taught her how to cast and let the spoon follow in their wake. She caught two pickerel. Roy threw the smaller one back and dropped the larger fish in a pail of water. That evening, he filleted the fish, dipped it in flour, and fried it in butter. They ate by candlelight, garnishing the plate with beans from a tin that Hope had found in the cupboards. She was twenty years old and she found it thrilling to be sitting across from this new husband, whose eyes in the flickering light turned from grey to green to black.

Earlier, as they had been returning to the marina, the Evinrude had sputtered, caught, sputtered again, and then died. The vast lake all around had turned calm, and as they floated and drifted Roy tried to restart the engine. He checked the gas and took off the engine cover and tinkered. He pulled at the starter cord for five minutes, but there was nothing doing. He sat and looked at Hope and said, "Well, we'll have to row."

He took the oars that were stored in the bottom of the boat and fitted them into the oarlocks. He sat with his back to her and as he rowed she observed the movement of his muscles through his shirt and the sweat forming on his neck.

"We're miles out, aren't we?" she asked.

"Well, at least we have dinner," he said. She couldn't see his face and so didn't know if he was joking or serious.

"Someone might come by," she said.

A loon surfaced nearby, studied them, and then dove back under the water.

"The silence is nice," she said. "At least we're not scaring the animals."

He grunted and pulled.

She thought of offering to take his place but she knew he would refuse.

They were saved by an old fisherman in a cabin cruiser. He pulled up alongside and when Roy said, "Engine trouble," the old man nodded and threw them a rope. "I've towed this coupla times already," the old man said. "Harry should get his shit together."

She hadn't been worried at all out there on that immense lake. She saw the breakdown as an adventure, as something out of the ordinary. She might even have felt a little disappointment when the old man's boat appeared, the last evening sun winking off the bright metal. Of course, had she been alone, she might have felt differently. As it was, she had Roy, and though he had been impatient and called the engine "stupid," she had never, at any point, thought that she was in any danger.

* * *

Six months into her first year of marriage, already wearied by domestic duties and not given to joining the typical women's groups in town, Hope began to pick up hitchhikers, something she kept from Roy. She was fond of driving the car Roy had given her, and at least once a week she motored alone to Winnipeg, forty miles away. She shopped for clothes and then rode the escalator to the restaurant of Eaton's department store, where she usually ate the same thing. A roast pork sandwich and a dessert of gingerbread and whipped cream washed down with coffee. She ate slowly and looked about at the other shoppers and was quite content. By early afternoon she would be on her way home, in her mind going over the possible supper options for Roy. He liked meat loaf and mashed potatoes. He didn't like salads or vegetables, though he would eat corn. Noodle casserole was his favourite. One day in April she picked up a couple from the East Coast who were heading home to see family, and on another day she gave an older man a lift to a town that she had passed through on her way to Eden. Both of these incidents had come off without trouble, and she had not mentioned them to anyone.

On one of her trips back to Eden on the Trans-Canada Highway in late May, it was raining and there was a hitch-hiker huddling against the wind a few miles out of the city. She slowed and pulled over to the side, watching him in the rear-view mirror as he ran towards her, his small suitcase banging against his leg. She almost started the car and left him, suddenly fearful, but then she calmed herself and said, "It's okay. You can do this."

He turned out to be more boy than man. He was nineteen and on his way to his parents' reserve in Northern Ontario. He lit a cigarette right off and then asked if it was okay. Hope said, "Please, yes. Go ahead." She was driving a brand-new Fleetmaster with soft corduroy seats and she imagined a cigarette falling onto the seat and burning a hole and Roy discovering it. He had rules about the car. The boy looked her over and asked where she was going. Water dripped from his baseball cap onto his lap. He was very thin. She explained that she was from Eden and had been in Winnipeg buying a few things for her home. He asked if she had any food. She said she didn't. It was quiet then except for the single wiper slapping against her side of the windshield.

She felt the silence and, trying to be civil, said, "My husband, Roy, he doesn't like me to drive in the rain."

The boy said that he would be glad to drive. "I've not driven such a beauty before." He looked around and patted the seat between them.

"Oh, no, Roy wouldn't want me to give the wheel over to you. Not because it's you, but he would be against me giving it to anyone. He owns a Chevrolet dealership. Well, he and his father own it. He plans to buy it someday. He takes his cars quite seriously."

The boy wasn't talking, and this made her nervous. She said, as if to solidify her position, "We were married nine months ago and plan to have a number of children. Actually, we're planning on building a new home."

The boy opened the passenger window a crack and threw out his cigarette. He settled back in the seat. He seemed to be thinking, but he wasn't speaking.

"I have family in Kenora," she said. "Uncle Ernie works at the sawmill, and Uncle Stan is a fisherman. You might know them."

"Doubt it," the boy said.

His answers to her questions were brief and almost harsh. Though she wasn't frightened. She said, "You could come for supper if you like. I'm making a noodle dish and there will be more than enough. Roy wouldn't mind. And then, after, we could drive you back to the highway. Are you in a rush?"

"Not going anywhere fast," he said.

She believed this meant he was willing, and she took the turnoff to Eden and they drove the remaining ten miles in silence. The rain had halted and to the south the sun had appeared. As she turned up the street to the house and pulled into the driveway she experienced a failure of will. She had never been in the house alone with a man other than Roy, and she thought now that she had perhaps chosen badly. She brushed these doubts aside and told him to come in. At the door, before they entered, she said, "My name's Hope." She held out her hand. He looked at it and grinned and shook her hand and said, "Harlin."

She had him take off his boots and sit at the kitchen table so that in this way she could keep an eye on him as she cooked. She didn't mistrust him, but he seemed nervous, taking off his cap and putting it back on and then off again, twisting it in his hands. He wanted to smoke again and she fetched him a saucer, as neither she nor Roy smoked, and she laid it in front of him. He said that he'd never been here before, in this town, though he'd passed the sign numerous times out on the highway. He said that maybe her husband was hiring. He knew something about motors, as he worked on outboards and such.

"Well, that's a thought," she said. "One of my cousins, Ian Macintyre, can tear down an outboard and put it back together in an hour. He lives near the marina in Kenora. You might know him."

He shook his head.

"He's a redhead. Can't miss him. He married Candace

Shand. Her family owns the movie theatre." She scooped elbow macaroni into the boiling water. Stirred it. Watched it come to a boil again. She felt uncertain, though she wasn't sure why. Harlin was just sitting and smoking and he wasn't even looking at her in any way that felt awkward, though when she had her back to him she was aware of her calves and the Band-Aid on her Achilles tendon. She'd put it there in the morning because the back of her shoe, the right one, was chafing and creating a blister. She wondered if the Band-Aid itself made her appear vulnerable.

She asked Harlin if he wanted to watch television. They had recently purchased one.

He nodded. But he didn't move, or indicate any desire to see the set. He crossed his right leg over his left thigh and rested a hand on his ankle. She went to wash and clean up her hair and change, and when she came back down he was still sitting as before. She was wearing a beige short-sleeved dress with a high neckline and light hose and tan pumps. She had pulled her hair up. She usually dressed up for dinner with Roy.

When Roy came home at six, she heard his car pull up in the driveway and she met him at the door. She took his suit jacket and kissed him on the cheek and said, "We have a guest for dinner." If he was surprised, he did not show it. The three of them ate quietly. Roy asked Harlin various questions. Had he finished school? He hadn't. Was he working? He wasn't, though he might fish with his father through the summer.

"I told him that Uncle Stan was a fisherman," she said.

Roy talked about his day, about the new 1951 Fleetline Deluxe. "The chrome is splendid. A V8. People have been asking for it." He gave the list price, but Hope didn't quite hear it. She was thinking that she had made a mistake.

She kept thinking about this through the cleanup of the dishes, which she was doing alone. Roy had driven Harlin up to the Trans-Canada. There had been no discussion of Hope going along. Roy had simply folded his napkin and moved his chair back from the table and said to Harlin that it was time to go.

She scrubbed the Dutch oven, removing the stuck-on noodles. When she drained the sink there was a large amount of soggy noodles in the drain and she removed these and put them in the garbage. She thought it would be nice to get a dog, though Roy disliked domestic animals. Still, the one time they had discussed the possibility, he did say that he pre-ferred dogs to cats.

She sat in the growing darkness of the living room. At eight she called her mother, who answered on the first ring. She told her about the hitchhiker and about where he had come from. The fact that he was an Indian did not come up, though her mother would have been interested. After her conversation with her mother, Hope read for an hour. She had planned to stay up until Roy returned, but it got to be eleven and she grew tired and so she went to bed, waking at 1 a.m. to discover that Roy was still not home. She panicked for a moment and then decided that he had gone to the office. He did that sometimes, working very late.

He returned early in the morning. She woke and held him and smelled the car on him and a hint of the boy as well.

She said, "Thank you." And he fell asleep. At the breakfast table he said that he had driven the boy all the way to Kenora. "I couldn't leave him out on the highway." He drank some coffee, put down the cup, and looked at her. "Don't pick up any more hitchhikers. It's too dangerous."

She said, "Did he attack you? Did he attack me or rob you?" She moved her hand from here to there and back again. "We're sitting here, eating breakfast. Nothing happened. Though it might have added some spice to my life if something *had* happened."

He grimaced. She knew that look. He said, "If you want spice, join the sewing circle. They have lots of work. Making clothes for the poor in Africa."

"I'm not interested in Africa. I had the chance to go to Africa. Arnold Dick wanted to marry me and take me to Africa. I could have married him, but I said no. Africa holds no interest for me." She had raised her voice and it shook and she felt the heat in her face. "Is it because he was an Indian?"

She could see that he disliked this accusation. He saw himself as fair-minded and civil, and to be accused of racism, which is what she was doing, hurt him. He did not answer. This was their first fight. They had been married almost a year and finally they were fighting. She had always wondered when they would fight, what would set her husband off, and she saw now that it was she herself who had needed to be set off. She wondered if this meant that she was too easy, too acquiescent, that perhaps she needed to be more headstrong. She stood and poured him more coffee. She said that she would not pick up any more hitchhikers. She was standing behind him and she placed her hands on his shoulders and smoothed his shirt and kissed the top of his head.

The following week she sped right by an older man who was hitchhiking. Two weeks later she drove by a man and a woman and a child standing in the pouring rain. Imagine that, a poor child who might catch pneumonia and ultimately die, all because Roy, stubborn man, was trying to protect his innocent wife. She decided that it was time to have a baby.

* * *

It took Hope several years to get pregnant, years that were full of doubt and anguish. She resigned herself to a life of barrenness, like Abraham's Sarah, and she cast about for various opinions on adoption. Roy, full of equanimity and calm, never complained or seemed worried. Instead, he built a house for his wife. It was a two-storey, in a new development close to the hospital, and it boasted everything modern and of the day: bathrooms upstairs and down, a grand master bedroom on the main floor with walk-in closets, three more bedrooms on the second floor for the children, a custom-designed kitchen with hand-built cherry cabinets and Floform countertops and two sinks, laundry on the main floor off the kitchen, a dining room that held ten easily, and a two-car attached garage that was fully insulated. She loved the house, but she wanted something more than furniture to put in it and when she finally became pregnant with her daughter Judith, in

1953, she began to relax and on winter afternoons she sat by the fireplace in the living room and looked out at the expanse of snow and caught glimpses of wild rabbits scampering across the front yard.

She did not breastfeed Judith. It was neither encouraged nor promoted. She had talked to other young mothers in town, at church, and at social evenings with the wives of Roy's compatriots, and no one was breastfeeding. This was a fact. Two years later Conner was born and Hope saw immediately that her two children, girl and boy, were completely different. Conner was an explorer. As soon as he was able to crawl he disappeared. She found him once in the neighbour's backyard, a block away. He had pushed the screen door open, edged down the back stairs and made it across their lawn and past the Nikkels' and the Tiessens', through the Friesens' tomato patch, and had come to rest by Mrs. Heinrich's tabby, who was lying near the begonias in her backyard. When Hope found him she kneeled in the grass and then lay down and saw the cat and the grass as Conner would see them. Conner thought that this was a game, and he climbed onto her head and clutched her ears as if he were a very tiny bull rider.

Judith, on the other hand, never strayed. She always looked to her mother for guidance and confidence and surety. When she began to speak she always said "Can I?" to her mother before acting. Years later, Hope would think that this was why she never married—because her mother hadn't given her the green light. The third child, born in 1957, was another girl. She was named Penny. Hope noticed immediately that Penny needed little attention. She rarely cried, ate when fed, slept copiously, and stared at Hope with an intense gaze that was disconcerting. Hope would bend over her and touch her nose and ask, "Who you lookin' at? Hey? Who do you love?" But this elicited no fondness, no cooing, no smile. The girl's face was serious. Hope wondered if the child was able to see some dark flaw in her mother that no one else had yet discovered. She took to talking with Penny from a distance. Without eye contact. Fearing a response. Not that Penny was difficult. She just seemed prescient, and old for her age.

Alone with three children all day, she had no idea if she was a good mother. Her own mother had had only one child, and in fact her father had taken care of her when her mother was at school, teaching. She recalled her father sitting in a chair, smoking, telling her stories, sometimes nodding off, or standing at the kitchen counter rolling out pastries on his mammoth bread board. She remembered helping him make cinnamon buns and then eating them with coffee in the late afternoon. She had been allowed coffee as a child. One day, with her own children, she attempted to replicate that scenario. She pulled out the yeast and flour and cinnamon and rolling pin, plunked Penny in a high chair, called Judith and Conner, and together they set to work. Conner's hands were everywhere, and he gobbled up the dough. Judith kept shushing Penny, whose fat little hands moved like pistons, demanding her own portion of dough. "Not too much, dear," Hope told Judith. "She'll choke." They ate the warm buns in the dim light of a fall evening. Judith had insisted that they wait for Dad, and so they waited and waited, until they could wait no longer. Hope said that perhaps they should place a bun on a plate and set it by Roy's place at the table and he could eat it when he got home. This is what Judith did, writing a note that said, "Dad, this is for you. We made it. Love, Judith, Conner, Penny."

That night, when Roy finally arrived home at nine o'clock, Hope sat across from him and talked about her day. She talked about Penny falling and cutting her chin, though she wouldn't require stitches, and she told him about making the cinnamon buns and how excited Judith had been to share one with him, and she talked about driving to Penner Foods for groceries and how difficult Conner could be—he was constantly running. "It's a good thing everyone knows him. If we lived in a big city he might just disappear, he's so elusive." She thought about this and then said, "Not that I want him to disappear, it's just he's so much work sometimes. How about your day?"

He looked over at the kitchen. "Is there dinner?"

She looked at him and then looked over at the kitchen as well, and then her face crumpled and she began to cry. She covered her face with her hands and she cried for a good number of minutes so that Roy, bewildered, finally reached out a hand and said, "What? What did I say?"

She lifted her head. "That's it. You're eating dinner. It's all the time I had. And then you were late, and Judith was disappointed that she couldn't watch you eat the cinnamon bun that she had made with her own hands, and Conner wouldn't go to bed properly, and Penny just sits there staring at me, and you don't like my legs anymore."

"What are you talking about? Of course I like your legs. What does that have to do with dinner, Hope?"

Earlier, after the children were in bed, she had bathed and shaved her legs and put on a yellow dress that hugged her hips and allowed some space for her stomach and hung just right, so that her legs, the best feature on her body, were exposed very nicely. Her legs were her pride and joy. She was aware of the extensor muscles on her calves, which were unusual and very defined.

"I was the fastest runner in high school, Roy. And I got the gold medal for highest marks at graduation. Don't forget that."

"Sure you did. I didn't forget."

"But you do forget. You leave me early in the morning and then return late at night, and you trust that I will still be here. Well, here I am. Your ugly and forlorn wife."

"Don't be melodramatic, Hope. You're tired."

"I'm not. I'm lonely."

He rose and sighed and came around the table and placed his hands on her shoulders and kissed the top of her head. "Don't be silly. You have three beautiful children."

"Am I? Silly?"

"Yes. Silly Hope."

"I could fry you some eggs. And there are a few potatoes in the fridge. I could fry those as well." She placed her hands on her lap, calmer now. Leaned her head back against Roy's stomach and looked up at his chin. "I'm sorry."

"Don't worry. I ate something at the diner. Come." And he pulled her to her feet and held her.

In the morning, when Judith came down for breakfast, there was a note waiting on the table. "Dear Judy. Thank you for the cinnamon bun. Good work. Dad."

She knew that Roy's days were difficult. He worked hard. He was gone from seven in the morning until six at night. And sometimes he went out to meetings in the evenings: the Chamber of Commerce, prayer meeting, town council. He usually did not sleep through the night, and sometimes she would wake and discover his absence and would get up and find him in the living room, drinking juice and reading a magazine or a crime novel. "Are you okay, Roy?" she'd ask, and he would look up and smile and say that of course he was fine. He said that he would come back to bed shortly. They made love at those times, when he returned to bed. The house was quiet, the night bottomless. After, he slept deeply and she lay awake and listened for danger. She wondered if any other married couple had made love at 3 a.m. in Eden, Manitoba, on June 14, 1959. She smiled at the thought.

* * *

In 1960 her father died of lung cancer. At the funeral Hope sat with her mother and held Penny on her lap. Judith sat between them. Roy was on the men's side with his father and brother. Conner, sitting on his lap, kept trying to escape. During the hymn "In the Sweet By and By" she saw

Conner flash by, legs pumping, and then Roy was out of his pew, his arms hung low and his shoulders bent as if to diminish himself in some way, and for the first time Hope noticed that her husband resembled a monkey. His arms were very long and he was stooped and his forehead was small. This made her nervous and she felt sweat drip from her armpits. She didn't want to ruin her dress and so she held her arms out from her body slightly and told herself to breathe slowly. Penny, in her lap, had worked one of her shoes free and dropped it on the floor and then leaned forward to discover into which particular abyss it had fallen. She giggled. Hope shushed her. Judith bent down and picked up the shoe and slipped it back on Penny's foot. She retied the lace and looked up at Hope when she was finished. "Thank you," Hope mouthed.

Penny untied her shoe and dropped it. Judith picked it up. The girls giggled. And so the game went on. Finally, Hope told Judith to take Penny into the back, by the boot rack. "Not outside, okay?" After the girls were gone, Hope slid over close to her mother and took her hand and held it, and in doing so she felt for the first time the sadness of her father's death. She was aware that she had loved him from a distance. And he her. Her mother did not radiate sadness, but then she never had. She remained eternally optimistic and was always more curious than spiteful. She liked Roy. She thought that he was strong and kind and she liked that he didn't drink. He had money, something Hope's mother had always struggled to achieve, and so Hope was fortunate. An only child who had found her way in the world.

Roy had organized for her a bank account into which he put a small amount of money on the first of every month. Groceries, clothes for the children and for her, makeup, general upkeep of the house—these things were paid for by Roy from his bank account. The other account was completely hers to do with as she pleased. Before the children were born, she found that the money went quite quickly. Now, because she was busy and didn't have time to drive into the city to shop for a new dress or to take a meal at Eaton's, the money began to accrue, and as the account grew, she wondered what she should do with it. She found an orphan in Vietnam through a church organization and donated five dollars a month to that child. The child's name was Trang, and one day there arrived in the mail a black-and-white photograph of Trang and a letter from her. The letter was in her own words, or so it appeared, and Trang described her house and her life and the school she was attending and she thanked Hope for the support. Trang's face was thin and she wore a white short-sleeved shirt and a blue skirt, a school uniform, and on her feet she wore rubber sandals. She was seven. Hope pinned the photo to the bulletin board.

Strangely, she had been experiencing morbid thoughts in the last while, thoughts of Roy dying and leaving her and the children bereft and poor. She had no occupation. On certain days she was sorry she had quit nursing to marry, but for the most part she had convinced herself that she hadn't enjoyed nursing to begin with. She liked the sound of certain occupations, such as law, and she had it in mind that she might want to look into the education required to become a lawyer. In high school she had always achieved the top marks in her grade, and there had been the sense, both from her teachers and from her mother, that she could go far. She had also been a top debater. And so, one morning, Hope arranged for Mrs. Tiessen, the neighbour, to watch the two younger children, and she drove to the city, to the University of Manitoba, where she had made an appointment to see a counsellor about studying law. The counsellor was younger than Hope and she wore a tight skirt to mid-calf and her hair was high on her head. She sat beside Hope and together they talked about Hope's having dropped out of nursing and Hope's burden of having children. At first Hope didn't understand what the counsellor was saying, this notion of a burden, and then she realized quite quickly what she was implying.

She said, "Oh no, I love my children. They're not a burden. I was hoping I might study part time, or be able to take courses by correspondence."

"Almost impossible," the counsellor said. "Have you written the LSAT?"

Hope shook her head. She felt suddenly lost. She pushed back her chair and thanked the woman and then wandered about the campus. Everyone was younger than she was. She found the bookstore and on a whim bought a Russian grammar text and workbook. Roy's father spoke Russian, had in fact come over from Russia in 1926 along with the second wave of Mennonites, and there was also the Cold War, something with which Hope had been keeping up, more out of fear than interest. She took the textbooks home, and for the first week she worked one hour a day at learning the Russian characters. One night Roy found the textbook and picked it up and said, "What's this? Are you planning on being a spy?" He said no more but she was slightly humiliated and saw the futility of her studies. Eventually, the books were relegated to a shelf near the fireplace, and finally they found their way up to the attic, where they sat in a box alongside Hope's high school diploma and her mortarboard.

One evening in late June, Hope asked her mother to watch the children and she drove over to the church for a counselling session with Pastor Ken. Ken was quite young to be a senior pastor. He had been educated at a seminary in California and he carried himself with tremendous aplomb and a certain arrogance. Some of the members of the church, especially the men, found him to be puffed up, but most of the women thought he was genuine. He had a mellifluous voice and he was a fine listener. On this evening, Hope found him in his office, reading. He was dressed in casual slacks and a short-sleeved shirt and he wore runners. He had just returned from a game of golf, nine holes with his wife. They didn't have children, not yet, and so their lives were more open, less structured. Hope found that she suffered a moment of jealousy as he described the round of late-afternoon golf. She herself had considered taking up golf, in order to be with Roy, but he had discouraged it, had in fact been downright impatient with her swing. And besides, she didn't have five free hours in her life on any given day.

She had called Pastor Ken the week before to arrange this appointment, and when she set it up she had been feeling unstable, she couldn't breathe properly. Even though she did not attend church regularly, Pastor Ken had sounded quite open to meeting with her. She thought that he might be able to help her. She hadn't mentioned any of this to Roy, who might have bristled. He saw Ken as an effeminate man who had too much time on his hands—time spent with the women of the church.

"Tell me what it is you would like," Ken said as he sat and leaned forward.

"If I knew that, then I wouldn't be here," Hope said.

Ken laughed. He was so easy-going she felt immediately that she could speak her mind and nothing would come of it, that there would be no repercussions.

She told Ken exactly this.

He said, "Who punishes you for speaking? Not Roy, certainly."

"No, no. Not Roy. It's just sometimes I feel mad. Crazy. As if my thoughts are the opposite of everyone else's. In church sometimes, I walk out and I swear under my breath. I say terrible things. But only to myself. But it's like I can't help it. Everyone's so perfect, so pious."

"Well, that's not true."

"But it seems so. Mr. Geddert was mowing his lawn the other day. Perfect diagonal rows. I wanted him to slip, to veer off. I imagined his foot getting caught and him losing a toe. Awful, isn't it?"

Ken smiled again. He asked, "You walk out on my sermons?"

She was embarrassed. "Sometimes."

He applauded silently. "Good for you."

"Why?"

"We don't need more sheep, Hope. And you are certainly not one of the sheep. Your thinking is vivid and
contradictory."

"Roy says it's crazy thinking."

"To him. He sells cars. He runs a business. Raising three
children is much more demanding and can lead to bigger
questions and ennui." He said this last word with a certain
flourish and though she didn't know the word she thought
that this was exactly what she was suffering from. "Don't get
me wrong. Roy's a good man. He is big-hearted and generous and I imagine he is a good father and husband." He lifted
his eyebrows.

She nodded.

"But that doesn't mean he understands your existence at
home. Be clear, Hope. If you need something, then ask for it.
The worst that can happen is he'll say no."

She wondered if he would pray with her, but he didn't.
Perhaps it was too intimate an act, something one did on a
grander scale with a congregation or alone in one's room.
Certainly not with a young woman, in the office, kneeling
side by side. Driving home that evening, she felt buoyed
up. Funny thing, she felt sensual as well, something that she
hadn't experienced for a while. She was looking forward to
seeing Roy.

Judith, at the age of nine, had become engrossed in painting and drawing, and for her birthday Hope bought her a
watercolour set of twenty tubes and three brushes of graduated sizes. Watercolours, to Hope's mind, leaned towards
soft bucolic settings and pastoral images: church bell towers, flowers, cows at pasture, or perhaps small birds on bare
branches that were beginning to show little green buds. Not
so with Judith. She preferred dark shades and darker subject matter. Her paintings were miniatures, almost requiring
a magnifying glass to discern the details. Every painting,
regardless of the setting, had at least one human in it, if
not more. The humans, however, were not normal. Their
limbs were elongated and out of proportion. The eyes were
much too large and resembled the sockets of a skull. Hope,
leaning over Judith's shoulder one Sunday afternoon as she
painted at the dining room table, exclaimed, "Isn't that arm
a little stretched?"

Judith shook her head. Her hair was fine and blonde and
cut short and she had pulled it back with bobby pins and there
was nothing especially pretty about her hairdo, but it was
impossible to suggest a different look for Judith. She would
just say, "I like it this way." And now, she shook her disor-
dered head of hair and bit her lower lip and set to, ignoring her mother. The skyline in the painting revealed storm
clouds, perhaps a tornado, while the girl in the foreground
was beneath a tree and she was reaching, with her elongated
limb, for the hand of another girl who was sitting in a topmost
branch. The girl in the tree was looking away.

Hope thought the whole endeavour was deeply depressing and she worried about Judith's state of mind. She showed Roy the painting that night as he was sitting on the edge of the bed, removing his shoes. She thrust it at him, as if it were to be feared, and said their daughter's name, "Judith."

He took it and examined it, holding one of his shoes in his other hand, and then he set the shoe down on the rug and said, "She's got talent."

She knew that many people perceived Roy as wise. "Wisdom" was another word for level-headedness or prudence, though in Eden it was wrongly used in place of "parsimonious." So Hope thought. Most people she knew were parsimonious, and this was not only in matters of money. Parsimony could be extended to narrow thinking, to religion, to the claim that baptism by immersion was superior to sprinkling or pouring—all nonsense, according to Hope. Not that she thought her husband was like that. He was far too reasonable. However, when it came to this painting and numerous other paintings like it that Judith had produced, Roy's "wisdom" was beginning to smell of indifference.

She snatched the painting from him, studied it again as if she might have missed something, and then pointed at the surreal outstretched arm. "It's like a vision of some other world," she whispered. "It's not realistic."

Roy had removed his other shoe and was standing now, loosening his tie. "What are you worried about, Hope? Is she eating?"

Hope admitted that she was.

"Has she run away from home?"

"Not yet."

"Has she talked of it?"

She shrugged.

"Are others worried? Mrs. Penner, for instance?"

Mrs. Penner was Judith's second-grade teacher, and yes, she had been troubled, but Hope decided at that moment, as Roy was hanging up his pants, standing with his back to her, his thin white legs sticking out of his shorts, that this was not something he needed to concern himself with. He worked far too hard as it was. And so she lied and said, "No, she's not." The previous week, though, at the parent–teacher meeting, Mrs. Penner had raised the issue of Judith's drawings and her clinginess to Angela. All of this, the disturbing drawings, the clinginess, had troubled Hope. In fact, the whole situation was so complicated that she could not make sense of it, which is why she had thrown it so desperately at Roy.

Angela was the daughter of Mrs. Emily Shroeder, a woman whom Hope had met at the beginning of the school year, and who had quickly become one of Hope's best friends. In fact, she would say that Emily was her only true friend. She loved her. Emily was witty and well read. She had recently presented Hope with a gift of a book: Pascal's *Pensées*. Emily had kept her own name when she married, a radical act. She worked part time at the local newspaper, writing obituaries, and with the money she made she flew to New York, where she went to the theatre and stayed up till all hours drinking in small bars. She travelled alone. Her husband Paul was an accountant who disliked travel. He made bird feeders and end tables in his woodshop in the evenings while Emily went to poetry readings in Winnipeg.

It was Emily who had handed her a brochure for the Book of the Month Club, saying, "You've got to expand your reading beyond romances." Hope decided to read *Lolita* and *Dr. Zhivago* and *Lady Chatterley's Lover*. She wouldn't normally have chosen books such as these, but they came highly recommended by the book club. *Lolita* was a stretch for her. She thought that the characters were mad and off balance and she couldn't identify with any of them and she found the general language of the novel very fancy. She thought that the author wasn't as funny as he thought he might be. She knew that she was missing many of the subtleties of the story and didn't understand the young girl, who was called Dolores, and various other things. Even though she couldn't relate to the characters, she had a perverse desire to keep reading, and when she was done she felt that the world of this particular novel was cheerless. *Lady Chatterley's Lover* she read very quickly and then she tore the book up and threw it in the garbage. Roy shouldn't know about a book like that. The one time he had perused it, when they were climbing into bed one night, he had asked in his bemused tone, "Who is the lady's lover?" She had snatched the book from him and said that it wasn't for him. He'd get ideas. *Dr. Zhivago* was more her type of story. She felt no guilt reading it in bed beside Roy, who usually fell asleep within three minutes of settling down beside her.

The girls, like the mothers, became immediate friends. After school, Angela came over and the two girls spent hours in Judith's room, the door closed, plotting whatever it was that nine-year-olds plot. One day, Hope baked cookies with Conner and Penny, and she carried up a plate to the girls. She paused at the bedroom door and was about to knock when she heard Angela say, "On the bum." Her voice was quite strident, almost shrill. Hope waited, thought she should enter, and then became frightened that the girls might be undressed, or that she would catch them in some sexual position. Again, Angela said the word "bum" and then there was the sound of a slap and a giggle, and then another slap. Hope set the plate down on the floor, knocked twice, and called out, "Girls, I've left you some cookies. They're fresh and waiting right here by the door." And she walked back downstairs.

Conner and Penny had finished most of the remaining cookies. Conner's hands were full of chocolate and he was washing himself at the kitchen sink, spraying water every-where. His hair stuck up. His pants were too short. Penny was swinging her bare legs at the table. She was humming to herself. Hope was mystified. She didn't know how a child made the leap from this kitchen scene to the spanking incident she had just overheard.

That night she tucked in Judith, brushed back her bangs, and asked how her day had been.

"Okay."

"Did you have fun with Angela?"

"Yeah. It was okay."

"What did you do?"

"Nothing."

"Did you like the cookies?"

"Yeah."

"It would be good to include some other friends some-times, don't you think? Sherry or Carolyn."

"They're boring."

"Sometimes it's good to open up your world." She moved her hands out as if the world were indeed the small space they were sharing.

"Well, you just see Mrs. Shroeder a lot. Don't you?"

Hope laughed and said, "I guess that's sort of true, isn't it? I'm a hypocrite." She paused and then said, "When you play with Angela, sweetie, you keep your clothes on, yes?"

Judith turned over and away from her mother.

Hope patted her shoulder. "I love you."

"Me too."

"Good night," Hope whispered.

"Night."

She decided to talk to Emily about the games the girls were playing. They had gone to the library and then dropped in at a local restaurant for lunch. Hope had Conner and Penny in tow, and so she had to talk *sotto voce*. Emily had taught her this term and she thought of it now as she leaned forward in confidence. "The other day I caught the girls playing a game, a sexual game." She stopped. Waited.

Emily lifted her eyebrows and smiled. "Good," she said. "They're nine. Developmentally, they're right on target."

"So you're not worried?"

"Not at all."

"Do you talk to Angela about this?"

"Oh, Hope, of course. You should be talking to Judith. Haven't you? People should talk openly about sex."

"Well, a little, I guess." She was embarrassed. "I will. Soon." And she changed the subject.

The confusing thing about this was the irony in Emily's life. Over the past year she and Hope had talked of everything, sex included, and it became clear that Emily did not have a good sex life with her husband. They rarely made love. Emily said that Paul wasn't interested. He didn't even want to talk about it. Hope, not given to hyperbole and not especially aware of what was "normal," said that she and Roy had sex two or three times a week and she always had an orgasm. She didn't try—it just happened. Emily had seemed surprised by this news, though she said that it was wonderful. "You're lucky." She paused, narrowed her eyes, and asked, "A vaginal orgasm?"

"I think so. Is that bad?"

"No. No. You're lucky." And this is how they left it.

And yet, now, when they were discussing their girls, Hope heard the criticism in Emily's voice and she felt angry. And sad. She didn't want to lose Emily's friendship.

Hope continued to worry about the future of the planet. Roy sometimes mentioned what was happening in the world—the building of the Berlin Wall, the communists in Cuba, the buildup of nuclear warheads in the United States and the Soviet Union—and she became especially concerned for her children. She imagined that everyone she loved would die in a conflagration, or that Russia would invade North America and there would be a diminishment of the wealthy and suddenly everybody would be equal. She had grown used to her house, her status as a businessman's wife, the new car she drove, the charge account Roy had arranged at the local res-taurant. Having grown up poor, she had never dreamed that one day she could have so many luxuries, and now that she had them, she was anxious that they could be lost, like a sock that suddenly goes missing, never to be found again. Some nights she woke and visited her children's bedrooms, and then climbed back into bed and told Roy her worries. He lis-tened, told her that she was safe and there was nothing to fret about, and fell back asleep. In the morning she was exhausted by her lack of sleep and by her anxiety.

And then Roy came home one day and flashed two tickets for a trip to Hawaii. They would leave in three days. He had arranged care for the children. Everything was set. Hope was surprised and upset, but she did not show it. She packed the suitcases and laid out a week of clean clothes for each child. She wrote a long note to Mrs. Tiessen, who was to take care of the children. She said, "Don't force-feed peas to Penny. She detests them. And Conner is allowed to ride his bike to the end of the block, but no farther. Judith will want to have Angela over for a sleepover. She may, but one night only, and her door must stay open." She erased the bit about the door. She taped the note to the fridge. She baked a tuna casserole and froze it. Emily called and Hope told her that she and Roy were going to Hawaii for a week and Emily said that was a very bourgeois thing to do. Hope didn't quite know what this meant, but she assumed it was a criticism of sorts. She said, "I didn't want to go, but Roy needs a holiday. He works so hard."

She had forgotten what it felt like to be alone. At the hotel on Waikiki, during the day when Roy golfed, she lounged by the pool and read, and then she lay down in her room, on the large bed, and she heard the surf falling onto the beach below. The first few days she kept thinking that she heard a child calling, but it turned out to be a seagull or the honk of a vehicle. She and Roy ate dinner late, often in the hotel restaurant, which bordered the beach. He talked about his golf game and she talked about the book she had been reading or the conversations she'd had with the maids or the bellhop. She said that the humidity was good for her feet. She had had a pedicure that afternoon. She was wearing sandals with high heels and she lifted one of her feet slightly to let Roy have a peek. She took his hand and said, "This is wonderful. Thank you." They shared a bottle of wine, though Hope drank most of it. She felt so free, so comfortable. She laughed at Roy, who was flirting harmlessly with the waitress. He was very handsome. That night she became pregnant with her fourth child, Melanie. She was slightly drunk, terribly content, hasty in making love, and careless.

Two months later, when her doctor told her that she was pregnant, Hope looked at him and said, "But I can't," and she began to cry. Doctor Krahn became flustered. He stood and sorted through his effects on his desk, and when she had wiped her tears, he asked if there was something wrong. Was she worried? She shook her head and waved him away. "I'm sorry. These days the tears just come out of nowhere." That evening she waited until Roy had eaten and was drinking his coffee, and only then did she look at him and say, "I went to see Doctor Krahn today. It turns out that I'm pregnant again." She had thought he might be distressed or upset, but then she often made that mistake, assumed they would share the same feelings. Roy raised his eyes and tilted his head. He got up from his chair and came around to her side of the table and kissed her cheek and hugged her. "That's wonderful news."

"How do you do that?" she asked.

"Do what, Hope?"

"How can you be so happy? Aren't you worried?"

The children had finished eating and were watching television in the next room. They were free to talk. He laughed. "Look at all the space we have. The children will love having a baby brother or sister. The more the merrier."

This was true. And yet, another little body terrified her.

"Sometimes it feels like so much. Have you noticed Judith's teeth? The gaps? She'll need her teeth straightened. Penny's an outright mystery. I can't make meaning of her. And Conner's been wild and unruly. The other day he got into a fight at school. Mr. Rempel called. I tried to spank Conner when he got home and he just laughed at me. I should have used a wooden spoon. I told him that his father would take care of it. He looked at me and said that you would never spank him. You told him never to back down from a fight. Is that true, Roy?"

"Why are you telling this to me now? I should have known the day it happened. I can't punish Conner now."

"So he was right. You're afraid of him."

"Hope, come." He took her chin and looked into her eyes. "Everything will be fine. What a delight, to have another child. Perhaps a boy."

"Yes, and then we'll have two boys who are boxers."

She hung on to that notion of Roy being afraid of his son. It might be true. He indulged the child, seemed to think that the sun rose and set on his head. If this continued the boy would become a rebel and ne'er-do-well. In the kitchen later, cleaning the dishes, she began to cry quietly. The dread hovering about her shoulders was forceful and strong.

What also worried her was her own body, and the fact that she was larger now than when she had first married Roy, and that with each subsequent child her stomach had stretched. Now she didn't look quite as good in her bathing suit. She didn't want to talk to Roy about this, because it would be like throwing a problem down in front of him that he might not even have been aware of. So she left it alone and sometimes studied herself in the mirror, and she discovered that if she focused on her legs, which were long and holding their great shape, she could imagine that she was still young, and that Roy wouldn't have to look elsewhere.

She called her mother, as she did at eight o'clock every evening, not because she wanted to but because it was her duty. You see, she could have told Roy, the children so consume me that I can't even talk to my mother or have her in for dinner or simply be there as a daughter. Not that her mother had any expectations. She was retired now and often dropped in to help with the children, though when Hope saw her crossing the backyard and approaching the house, the weight of another body to talk to and feed and care for overwhelmed her.

On the phone now, she said, "I'm pregnant, Mom."

"Oh, Hope. That's wonderful. Isn't it? Are you happy?"

"I've been too worried, Mom."

"About what, Hope?"

"Everything. About my plants, that they will die. I worry about the kids. I hoard cans of food for the apocalypse. I worry that Roy will be unhappy with me. I worry that I worry too much."

"Oh, Hope. I'm sorry. Do you have someone to talk to?"

"You mean friends? I talk to Emily."

"I mean a doctor, someone who won't let you make excuses. Someone who's objective."

"I can't talk to Doctor Krahn about this."

"There are pills that can help. But first you should talk to someone. How are the children?"

"Judith wants to visit you Friday night, as usual. Conner is going to a birthday party Saturday. Penny is her usual silent self, slipping through the world. She waxed the kitchen floor yesterday. Just like that. I worry that she senses the craziness in the house."

"She's such a sweetie. They all are. Talk to Doctor Krahn, okay? Promise?"

"I will."

But she didn't. She had little faith in Doctor Krahn, who had helped her birth all her children, who would be there for the birth of this child, but who wasn't terribly smart when it came to conversation. He seemed frightened, or perhaps a bit thick. Why would she talk to him?

Emily, when she learned of the pregnancy, thought Hope was mad and was digging herself in.

"What do you mean, 'digging myself in'?" It was one thing to feel sorry for oneself and admit to the vast responsibilities in life, and it was another to have a best friend criticize and imply failure. "I like children. I'm a good mother. It's just sometimes I get tired."

"Well, sure you do. Four sets of diapers, all those nights getting up, four times you toilet train, four times you send them off to grade one, four times you teach them to ride a bike. By the time they've all left home, you'll be four times worn out."

Emily's voice was shrill. Hope looked at her and wondered if she was jealous. She'd had only one child and she'd implied that she would never want another, but what if that wasn't true? What if Paul was incapable, or Emily was incapable? That might make her more strident.

She often saw herself as beneath Emily. Emily was smarter, she spoke French, she owned Great Books and had just read Rachel Carson's *Silent Spring,* from which she read long passages out loud to Hope, and then paused and raised her head as if to say, *See?* Emily had an opinion on everything, and she was constantly talking about "running away" as if Eden were a curse from which she needed to escape. Roy, only once, wondered out loud if it was healthy to spend time with a woman who so hated the town she lived in. "Sometimes," he said, "negative thoughts land in our lap and they sit there and we don't know how to chase them away. Emily's like that. She drops those thoughts in your lap, Hope. She's full of dissatisfaction."

Emily said now that she was taking a psychology course at the university once a week, Thursday evenings, and she was reading a book by Betty Friedan. It was very important. Hope thought that she had said, "Betty Friesen," the woman who lived on Third Street, a woman their age, and she asked Emily if it was true that Betty Friesen had written a book. "I never imagined that she was a writer."

"Come on, Hope. For goodness' sake. Betty Friedan. She's from New York. She says that women need to be emancipated. It's brilliant."

Though Hope didn't believe herself trapped in any way, she resented the implication. So what if she hadn't heard of Betty Friedan? Emily was still talking about her course and about the professor, a youngish man who wore a beret to class and who was American and lived with an American woman who was also a professor of psychology. "They aren't married," Emily said. "Just lovers."

Hope wondered what "just lovers" meant, but she didn't ask. She felt suddenly old and stupid. She didn't *know* anything, and this was a depressing thought. On the other hand, she wondered if there wasn't entirely too much thinking going on and not enough work. Work was good for the soul. Thinking sometimes just confused the heart. Leisure, as Roy said, was a luxury that shouldn't be overindulged, and for once Hope agreed.

One day there was a knock at the door and when Hope opened it she discovered Harlin, the hitchhiker, standing there, and beside him a young woman.

Hope tilted her head, unsure why Harlin was visiting, and then she laughed and said, "Do you need a ride somewhere?"

"Just got one," Harlin said. Then he said, "Joking," and he pointed at a Studebaker sitting in the driveway. "Got my own ride now." He waited.

"Well," Hope said, "do you want to come in?" She was showing already and she saw the young woman studying her stomach, and in order to make everyone comfortable, she said, "I'm pregnant," and she made a little curtsy right there on the green linoleum.

Conner walked in holding a toy gun and he pointed it at Harlin and shot him.

"Got me," Harlin cried and he stumbled across the kitchen holding his chest. Conner thought this hilarious. So he shot him again and again, and with each bullet Harlin writhed and groaned.

Hope pulled Conner's arm and said, "That's enough, Conner. He's dead." She told him that these were friends from long ago.

"Eight years. Maybe more. This is Ella, my fiancée."

Hope shook Ella's hand. Ella nodded but didn't say anything. Conner pulled his mother down to whisper in her ear.

"They're dark."

"Yes, they are," she said.

"Why?"

"Off you go." She pushed him towards the back door.

"See ya, buddy," Harlin called out.

Hope didn't recall him being so talkative and she said so. "Last time I saw you you said maybe three words. I did all the talking."

"And your husband."

"What do you mean?"

"He drove me all the way back to Kenora and he talked and talked. He talked about work and honesty, and he talked about everybody getting a kick at the can. And he offered me a job at his garage. I told him that I couldn't live in a town that was all white." He looked at Ella and then Hope and he grinned. "Still is white. I told Ella that there wasn't a single Indian in this place. Or Chinese, or black man."

She wasn't sure what Harlin wanted. She didn't like his take on the town, though he was absolutely right. She said, "So you want a job now? After all these years?"

"Hell, no. I'm a roofer in Kenora. No, me and Ella were passing by and I said you want to see a town in a time warp and she said yeah and so we took a detour. We went shopping, by the way, at your second-hand place. Lady there told us where your new house was. Ella's looking for a wedding dress."

Harlin stopped talking and pulled out a pack of cigarettes and lit one and exhaled. Hope fetched a saucer and laid it before him. He waved the smoke away and said, "You're looking good, Hope. I was nineteen back then, and I told Ella that you were quite a looker. It was very different, you inviting me in like that. I thought that you were either nuts, crazy, or didn't care."

"Oh, I care. Thank you very much. I trusted you."

"That's what I said to Ella." He grinned.

Hope turned to Ella and said, "I've got a wedding dress. And we're almost the same size, don't you think? Except I'm bigger at the moment." She stood and indicated that Ella should stand as well. She stepped towards Ella and faced her. They were eye to eye. "Pretty close, don't you think?" She looked at Harlin.

He put out his cigarette and nodded. "Whaddid I tell ya, El? Isn't she a wonder?"

"I'll go upstairs and look. It's in the cedar closet."

She climbed to the second floor and passed by Penny, who was sitting on the stairs with her notebook and pen. "Are you eavesdropping again?" Hope said good-naturedly. Penny's habit over the past year, since she had learned to read and write, was to listen in on adult conversations and take notes. Penny shrugged and closed her notebook. Hope found the dress in the back of the closet, covered in plastic, and she carried it back downstairs. On the stairs, Penny said, "You're going to give it to them for free?"

"To borrow. That's all. Don't worry. Are you worried?"

Penny had a long face and a mouth like Roy's, and whenever she was uncertain, her mouth went downwards in an unhappy way, like Roy's, and it was doing that now.

"They'll bring it back, sweetie," Hope said. "What am I to do with it? It's just sitting there, in a bag."

She continued to the kitchen. She removed the plastic and held up the dress and said, "So?"

"It's a beauty," Harlin said.

"You could try it on," she said, and she took Ella back up the stairs, past Penny, and closed her in the master bedroom. Ella came back downstairs wearing the dress, no shoes, and for a moment, when Hope saw the manner in which Ella's long dark hair fell over the bone-coloured buttons at the back of the dress, she suffered a pang of regret. She said, "It fits you. Very nice."

"Better than nice. Sexy," Harlin said and he pulled Ella onto his lap.

Hope had the strange sense that Harlin had just pulled *her* onto his lap, this being her kitchen and that being her wedding dress. Even Ella seemed uncomfortable. She stood and brushed lightly at the front of the dress and asked Hope if she was sure.

"I'm sure," she said, though she wasn't sure at all. "Don't bother cleaning it. I'll get it dry-cleaned."

Later, after Harlin and Ella were gone, Penny appeared and poured herself a glass of milk and then sat at the table and watched her mother prepare supper. Penny didn't speak— she just watched. She was empty-handed, her notebook was upstairs. Sometimes, Penny made Hope nervous with her silences and long gazes and this was one of those times. She looked at her daughter and then went back to her work and finally Penny spoke.

She said, "What will Daddy say?"

"About what?"

"The wedding dress. That you gave it away?"

"I didn't give it away. I loaned it to them. They were in need. Daddy will understand."

Penny got up and wandered into the living room. Then

the side door opened and closed and from the kitchen window Hope saw Penny in the backyard, on the swing, and Conner was aiming his pistol at her and shooting her. Penny kept swinging and Conner kept shooting.

At supper, which was roast chicken and mashed potatoes and gravy and corn from a can, she came right out and said that Harlin and his fiancée had visited and she'd given them her wedding dress. "You remember Harlin, don't you?" she asked Roy.

He looked at her and said that he did. "I thought you were saving the dress for the girls. For Judith."

"For me?" Judith asked. "I'm never getting married."

Hope wondered where such disdain for marriage came from. What did she see in her parents' world that made her talk this way? Perhaps she had been unduly influenced by Angela and Emily.

"Never say never," Hope said.

"You just did," Penny said.

"Did what?"

"Said 'never.' *Never say never.* You said it."

"It's a saying. It's meant to be ironic."

"What if they don't bring the dress back?" This was Conner. He was studying the piece of chicken on his plate, picking at it, moving it from side to side.

"Well, then, that means they needed it more than I did." She looked at her eldest daughter. "And Judith, should she get married someday, will have to get herself a new dress." She smiled, as if in cahoots with Judith, but Judith didn't smile back.

"What's 'ironic'?" Penny asked.

"Daddy will tell you," Hope said. "I'm tired." She got up and walked up the stairs and removed her clothes and climbed under the covers. She lay there with her eyes open, listening to the movements and mumblings of the family downstairs. It wasn't fair just to throw everything onto Roy's lap—he was tired too—but she wasn't able to keep her shoulders square anymore. She slept, and when she woke Roy was snoring beside her. She got up and walked to her children's rooms and found them all safe in bed and sleeping. Conner had thrown off his covers, and his left foot had tumbled off the bed and was dragging on the floor. She tucked him back in and kissed his damp forehead. He smelled of soap and talcum powder, and she realized that Roy had bathed him, or Conner had bathed himself, before bedtime. She imagined that if she should die, the children would be fine. They would eat and dress themselves and go to school and fight and come home and shampoo their hair and Roy would perhaps hire a woman to come in and wash the clothes and the floors and make meals and the woman would be young and pretty and efficient, with a flat stomach and a perfect body, and Roy, gullible and flirtatious, would fall in love with the woman and marry her and the kids would adore the new wife. Everyone might be happier if Hope weren't around. But then who would understand Conner's obstreperousness, or Judith's eccentricities, such as her desire never to marry, or Penny's dark and brooding silences, her piercing and all-knowing eye. Some strange new wife could never guess at these oddities. No, Hope would have to raise the children.

In the morning, a bright blue sky welcomed her. Roy had left for work and Judith was already at school, and when she came down to the kitchen, she saw Conner and Penny at the table eating oatmeal. There was a strange woman at the stove. Well, not so strange. It was Heidi Goosen, Roy's cousin's child, a buxom girl of twenty-two whom the children already knew from family gatherings, and whom they adored.

"Why are you here?" Hope asked.

"Oh, Auntie Hope, good morning. Roy called me early this morning and said that you weren't feeling well and could I come over and watch the children."

"I'm fine. I'm well."

"Okay." This girl with the large bosom was not to be deterred. "I'm glad to hear that. I packed Judith a lunch. She's going to Angela's house after school. Later, I'm taking Conner and Penny to the library and then out for grilled cheese sandwiches and fries."

"Really."

"Don't worry. Uncle Roy gave me money for lunch."

Conner was chanting, "Grilled cheese and fries," and spinning his spoon in his porridge.

"All right then," Hope said and she turned and walked back up the stairs and lay down. She had nothing against Heidi Goosen: she was lovely, and she was family. She wasn't the girl of Roy's dreams, that was certain. And Roy was simply trying to give Hope a break, she could see that. She heard the children leave with Heidi. She rose and went to the bathroom and ran a bath. She lay for a long time in the water, refilling it, heating it up. She shaved her legs and under her arms. She lay back and studied her belly, which from this perspective appeared not at all large. She placed her hands on her stomach and waited to see if the baby would move. There had been a few bumps over the last while. Nothing at the moment. She got out of the tub and dried herself and then walked about the house in her housecoat. In the kitchen she removed the calendar from the fridge. Put it in the garbage. She took the calendar in the dining room, the one with the photographs of Paris, and she threw that out as well. She took the clock hanging above the piano and carried it to the garage and laid it down on Roy's worktable. The grandfather's clock in the living room was too large to move, so she found a sheet and hung it over the clock face. The clock on the stove was permanent—nothing to be done with that. She taped a piece of blank paper over it. The bedroom clock and the upstairs hall clock were portable and she moved those into her shoe closet, tucked away in a box with a lid. Then she found a suitcase and packed a few things—an extra skirt and blouse, some underwear, a second bra, pantyhose, a second pair of shoes, her makeup, her hairbrush, her Bible, a few books—and she carried the suitcase down to her car. She went back inside and wrote a note to Roy. She said, "I'm going away for a little while. Maybe two days. Thank you for asking Heidi to help out. She's a godsend. My head is above water. Love, Hope."

She drove to Winnipeg and took a room at a hotel close to the train station. It was spring, the trees were greening, the earth smelled new, and the streets were busy with couples strolling arm in arm. She decided to take a walk herself and made her way down towards the river, where she watched the ducks and the geese. She decided that she would smoke, so she went into a little store and asked for cigarettes. The man behind the counter asked what kind of cigarettes did she want and she said calmly, "Just give me the most popular." The man raised an eyebrow and handed her a package of du Maurier and she paid and walked out. She sat in the bar of the hotel and ordered a glass of wine and she smoked, though she didn't inhale because it made her dizzy. A man in a grey suit and a grey hat tried to talk to her. He leaned towards her and asked if she was alone and she looked at him and said that she was waiting for her husband. He said sorry and left.

That night she wanted to call home, but she didn't. She thought Roy needed to be punished in some way, and if this was it, then so be it. He had all the pleasures, all the freedom, and now, for two days, she was going to be the one to demand certain pleasures and freedoms. She hoped the children would remember to brush their teeth before bedtime. Conner liked a warm glass of milk, and Penny liked to read till nine. This was allowed, but Roy wouldn't be aware. But the kids would make him aware, certainly. She had raised them to be clear and headstrong and forthright. Poor Judith, probably believing that her mother was gone for good—because it would be Judith who would suffer doubts and fears. She needed her mother the most, and thinking of this now, Hope felt an overwhelming love for her oldest child.

Earlier, she had unpacked her suitcase, hanging her blouse and skirt in the closet, placing her other articles in a drawer of the dresser. The room was dimly lit and the open suitcase, now empty, frightened her for some reason, as if it were the gaping mouth of a large beast. She closed it and snapped the locks. Placed the suitcase in the closet, next to her shoes. Now, at night, lying on the bed, she wondered how it was that women in books were able to travel so well and so far and to have full and confident emotional lives. Like Adela Quested, the character in the novel she was now reading, *A Passage to India*, given to her by Emily a year ago. Hope had just recently picked it up and she thought the story of Adela and her mother-in-law was so unlike her own life, so exotic and untamed and full of possibility, that this might be why she had run away from home. She needed to feel the threat of danger, and the movement of time. Time. What a horror, especially when she was at home with the children and the ticking of the clock on the kitchen wall was like a prisoner knocking on the wall of a dungeon. There were no women in plays or books or movies who spent their days bleaching sinks, ironing clothes, and holding children. Of course not. That would make for an agonizingly empty story.

In the morning she felt better. She ate breakfast in bed and then slept some more and read and in the afternoon she went shopping for a dress that would carry her through this pregnancy. She found one at the Bay, and while she was at it, she bought a fur coat that was on sale and she had it stored till the winter. She bought a two-piece bathing suit for Judith, a notebook and fountain pen for Penny, and a slingshot for Conner. For Roy she bought a pair of cufflinks and for herself a small bottle of perfume, which she imagined she would share with Roy at some future intimate moment. These purchases left her feeling hopeful and buoyed up. So buoyed up in fact that she checked out of the hotel and drove home, arriving to find the house empty of children. It was a Saturday. She phoned the dealership but Roy wasn't in his office, though the dealership would be open on a Saturday. She got in her car and drove around town looking for Roy's car, and saw it parked outside Gertrude's Inn. She found the family inside eating dinner and when Conner, who saw her first, called out, she went to them and sat and the waitress brought another plate and a setting of cutlery and she ordered steak, medium, with a baked potato. She touched Judith's head. Penny studied her and asked, "Where were you?"

"In the city, buying a few things. I have something for everyone."

"The calendars are all gone," Penny said. "But we found the clocks."

"Yes, well. We'll buy new calendars on Monday. How about that?"

She took Roy's hand and squeezed it. He let her hold his hand and seemed entirely pleased to have her back.

* * *

The following November, when Melanie was a newborn and John F. Kennedy had been dead for merely two weeks, Emily Shroeder left her husband, Paul, and moved with her daughter to Winnipeg, where they settled in a dingy apartment on Young Street. Divorce was infrequent in Eden, and no woman that Hope knew had left her husband to live on her own in a small apartment in the city. Emily, however, seemed

THE AGE OF HOPE 79

happy with her circumstances. She found work at one of the city papers, writing book reviews and covering community events, and Angela went to a nearby public school. One weekend, on a Saturday, Hope and Judith and Melanie drove into the city to visit the Shroeders. Judith held Melanie in her lap during the drive, and at some point, when Hope looked over at her eldest daughter holding the infant, she was astounded to realize that Judith was very mature for her age.

The apartment was small and crowded, a complete contrast to the spacious house Emily had left. She had walked away empty-handed and so her dishes and cutlery were a mishmash. A folding card table was used in the kitchen. "Very bohemian," Emily joked. There were unframed prints taped to the walls in the living room, bright images of nothing but paint splotches, though there was one larger poster of a dark-haired woman displaying her bosom as she lay back on a long narrow couch. Hope felt a slight thrill as she glanced at the poster. No one in Eden put pictures like this on their walls. A single fat candle burned on the hearth of an electric fireplace. Emily had created a bookshelf from planks and bricks, and Hope was drawn to the spines of the paperbacks, as if hidden there was the promise of something grand and mysterious. Emily and Angela shared a bedroom—in fact, they shared a double bed—and Hope tried to imagine sleeping with one of her children, rather than Roy. She thought that there might be something cozy and safe in that. Emily's new lifestyle both horrified Hope and made her jealous. Emily confessed that she had gone on a date the other night with a younger man named Karl from her university class. They had gone to a concert.

"The symphony?" Hope wondered.

And Emily said, "Oh, no. It was an impromptu sort of thing in a bar. A folk band, friends of Karl's."

Hope looked around helplessly. "Have you seen Paul? Do you talk?"

"We talk. He comes into town to pick up Angela, and she goes back home for weekends sometimes. Which leaves me completely free. I forgot what that feels like. You should try it sometime."

"Yeah. Okay. I'll just up and leave this one with Roy and I'll find myself a young man who plays in a folk band."

"Oh, I know. I'm the scourge and the pariah." She shrugged. "I'm happy."

"And Angela?"

"She loves her new school, though they don't work her hard enough. She's making friends."

Hope noticed that Angela had changed. The girl looked at Judith and shrugged, and the two of them stood in the kitchen with their mothers for the longest time, as if they didn't recognize each other, until Emily pushed her daughter towards the bedroom and said, "Show Judith your record albums."

They were in the bedroom now, adjacent to the kitchen, and Hope could hear them talking, or she could hear Angela doing most of the talking, and there was music playing. She felt sorry for Judith.

They ate a small lunch together, fried rice and raw carrots, and then the girls watched TV in the living room. Emily had taken up smoking, and she liked to sit in her jeans and loose top and blow smoke rings at the ceiling. Her hair was longer and she wore silver jewellery on her wrists and a beaded necklace around her neck. She leaned forward and asked if Hope would like to smoke some marijuana. "It's very relaxing," she said.

Hope made a face that was noncommittal. She was shocked, actually. This was not the Emily she knew. What was next? Road trips and dropping acid?

Emily stood and found her purse and took out a single cigarette and lit it. Her eyes closed and such a display was made of everything, the inhalation, the breath holding, the exhalation, that Hope thought of the word "exaggeration." Everything seemed to have become big and important. And this made her feel very unimportant.

"Wanna?" Emily held the cigarette out for her.

Hope shook her head. "No thanks."

"It's all right. You'll find your way."

Melanie was pushing her face against Hope's breast, looking for a drink. She had decided that this one would breastfeed, regardless of the stigma. She lifted her sweater now and unhooked her bra and offered Melanie the breast. Emily said, through the haze of smoke, that Hope was doing the right thing. "This opinion about breastfeeding being wrong, what stupidity. Good for you." She dipped her small chin and nodded, as if to affirm Hope's decision. The girls came in and Judith watched Emily smoke and Angela looked at Hope's bare breast and the baby sucking on it and said, "Ewww."

Emily laughed and said, "There's something you never had, young girl."

Hope cast about, looking for something to say. "You know how everybody is always asking, 'Where were you when you heard about JFK?' Well, I just say I know exactly where I was. Having a baby. I remember holding Melanie in the hospital, trying to nurse her, and the nurse came in and said that he was shot." She paused. The girls were pensive, as if waiting for a punch line. She felt breathless. She stumbled along, adding to her story. "And then Jackie's pink suit. Blood everywhere."

Emily put out the joint and smiled. "Karl says it's all middle-class anguish. And then this fear that it was the Communists."

"Well, what if it was?"

"Well, that's just silly," Emily said. She waved dismissively, as if there was no more to say about that.

Later, driving home, Melanie slept in the back of the car while Judith sat silently in the passenger seat and looked out at the fields and the blowing snow. Hope's heart felt heavy as she attempted small talk.

"Does Angela like her new school?"

"I guess. Her teacher's a man."

"That's fun. Has she made new friends?"

"Sure she has. Lots. On the weekends they have dance parties."

"You can have a dance party."

Judith didn't answer. Then she said, "Angela thinks that our interests have *diverged*."

"That's what she said? Hmm."

Judith turned to look at her mother and said, "Why don't *you* get a job? Like Emily."

"Well, I don't know. Emily works because she needs the money. She has to pay rent."

"Angela has a boyfriend. His name is Jarrod."

"Well, that's nice. Is she going to marry him?"

"Why do you feed the baby like that? You look like a cow." She began to cry. Little hiccups interrupted by sniffling, her face turned to the window.

Hope let her cry for a while and then reached for her hand. She held it while she drove. "Everything will be okay. Emily and Angela are just finding their way in a brand-new world."

"Our world is so square," Judith said. She wiped at her face.

"What are you talking about? What a strange word. Did Angela tell you that?"

She shrugged.

Hope was angry. "Goodness. That girl's head is swollen. She should be a better friend. You know what a friend does, Judith? A friend accepts you, no matter what. A friend doesn't fly off to greener pastures, and a friend is not ashamed to be seen with you, and she is proud of you and loves you."

Judith pulled her hand away and laid it in her lap. She didn't speak. It seemed that Hope's speech had frightened her a little. It had frightened Hope.

That winter, the three older children were in school and she was alone with Melanie, who turned out to be the calmest and least demanding child she had ever birthed. She found that she could put Melanie in a high chair with a few toys and leave her there for two hours and Melanie would happily play and coo. Hope wondered if this was a problem. She believed that a feisty child was a healthy child. She did not want her fourth child to be simple.

According to Doctor Krahn there was nothing wrong with Melanie. "The last born is often like this. Even at her age she knows her place. She's privileged. She's surrounded by older siblings who are blazing a trail for her. No, this girl is a healthy specimen. She'll probably be an Olympic athlete."

"Well, we don't want that," Hope said.

Because Melanie was so easy to cart about and because she was so charming, almost like a doll one might buy at Eaton's toy department, Hope found herself going out more. Though mornings were still difficult. She found that she just wanted to stay in bed, and sometimes she did this. Melanie, so quiet and independent, lay on her back in the crib, babbling at the mobile above her. Hope woke occasionally, her head in a dark cloud, aware that her daughter might be in danger, and then hearing Heidi downstairs with Melanie, she promptly went back to sleep. By noon the cloud had mostly dissipated and she found then the energy to bundle Melanie and put her in the car and go out for lunch or visit a friend or two in town. Sometimes they drove to Winnipeg, but Hope found the return trip increasingly difficult. She envisioned herself driving past the Eden turnoff and on into Ontario and up through Thunder Bay towards Toronto. These thoughts and feelings frightened her. She did not share them with Roy, who, having decided to buy out his father and expand the business, had enough on his plate.

She did not love Melanie as she had loved her three other children at birth. There was no joy, simply the plodding heaviness of changing diapers, giving her the breast, burping her, laying her down, picking her up, doing the laundry, giving her the breast again. She was grateful that her three older children were in school, because if she was overwhelmed by one child, what would she do with four all day?

One evening, Roy asked if she needed a holiday, or if she needed to talk to someone. She said that she was fine. Winter had been very long that year and she'd been shut in. They were sitting at the dining room table. Supper was finished. The kids were upstairs and downstairs. Conner had run outside to work on a fort in the backyard.

"Jim Martin's wife, Liz, was put in the Winkler Mental Health Centre last week."

Roy had a way of saying things, as if he didn't quite understand the subtlety of language. She wondered how he managed to run a business with thirty employees.

"Put in?" she asked. "It sounds like she's some sort of rabid animal that's been locked up."

"She went voluntarily. Jim said that one morning she woke him up and asked him to drive her to Winkler."

"Oh, so now you have *me* going crazy. I'm not going crazy. I'm fine." She wondered if Liz had seen the breakdown coming. Was it like a train on a track, far in the distance, and it just kept coming, slowly and implacably, until at some moment it arrived? How did she know to ask? She found herself envying Liz in some small way. Liz would be by herself, in a room, with no one making any demands. Hope looked down at her thighs and smoothed her hands across her skirt. She had dressed for dinner at 4 p.m. Up until that hour she had wandered about the house in her nightie, moving clothes about, lifting a dishcloth and putting it down, sitting and staring out the window. She felt better now that she was dressed and the children and Roy had been fed. She said again, "I know that if I can swim through the mornings then I'm good to go. I'm very contented right now." She sighed and stood and went to fetch Roy more coffee.

He touched her hand just as she was moving back to the kitchen and he said, "You shouldn't have to swim through any part of the day. Maybe you need to join a club, or set up a breakfast group with some friends."

"We can't both be going out to breakfast every morning with our acquaintances. Who'd get the children off to school? Who'd make lunches?"

"Heidi does that now, doesn't she?"

She was quiet. She knew Roy saw her as a complete failure. She was incapable of raising the children and taking care of them. She said, off the cuff, as if she'd just thought of it, "Do you love Melanie?"

"Why sure. What a question."

"She's different, don't you think? She just sits there."

"She's happy. You want unhappy, like Judith?"

"You don't love Judith?"

"Of course I do."

"Judith is sensitive. She broods and thinks. She's reflective."

"As a baby she just cried. I'm quite happy that Melanie doesn't cry."

Her mother took to coming over mid-morning. She walked in and picked up Melanie and kissed both cheeks and then she helped Hope get dressed and sent her off. Hope

would go directly back to her childhood home, undress, and climb into bed. She slept the days away and returned to her own place in the late afternoon to discover that the house had not burned down, that the children had returned from school, and that her mother had prepared dinner. She would sit with her mother then, at the kitchen table. This was the best time of day for her, a time when there were just a few hours of daylight left and then the children would be off to bed.

One afternoon, her mother said that Penny had come home early from school. She had a stomach ache.

"Well, she's like me that way. The worries of the world end up in her stomach."

"She might be unhappy in her classroom," her mother said. "It happens sometimes with young girls. They get caught in a triangle or they have difficulty finding their way with friends. I saw a lot of that when I was teaching grade three. Sometimes the child just needs a break. I don't mind helping out."

"Do you think so? She already spends after school cleaning the house. That's what she does. And writing in her notebook. If she stayed home, the house would vanish from cleanliness."

"She's such a sweetheart. Don't worry about her. I could teach her at my house. A bit of math, social studies, and I could read to her. Even though she's a fine reader, children like to be read to. In this way she could stop worrying."

Hope felt a kinship with her middle daughter. Poor thing, lost in a jumble of siblings. She told her mother that she would consider it. She would even talk to Penny, try to find

out what she wanted. Perhaps Penny would know what she was suffering from.

In spring, when the fields were still full of water and the lilac bush in the back was pushing out new buds, Hope travelled to St. Anne, a neighbouring French town, where she had arranged for a room at the community centre. She had put up posters announcing that a Friendship Club would be meeting at 2 p.m. every Thursday, Hope Koop presiding. She carried some board games and an article from *Reader's Digest* that she imagined might start a conversation. She also carried her Bible as something to fall back on should there be a difficult discussion or a need to go to a source.

The first day, one woman showed up. Her name was Annie and she smelled of alcohol. She was slightly younger than Hope, maybe thirty, but appeared to have lived harder. They talked about their personal lives, swapped stories about children, shared a recipe or two, and said goodbye. Hope, driving home, thought that the first meeting had been a tremendous success.

At the second meeting, three people appeared. Annie, her cousin Linda, and an older man named Frank who showed an obsessive fascination for Hope's breastfeeding. In the end, she left the room to feed Melanie, and returned with the child draped over her shoulder, patting her back, seeking the elusive burp. Frank wanted to talk about Armageddon and the end times. He took Hope's Bible and read from Revelation and went on a long rant about Richard Nixon being the anti-Christ. Linda waited impatiently for Frank to finish and then she said

that the hardest thing in life was to accept one's lot. "All this nonsense about the world coming to our doorstep and destroying life as we know it is just fearful people blowing smoke up your ass. Take control of your own life. Make smart decisions. Realize that this is it, this is all you have, this life, in this little place, on this planet, in this corner of the world." She paused and looked at Hope and for a brilliant moment Hope saw that what she was saying was absolutely true, and then the window that looked out onto that clear space slammed shut.

As she drove home later, Melanie slept on the floor, wrapped in blankets. Hope didn't intend it—in fact she would think later that there hadn't been a plan and it was almost as if someone else were driving her car, but she pulled off onto a side road and turned the ignition off, and she sat and listened to the wind blow, rocking the car slightly. The field to her right was bare, with patches of water, and she saw a path made of flowers and sunlight winding its way between the puddles. She got out of the car and left Melanie and she walked down through the ditch and out into the field. Her shoes were immediately wet but she did not notice. The temperature was near freezing, but the sun was warm and fell on her head and shoulders. She walked the golden path between the bright puddles and found, deep in the field, a bed of straw that had been laid out for her, and onto this pallet she first kneeled and then lay down. She heard high above her the cry of a bird that sounded very much like the call of a child. She sought out the bird but the light was brilliant and blinding and so she closed her eyes and thought that she might take a little nap before returning home.

2

Age of Despair

Her room had two windows, both of which looked out onto several apple trees that were, at some point during her stay in Winkler, replete with bright pink blossoms. The view and the blossoms were such a deliberate mockery of her state that she had the nurses draw the blinds closed when she was alone. Visitors, when they arrived in the first week, often opened the blinds and exclaimed, and so she felt she had to exclaim as well in order to appear to be well on her way to health and happiness. This facade, and her utter capitulation, disheartened her and she grew to dread visitors, especially the women who arrived from Eden bearing gifts of food and cards with Bible verses. Many of these visitors were distant acquaintances, women from the church or the community who knew Hope only in passing, and she knew that they had come to inspect her, to fill their own little lives with possible gossip of what a crazy woman looked like. It was important to be the first to know. After a week of this, she asked Doctor Janzen if he could bring to a halt all visitors save her own family and Emily Shroeder, who was her best friend. She also said that she hated the craft times in the afternoons. "I'm not a child and I'm not simple," she said. Her doctor said that the point of doing crafts was to take her outside of herself. But if she insisted, he would talk to the staff. "I insist," she said. And so she settled into her stay at Winkler, and she found that with time and medication and, ultimately, electric shock therapy, she was beginning to arrange her thoughts more logically, or to simply let go.

Her doctor told her that electric shock therapy would be necessary and she did not argue. Neither did Roy, though he was concerned about the side effects. Her mother visited on Sunday afternoon, the day before her first treatment. Even though her mother had come two days earlier, on this day Hope was so pleased to see her that she cried for a bit as they held hands. She thought she might be relieved that she did not have to behave herself, that she did not have to project strength and courtesy. "I'm sorry," she said.

"Oh, no," her mother said. She brushed a stray hair from Hope's brow.

"I think I should feel ashamed. But I don't. I'm just tired." She twirled a finger near her temple. "Hope Koop goes nuts."

"Your body knows when enough is enough. I'm sorry that I didn't help you more with the children. And you must stop worrying about what people think. About Roy. The children. Me. You'll drive yourself crazy." She raised her eyebrows, acknowledging her false step, and said, "Everyone is fine. The children are very happy. What an awful colour these walls are." Her mother frowned at the bright green paint. "How do they expect people to get better?"

"The doctor thinks that I will get better only if he electrocutes me." She tried to make her voice light and inconsequential.

"Well, that's one way to put it, I suppose. You were always a little extreme, Hope. Even as a child, a little burn on your finger produced intense theatrics."

"It doesn't frighten me. Not a bit. As long as the darkness goes away."

On Monday morning, the nurse who prepared her before wheeling her down the hallway to the treatment room was a stout Mennonite with a slight lisp and a Low German accent. Later, on the gurney, as the rubber clamp was being fitted into her mouth and just before she fell asleep, she reached up and tried to straighten the stout nurse's cap, which was crooked, sweet thing. When she woke, she did not recognize her room or her own hands lying on the bed. She wanted to cry out but thought that might be inappropriate. Her arms ached, and her mouth tasted of tin. Two mornings later she went for another treatment, and so it continued for two weeks.

At first there was little change in her spirits. And then, imperceptibly, her mood changed, and she found herself looking forward to seeing her children. When she had first entered the hospital, she did not know who was taking care of them, and she did not care. When she finally asked Roy, he said that there was nothing to worry about, that Heidi was living at the house and the children were thriving. "They love Heidi. They see her as a sister."

"What about Melanie. Is she eating?"

"She's taking the bottle just fine."

"Who found us?"

"A man named Hugo Bertrand, from St. Anne. He found Melanie, and then followed your tracks out into the field."

"That was very good of him." She heard the words come out of her mouth, but she did not recognize them as her own. Her tongue felt thick, and she realized that the conversation with Roy was very formal, but she could not stop herself.

Roy smiled.

"Was Melanie still sleeping?"

Roy shook his head.

"She was crying?"

"A little. She's no worse for wear."

"Poor thing. I'm worried, Roy."

"What are you worried about?"

"That I don't love her."

"You do, Hope. It's just the sadness talking."

"Do you think so? Tell me about Melanie."

"She's getting fat."

"Is she? I want to see her."

"Are you sure? And the other children?"

"Do you think I could? Do they want to see me?"

"They're always talking about you, asking. The other day Conner pretended to be you. It was rich."

"What did he say? What did he do?"

"He was flipping pancakes and wearing your apron. He told Penny to put her notebook away, that she wouldn't get any food until it went under her chair."

"He's such a card. So wild and original. What will happen to him?"

"What do you mean?"

"And Penny? She's still obsessing over her diary?"

"She's making a comic book now. About a crazy woman."

"Bring the children here, okay? I want to see them."

And so the weekly Saturday visits began. The girls sat on either side of her and watched vigilantly as she held Melanie, who, as Roy had promised, seemed no worse for wear, and in fact seemed to be doing better without a mother. Hope did not speak much, other than to ask the girls questions about school and friends. The responses were monosyllabic on Penny's part and produced, from Judith's mouth, long soliloquies on life in Eden, in grade six, where her teacher Mrs. Highbottom had declared that dinosaurs had lived millions of years ago and that the world had not been created in six days and suddenly Mrs. Highbottom had disappeared for a week—the substitute said she was ill—and then she returned and changed her story slightly, to say that it was quite possible that the six-day creation might have occurred, though she still stuck to the dinosaurs, just go and see the bones in Drumheller, and also Angela had visited her father last weekend and she'd got her period.

Penny was listening intently and writing all this down in some sort of pictograph shorthand. Judith shrugged.

"Good for her," Hope said. "She *is* young, isn't she?"

"She might skip a grade."

"Does she still have that boyfriend?"

"Oh, no. There's a new boy, Pascal."

"That's interesting. It won't last." She didn't know why she said that, or how she thought that might help the conversation, but it just slipped out, perhaps because tales of Angela were always so large and she required so much attention, dating now a boy with a French name and getting her period to boot. "I'm sorry," she said. "I don't mean to be small." And all that time, she kept glancing down at Melanie, trying to ascertain what her own feelings were, or if she had any feelings at all, and though she was pleased to find that she did not resent the child, she felt no love for her. Melanie chewed on a fist and stared back into her mother's eyes darkly, and she wondered if her child was accusing her of abandonment. She tried to lock in, to will love, but her heart was empty. She gave Melanie to Judith and said, "Here, you take her for a bit. She's heavy."

Judith held Melanie on her lap and leaned forward to tickle her under her chin. Melanie gurgled and squirmed. Punched her fat fists in the air. "Who are you? Whatcha doing?" Judith said.

Hope turned away, ashamed by her own insufficiency and amazed at the ease with which her eldest daughter accepted this child.

Conner had slipped out of the room much earlier. Roy found him playing checkers with an elderly man in the games room. When they returned Conner stood at the foot of the bed and said, "This place is pretty nice."

"Really?" She smiled bleakly.

"Okay, kids, let's go," Roy said, and he bent to kiss the top of her head. "I'll come tomorrow."

"You don't have to. I'm fine. You have so much to do."

"I'll come."

But he didn't come. Emily, wearing a bright pink raincoat, arrived instead, perhaps sent by Roy, perhaps arriving of her own volition. Hope didn't have the courage to ask. She was very pleased to see Emily, who came with books—a spy novel by John le Carré and *The Winter of Our Discontent* by John Steinbeck—and with these gifts she had included a small framed print of a Degas painting (she made a point of saying the painter's name), in which a young woman wearing a white chemise was bent over in a dark room, and behind the woman on a small table was an open suitcase beside which rested a string of pearls. Emily placed the framed print beside Hope's water glass. It would remain there for the duration of Hope's stay, though she rarely looked at it, and when she did, it was merely to glance at it and then turn away. The open suitcase held some message, she was sure, but the thought of interpreting that message frightened her.

Emily told her to get dressed—they were going to walk outside for a bit. She had received permission from the staff. And so they strolled, arm in arm, around the block, and as it was Sunday and everyone was at rest, there was very little traffic, though children played in a nearby park, their voices lifting and then falling and then dissipating, and to Hope

the sounds of children were like the cries of birds. She listened to Emily talk about her life, an existence that now
included an older man who owned a restaurant that catered
to a high-end clientele and served dishes such as trout and
mussels and beef tenderloin on skewers. She had met him
at a parent–teacher meeting at Angela's school and they
had immediately formed a bond. He was witty and intelligent and well-travelled. "He has two sons. His wife died
last year." Emily said his name, Sam, and then said that Sam
thought the apartment she lived in was deplorable. He was
looking for something more fitting. "Not that I can afford
it. But he wants to help me out." She squeezed Hope's arm.
"He's quite the catch."

Hope said, "I'm so happy for you."

"I know you are," Emily said. "You're such a good friend.
That's why I know you will soon be home again, and that you
will persevere. You're faithful. I envy that. I wish I was more
faithful."

"But you are. Look at you now, visiting me."

"Oh, I know. But I left Paul in the lurch. Just walked
away."

"Does Paul know? About Sam?"

Emily shook her head. "It would kill him."

"He must suspect something. He's not naive. And let's be
clear. I am not absolutely faithful. I left my youngest daughter in a car and walked away from her."

"That wasn't you, Hope. That was some other person
who wasn't well."

"Yeah, Crazy Hope."

"Not much more crazy than me, sweetie. I've just been lucky."

She didn't like it when Emily called her "sweetie." It made her feel trivial, like Emily was talking down to her. "Did you ever look at Angela, when she was a baby, and wonder who she was? And feel nothing for her?"

Emily took her hand and said, "No, but then I didn't have four children either. Look at me, barely able to keep up with one."

"Judith told me that Angela is a woman now."

Emily laughed. "Yes, she is 'a woman' now. And that presents us with a whole new kettle of fish. Fits of anger, raging independence, the possibility of pregnancy."

"Oh, she's only thirteen."

"Going on thirty." Emily seemed proud of this, and it was up to Hope to make sense of what she thought was a misplaced self-importance.

When they said goodbye in the lobby, holding each other for a long moment, Hope felt that she was suffocating and she did not understand why Emily's visit had pushed her into a deep despair.

That evening she prayed that the morning would arrive not too quickly, and that when it did, she would manage to swing her legs out of bed and step into the slippers near the bathroom door. This was all she asked.

* * *

When Hope was discharged from Winkler and returned home, she entered a house where she was a stranger. Small things that Heidi had implemented left Hope discombobulated. The milk was stored on the wrong side of the fridge, the towels were folded in half rather than in thirds, the kitchen floor needed waxing, and Melanie demanded Cream of Wheat before bedtime. Even though it was now summer holidays and the children's routines had changed, Heidi still appeared every morning at seven, scooping Melanie out of bed and dressing her, talking all the while. Hope, waking, heard the domestic noises around her and felt immediately inadequate. Enormous social changes had occurred during the three months she was gone. Conner's hair had grown and his bangs hung down over his eyes and his ears had disappeared and his habit was to swing his head constantly to the left in order to clear his vision. Roy had bought him a drum kit, and every day Conner descended to the basement to make noise. Judith was now wearing miniskirts and high boots and she spent an hour each morning assessing her wardrobe and tossing clothes here and there, so that when Hope passed by her doorway mid-morning she saw the maelstrom, paused, considered cleaning it up, and then kept walking. One afternoon, when Judith returned from the swimming pool and left her wet bathing suit on the bathroom floor, Hope pulled her back upstairs and told her to tidy up after herself. "This isn't a farmyard, young girl. Heidi might not care how we live, but I do."

Judith stared at her mother. "You were gone, Mom, and nobody died."

She wore a light cotton top and Hope noticed that her chest had matured. She was wearing a bra now. When had this happened?

"That's true. And I'm glad. But your mother is back."

She realized that she would have to tell Heidi she didn't need her anymore. She mentioned this to Roy one evening as they prepared for bed. "I want my house back. And my children. Heidi's been wonderful, but I can manage on my own."

"Are you sure? She's very good with the kids."

"We can arrange for her to baby-sit one night a week. Right now, the kids need their mother, and with Heidi around that isn't going to happen."

And so she tumbled back into the world that she had left. At first Melanie constantly asked after Heidi, but within a week, she seemed to have reattached herself to Hope, who managed to rise early every morning, have breakfast with Roy if he wasn't off to a golf game or a meeting, and then start the laundry and dust the furniture. She felt that she was letting everyone know who was in charge.

In early August, over a three-week period, the family went on vacation, driving down to the States, staying briefly at Detroit Lakes, and then heading southwest towards Las Vegas and California. They pulled an Airstream that Roy had acquired through a trade-in with a customer. Hope's mother joined them, and so there were seven of them crowded into the Oldsmobile. Hope was delighted to be on the road. She loved the open sky, the horses running across the grassland, the approaching mountains, and she especially loved the proximity of her family. And the lack of routine. And she loved that

Roy was nearby, that he could help with the children. She was particularly pleased that Conner could spend three weeks with his father and have a model for how to be a young man. She worried about him: that he wasn't as bright as his sisters, that he hated school, that he would lose his way. The presence of her mother also pleased her, even though she required more attention and wasn't terribly nimble as the family hiked through the Redwood Forest or wilted on the streets of Vegas. During the return trip, on an early morning after driving through the night, they descended to the plains of Montana. The children slept and Hope reached out and held Roy's hand. "It's been wonderful," she said. "I wish we could just keep travelling."

"You'll be fine, Hope. The kids are happy to have you back."

"It's just so free out here. There aren't any walls."

Roy smiled, but he didn't say anything more. He squeezed her hand. She knew that he was eager to get back to his business, his routines, and his regular breakfasts with the men. She knew that a trip like this exhausted him, that he tired of the children and her mother, and of her as well. He needed to return to the world once more and plow through it.

"I wonder what kind of man I would have been," she said.

"You're very strange sometimes, Hope."

"Yes. That's why you love me."

"Yes. And because you're a woman."

"Do you, then? Love me?"

"What a silly question."

And a voice called out from the back. It was Judith, who must have woken up and heard the last bit of their conversation. "You love her, Dad."

Hope turned and saw that Judith's eyes were closed again. Her head rested against her grandmother, who was sleeping. Conner's head was in Judith's lap. Melanie was stretched out on the hat rack, one of her arms falling across Judith's chest.

"She's talking in her sleep," Hope said. "Sweet thing."

The sun rose and the grassland, the tiny shrubs, turned from purple to orange to yellow. The sun was gigantic.

She sighed. "It makes you feel small, doesn't it? I love it."

* * *

Over the year that followed, there was a set date for Friday evenings when Roy and Hope tried to go out alone together for dinner or to a movie in Winnipeg, and on this evening Heidi took care of the children. Heidi's brother, David, who was fifteen, often joined her on those Friday evenings, and together with the Koop children, they would make pizza and play games or watch television. One Friday evening Hope and Roy returned early from dinner because Roy was tired and feeling nauseated. He went straight to bed and Hope tidied the kitchen and then went down to the basement, where the children were watching TV.

"Where's Penny?" she asked.

"Upstairs with David," Judith answered. She looked at her mother and then looked away. Heidi was holding Melanie, who was now two.

Hope climbed the stairs to the second floor and went to Penny's room and opened the door without knocking and found Penny lying on her bed without a blouse on. David had his hand on her stomach. He sat up quickly.

"Auntie Hope," he said.

"What are you doing?" Hope asked. She moved forward and pulled David to his feet and pushed him backwards. She found Penny a blouse and gave it to her and said, "Put this on." How had she not known this? Where had she been?

David was trying to explain. "She had a sore stomach, something she ate. That's all."

For a moment, because her husband was also suffering from nausea, and because Penny suffered stomach aches, Hope almost believed him, but then she shook her head and said, her voice firm, "She's eight years old, David, and a sore stomach doesn't require removing her top, and besides, Heidi could have been taking care of her."

"Mom, it's okay. It was nothing." Penny was sitting up now, blouse back on, and she seemed so calm and insistent that Hope stepped back briefly, surprised by her own panic.

"I think you should go home, David. Okay?" She motioned to the door and David left immediately.

She went to sit beside Penny, who was, as usual, impenetrable. "Mom, you always make such a big deal of everything. It was nothing. David didn't hurt me."

"I didn't say he did. Was there a possibility that he might hurt you? Did he threaten you?"

"No. Nothing."

"Have you done this before? Spent time alone in your room with him?"

She shrugged.

"Did he touch you?"

"What if he did?"

"Oh, Penny."

"He didn't hurt me." She began to cry, and Hope took her daughter in her arms and held her.

"It's not your fault," she said. "You're young. My goodness, you might have feelings for David, but he's older, and he should know better." She held Penny's face between her two hands and waited until she had finished crying. She imagined the wretched possibilities. "He didn't touch you, did he?"

Penny's eyes were large and wet. She didn't answer.

"Down there?"

Penny nodded. She didn't look away.

"With your pants on or off?"

Penny shrugged.

Perhaps she had no sense of what was right or wrong. She was far too young. It was probably presented as a game.

"Did you touch him?"

Penny nodded. "He said it was okay."

"Were you afraid?" Oh my, what a question. Of course she wasn't. And now she would be. Because her mother was making sex out to be a dirty fearful thing. "David is older, and he should be playing with older girls."

"Like Judith?"

"Well, Judith would probably say no to David."

Penny narrowed her eyes, considering this. Hope imagined that she might have felt special, and now the special feeling would be gone. Because of her.

Hope swallowed. "Did he put anything inside you?"

"No. No."

"Did he try?"

"No, Mom. Why would he? He was very nice."

"How long has he been nice?"

She shrugged. Finally looked away.

"He's played with you before?"

She nodded.

"Okay." She kissed the top of Penny's head. "You're a sweet good girl. Don't worry."

"You won't tell anyone? Daddy? Or David's parents?"

"I don't know."

"Please don't."

She paused, suddenly lost. She took Penny's hand and patted it. "Should we make some popcorn? Can your stomach handle it?"

She nodded and then asked if she could eat the popcorn in her room. She didn't want to go downstairs.

"Okay," Hope said.

In the middle of the night, unable to sleep, Hope got up and went to Penny's room. She was sound asleep, an old toy dog pinned under one arm. Hope leaned over and listened to her breathe. She stood there for a long time, then touched Penny's head and went back to bed.

She did not sleep well and by morning had deduced that Penny was suffering as the result of her evenings with David. Since September and the beginning of school, Penny had experienced phobias and often had to be picked up by 10 a.m. because she had diarrhea or was vomiting. Also, Penny had taken to cleaning the house, waxing the kitchen floor, scrubbing the bathroom, and washing bedding. Poor thing. This would all certainly be related.

On Monday, under the pretext of Penny's phobias and her upset stomach, Hope took her to see Doctor Krahn. She left Penny in the waiting room and asked to speak with Doctor Krahn privately.

"Of course, of course." He was a big man with a too-large head and Hope wasn't sure she could trust him with all of her information and so she waded in carefully, spelling out her desire for Penny to have a physical.

"As you know, she's been suffering stomach pains and I just want to cover all the bases, you know? I'd like you to do an internal."

"Has there been some trauma?"

"Not that I know of, and I don't want to seem over the top, but she worries me."

"Is she eating?"

Hope had to admit that she was eating well.

"And sleeping?"

"Yes, she is. She's doesn't talk much, not to me at least, and I was hoping you might get her to open up."

"Of course. And you, Mrs. Koop? How are you feeling?"

Hope was holding Melanie on her lap, and as Doctor Krahn asked this question he chucked Melanie softly under the chin and it felt so intimate and so strange that for a second it seemed that the doctor had touched Hope's chin. She pulled back and said that she was much better, thank you. She stood and went to fetch Penny, who was reading a book, her bare legs swinging.

When Penny re-entered the waiting room, she blew up her cheeks and rolled her eyes at her mother. Hope returned to the examination room to talk to Doctor Krahn.

"Okay," he said. "It appears that Penny is suffering from anxiety. She's worried that you will disappear again. She's worried that the world will end. She's just generally worried, which is a big burden for such a child. Do you talk to her about world events?"

"Never. Rarely. The newspaper is available and there is the news on television, but we don't make a habit of discussing what's going on in the world."

"Maybe you should. She's very aware of politics. She knew about the Bay of Pigs, about the Kennedys, Khrushchev, and she believes that there will be a nuclear war." He lifted his outsized head. "A child her age should be playing outside, with friends. She shouldn't be so aware of the problems of adults."

"Did you do an internal? Has she been damaged?"

"No, I noticed nothing untoward. She has the physical prowess and constitution of a child her age. She has not been 'damaged.' Is there something I need to know?"

Hope shook her head. She was very relieved. She kissed the top of Melanie's head and stood and thanked the doctor.

In the car, driving home, she said, "The book I loved as a child was *The Wind in the Willows*. Maybe you should try it."

"I think I'll go to school again. Every day." Penny took a deep breath, and exhaled.

Hope looked at her. She was holding Melanie on her lap. "Okay. That's fine. I'll walk you."

"I want to walk with Judith."

"That's an idea."

"I wish I were old, like Judith."

"Oh, Penny. You have lots of time to grow up. Soon we'll have to have a little talk about your body and becoming a young woman."

"Judith already told me."

"About sex?"

"Yes, Mom."

"Oh."

"Does Doctor Krahn know about David?"

"No. Of course not. Why?"

"It's none of his business."

"Well, it is if you were hurt."

Penny turned away to look out the window.

Hope was perplexed. If Judith had told Penny about sex, perhaps she had been experimenting with David. Trying things out. Hope told herself to breathe. All would be well. She just needed to be more vigilant.

That same afternoon, after Judith and Conner had come back from school, Hope left Judith in charge of the children and drove over to the Goosens' house on First Street. She was driving a Chevy Biscayne, a two-door sedan, dark green. Roy had brought it home two weeks earlier and handed her the keys and said with a smile that he had a hot rod for her. She didn't like two-doors, as it was difficult to move groceries and children in and out of the back seat. And now, sitting by the curb in front of the Goosen residence, she thought that the car itself was very conspicuous and everyone would know who she was. She was dressed in slacks and pumps and she wore a light cashmere sweater over her blouse and she had pulled her hair back in a ponytail. She wore sunglasses because she was nervous. The fact was that there had been no damage to her daughter, nothing physical, and perhaps she was simply pushing the issue because ultimately she blamed herself. And now she was about to take it out on the Goosens' fifteen-year-old boy. When Hope was a child, Hope's mother had produced a word a day that Hope was to learn and use. One of those words was "pusillanimity" and she still knew the definition: the quality or character of being pusillanimous; lack of courage; timidity. And now, remembering this word, she got out of the car and walked up to the front door and rang the doorbell.

Mrs. Goosen became more and more disdainful as she heard Hope's explanation. Perhaps it was her delivery, Hope thought later, the fact that her story went in circles and wasn't terribly clear.

"You're telling me that my David molested your daughter, Hope? Nonsense."

"Well, molested is perhaps too strong, but I found him touching Penny's bare stomach in her bedroom."

"She was naked?"

"Her top was off, yes."

"Well, don't you think she's old enough to know better? Please, Hope, you're being hysterical. This is impossible."

"No, it's true."

"And you talked to Penny."

"Yes, and she confirmed it."

"Confirmed what?"

"That she touched David. Down there. And he touched her."

"Nonsense. Girls her age make up stories. You frightened her, Hope, and she had to make something up."

"I walked in on them, Doreen. They were on her bed. This isn't just a case of two children the same age playing doctor."

"Why did it take so long for her to tell you this? And where were you all this time?"

She had feared it would come down to this. Her own sanity would be called into question. She said, "This isn't about me. I've been back from the hospital for over a year now, and really my sanity is not the concern, and the fact that your son is touching my daughter has nothing to do with my sickness. Besides, I'm not sick. If I were, I wouldn't be standing here in your house."

"Hope. Hope. Your whole family was here for a family gathering at Christmas. Ian and Roy are cousins. They sit on town council together. David works pumping the gas at Roy's business. Why are you doing this?"

"I know all those things, Doreen. Don't talk down to me. I'm doing this for Penny, who is eight years old, not fifteen. The fact is we won't be coming to your house for Christmas anymore. David is not welcome at our house from now on, and I will talk to Roy about all of this."

She turned and left, and as she walked down the sidewalk to her Biscayne, she thought that what she had just done and said was completely uncalled for and she feared that Roy would be very angry, and she imagined that Penny might be more damaged by her mother's behaviour than any kind of sexual play with a second cousin. She was a failure.

That night, in bed, she held Roy's hand and told him the whole story. She finished with the visit to the Goosen house, and Doreen's outrage, and her own shame. "I felt bad, Roy. For you. For Penny. I should have talked to you first. I'm sorry."

Roy cleared his throat and asked softly, "Doreen took no responsibility? She said that David was innocent?"

"She didn't say he was innocent. She said that Penny had some responsibility for this as well. If any of this was even true. She didn't believe me."

"So the fact is, she didn't believe Penny."

Hope hadn't thought of it in that way. "Yes," she said. "She didn't believe Penny." She waited. "What will we do? Should we give David a second chance? I feel sorry for him."

"This isn't about David. This is about Penny. We need to help her."

"She didn't seem ashamed at all. Though she did say that I shouldn't tell you."

"Why should she be ashamed, Hope?"

"I don't know. I feel so embarrassed. I feel as if I can't protect my own children."

"Nonsense. I'll speak to David tomorrow and give him his two-week notice. There are lots of other jobs in town. I'll talk to Ian and explain why David will no longer be working for me. And why David should not visit our house anymore. And we should both talk to Penny and help her understand that this is not her burden. That she should not be ashamed." He took her hand. "And you have no reason to be embarrassed."

"She's my child, Roy. I raised her."

"A child, yes. Exactly."

"I thought you would be angry with me." She squeezed his hand.

"That's an insult, Hope, to think I would want to call Penny a liar. Who do you think I am?"

"You're right. I know who you are." Though she thought, as he fell asleep and she lay there, that she didn't know him in every way. His vehemence, his clarity, had been unexpected.

She fell asleep clutching him to her, grateful that he could surprise her, yet still worried that Penny had acquired her mother's nature.

* * *

She loved Roy. When they first married, she was smitten by his kindness and his soft nature. Even now, after many years of marriage, she still loved him, though she wondered sometimes if she didn't simply admire him because he had so few flaws. He was a good boss, one of the first business-men in Eden to set up an employee pension plan. He paid overtime, incorporated an employee complaint system, held regular staff meetings and parties, and handed out Christmas bonuses. Being stingy was not the path to success—satisfied workers and customers was. Failure, of course, was always possible, and both Roy and Hope knew that failure was not looked upon favourably. When Hope became sick, there was an underlying sense, conveyed through conversations and hints, that she was perhaps not strong enough in her faith, and that both of them were in some way tainted. As if to prove it wrong, Roy threw himself with increased gusto into his business, and because of this added energy and vision, the business grew and Roy spent more and more time at the dealership and she became more and more lonely. She had her mother, but this was not like having a friend. Emily rarely came back to Eden, and Hope was too busy these days to visit her in Winnipeg. As for the women in Eden her age, they too were occupied with children and keeping house and shopping for groceries and cooking large dinners. The few times Hope had attempted to insert herself into a Ladies' Auxiliary or Wednesday evening Bible study, she had come away feeling inadequate and different. She was different. She had had a nervous breakdown, and this was perceived as "dangerous," as if it were a disease that others might catch.

And so, once a week, in the evening after dinner, when Roy went out to town council meetings or returned to the dealership, she tucked the younger children into bed, asked Judith to keep an eye on them, and went to visit Emily's ex-husband, Paul Shroeder, who spent his evenings in his woodworking shop building end tables and hutches and smaller pieces he gave to the Goodwill store. She would sit in a lawn chair that Paul provided and watch him bend towards the lathe or the drill press, and because the machines were quite loud, the conversation was often broken up, though neither seemed to mind. She loved the smell of freshly cut wood and she liked to see a piece of furniture come together, section by section.

Following the first visit, when she left with sawdust on her slacks and woodchips stuck to her sweater, Paul presented her with a pair of coveralls. The coveralls were grey and orange and slightly large for her, but she wore them in any case, rolling up the sleeves so that her thin white wrists protruded like two bare branches of a tree. When they spoke, it was at first of Paul's work, and when that subject was exhausted, she talked about the children and Roy, never divulging much, keeping it safe, and then she sat, quietly waiting. She did not know what she was waiting for, but she did not mind the silences, and she liked the manner in which Paul moved so surely about his shop, his hands picking up a tape measure, and then a chisel, and then a piece of rough oak, readying it for the planer. Sometimes he asked for her assistance in clamping two pieces of wood, and during those moments, when he was spreading the glue and telling her which end of the wood to hold, she wondered if she too could possibly build something. She asked him this, and he seemed surprised, though in the end he suggested she might want to build a breadboard, how about that?

That evening before getting to work, they had talked about Emily and Angela. Paul said that Emily had a lover now, and the way he said it indicated that he was angry and bewildered. "Did you know?" he asked.

"I did. I knew this quite a long time ago. I thought you were aware."

"Why should I be? I work, I pay the bills, I give Emily money, I help out with Angela. Nobody tells me anything."

Hope, attempting to mollify, said, "Well, Paul, nobody's stopping you from finding someone. You're young and handsome. And available." She smiled. She herself didn't find Paul particularly handsome—his face was bulbous—but he was kind and generous, though agonizingly shy.

He didn't respond, simply handed Hope her coveralls and turned away as she slipped into them, as if allowing her some privacy, even though she was pulling them over the clothes she was wearing. This amused her, his modesty. Perhaps his imagination was greater than he let on, otherwise he wouldn't be so careful with her. And at the end of the evening he did the same thing, turned away as she removed her coveralls. "Okay," she said, perhaps too lightly, "I've got my clothes on," and she laughed. He turned back to her and she saw something dark in his eyes and then he reached for her and took her jaw in his hand and he leaned forward and kissed her. It was a rough intemperate kiss, very clumsy, and she felt his teeth bang hers as he pushed his tongue into her mouth. She tried to shove him away and mumbled, "Paul, stop, don't," but he was very strong and his left hand held her right forearm, clamping it, and his breath was hot and she felt his evening whiskers against her lips and mouth. She was leaning back against the table saw and her left hand scrabbled about, seeking support. She felt the hard square of the tape measure and she gathered it up and swung and hit Paul on the side of the head. He let go of her and put a hand to his head, turning away.

"What are you doing, Paul? Why?"

"I'm sorry."

She was shaking. "That's just stupid. Did I say something? Did I ask you to kiss me? Is that why you let me come here, because you thought this was more than it was?"

He turned to face her and she saw a trickle of blood on his temple. He said, "You should be more careful, Hope. You flirt and laugh and you leave your husband once a week to spend time with me and then you talk about having your clothes on. What am I supposed to think? That you're simply naive?"

"We're friends. That's all."

He waved a hand, then turned away again. She took this to mean that she should leave, and so she slipped out of the woodshop. She drove around town, not going home quite yet, aware of her beating heart and the humiliation that floated at the edges of her confused thoughts. Perhaps she was naive, going over to another man's house in the evening, talking and laughing with him. Maybe she hadn't wanted to recognize the feelings Paul produced in her, of being appreciated. He had paid attention to her. And she had accepted the attention.

That night, after Roy came to bed, she waited until he had settled in, and then she said, "You're gone too much. I want you to be at home more in the evenings. The kids miss you. I miss you." She had showered but she imagined that the smell of sawdust still hovered in her nostrils and she wondered if Roy could smell it as well. "Everything feels topsy-turvy."

"Are you taking your pills, Hope? Are things dark?"

"No darker than usual. And I *am* taking those pills. Though I'm gaining weight, haven't you noticed?"

"Not really."

"Maybe if you were here, watching me get ready for bed, you would see that I'm fatter."

"Don't be melodramatic, Hope."

"Am I? Melodramatic? Hmm. Am I a flirt as well? When you see me talking to other men, do you think I'm a flirt?"

"I don't know. When do I see you talking to other men?"

"Oh, Roy. You're impossible." She went up on one elbow and turned towards him and saw the dark shape of his head against the pillow. He was looking at the ceiling. She knew that he hated these late-night talks. He was tired and wanted to sleep. She said, "Men find me attractive, you know."

He chuckled. "Sure they do. What's going on?"

"Nothing." She was seated on the bed now, legs crossed. "When you meet other women, at work or at meetings, or you're served by a certain waitress, do you wish you were with them instead of me?"

"Don't be silly, Hope."

"Oh, now I'm silly. Have you ever kissed another woman, Roy? Since we were married?"

"Judith, Penny, Melanie, your mother. Just on the cheeks though. Hah."

"Emily has a lover, a man with lots of money and his own restaurant."

"Is that what this is about? You want to be Emily, to have her life?"

"When I was in the hospital for three months, you must have been lonely."

"I was too busy to be lonely."

"And now? You never get lonely?"

"I don't, I'm sorry." He sighed. "Can we talk about this in the morning?"

"Sure. Go to sleep."

She sat there and did not have to wait long for Roy to fall into a deep sleep. She wondered again what she had said or done to Paul to make him act like that. Perhaps she *was* a flirt. Perhaps she did not know the strength of her own sexuality. She was thirty-five years old. The years were picking up speed, beginning to fly by. How long had it been since she bought a new bathing suit? She recalled that lovely romantic week in Hawaii with Roy. Or was it just romantic in hindsight? Was everything better when tinged with nostalgia? There was even something nostalgic about her time at Winkler. It was a shadowy corner of her life, a dark painting that had lost its darkness with time, become even a little unreal. She had come to understand that everything in life, even sadness, eventually flattened out and floated away.

In the morning Roy had a men's breakfast and had left the house by the time she rose and walked downstairs. The week following, on a Thursday evening, she opened the front door to go outside and place the garbage cans at the front of the driveway, and she found a breadboard leaning against the doorjamb. There was a little note attached that read, "To Hope. From your friend, Paul." She saw him on the streets of Eden as well. It was inevitable, the town was small and crowded. Once, she saw him walking towards her and she scuttled into a nearby shop. She felt bewilderment and shame, as if she had done something wrong, though she wouldn't have been able to say what her error had been.

* * *

As the children grew over the next five years, they became more and more foreign and at times downright intractable, and Hope longed for the time when they had been innocent and malleable. Judith, now a young woman of seventeen, brought home various boys who sometimes ended up at the dinner table, and Hope did her best to make each consecutive boy welcome, though they frightened her, with their long hair and monosyllabic grunts. For a time, she disallowed these boys entrance to Judith's bedroom, insisting that the rec room was a fine place to hang out, but inevitably Judith would end up in her bedroom, and there were times, late at night or after school was out, that Hope would stand outside her eldest daughter's closed bedroom door and listen to the music from the stereo and strain her ears for the sound of voices. She imagined that if her daughter wasn't talking, she was having sex. She arranged for Judith to see Doctor Krahn, in order to receive a prescription for the Pill. She had told Doctor Krahn that Judith suffered horribly from menstrual cramps, and it was he who had suggested the Pill. When she spoke to Judith about this, she told her daughter that she shouldn't see this as licence for licentiousness. She actually used this phrase and smiled as she spoke, hoping that Judith would appreciate the humour. She didn't.

Judith had become callous. If she was ruthless with the boys, she was even more so with her mother, whom she saw as the enemy. She had little respect for wisdom or experience. At some deep and unspoken level, Hope applauded her daughter's rebelliousness, though she would have vigorously denied it. She wondered if she was envious of Judith's freedom.

Hope, after all, was only forty. She was not dead yet. She was still beautiful. At 3 p.m. every afternoon during the school week, she changed into a blouse and skirt and rearranged her hair and put on makeup, and then she descended to the living room where she landed on a chair, bare legs up on the ottoman, and picked up a book and pretended to read. And always, though it happened only once or twice a week, she found that she was excited when Judith entered with one of her boys. And inevitably, because the boys were polite and well brought up, they called out, "Hello, Mrs. Koop," and she raised her head, as if in surprise, and she waved hello, or she asked if Darren or James or Cass or Daniel would like something to drink, perhaps some pop, and if he wanted, he could stay for supper. She rose and walked to the kitchen and stood at the edge of the linoleum, as if she had been banished from her own personal space, and she *presented* herself. Judith ignored her. And the boy, aware that Hope was extraordinary in the way that mothers of forty are to teenagers, hovered for a while and addressed her in an enthusiastic manner until Judith pulled him impatiently towards her bedroom.

She found that it was best not to be too analytical about all of this. She had brief and fleeting images of Judith's small breasts in the hands of Darren or James or Cass or Daniel, and she knew the various designs of Judith's underwear because she had helped her purchase them, but this is where her mind stopped, at the design of the underwear, and perhaps the colour. What was the point in driving yourself crazy? She asked Judith one day, as they were driving into the city, if she was, you know, active with boys.

"What are you talking about?" Judith asked.

"Are girls your age having sex?"

"You mean, am I having sex."

"Yes, I guess that's what I mean."

Judith looked at her in horror and said, "If I were, I certainly wouldn't tell you."

"Of course not. I'd be surprised if you did."

"But you thought you'd ask anyway?"

"It was hypothetical, in a way. Sort of like, 'If you were having sex, even though you probably aren't, are you aware of what you are doing?'"

"You're not making any sense, Mom. I don't want to talk about it."

And so, based on that short and absurd conversation, she assumed that Judith was sexually active.

She told Roy none of this. He was building a brand-new dealership at the edge of the highway that led out of town, and so he was too preoccupied to have thoughtful discussions about the children, though had he known that Judith might be sleeping with Darren or James or Cass or Daniel, he would be nonplussed and then he would try to foist himself upon the situation, as if it were some sort of business problem, and then, failing to get anywhere, he would throw his hands in the air and call it impossible. And then forget about it.

She understood that Roy, like all men, believed circumstances and events could be controlled. This is why men went to war, and this is why they married, and this is why they invented machines, and all of this in order to stave off a fear of failure. The failure of a marriage or a business, or the failure of a child, was a symptom of some deeper personal collapse. Hope, on the other hand, was quite capable of accepting her limitations, her insignificance—though it wasn't exactly insignificance, which implied irrelevance. She wasn't irrelevant. She just wasn't that important in the larger world, which was spinning faster. She felt helpless. True, she had her children, but Judith ignored her, and when she didn't ignore her, she treated her as invasive and disgusting. And Conner was always outside riding his dirt bike or snowmobile, or he was down in the basement tearing an engine apart. And Penny deliberately and neatly disappeared between the cracks of the house, silently sliding from room to room, always with a book in hand. And so Hope tried to focus on Melanie, who was six and had just started school, and who seemed willing to listen to her mother talk. Hope made a point of baking cookies and making tea for an after-school snack, and when Melanie arrived home, the two of them would sit at the kitchen table and talk about their days.

Melanie was a mystery, the girl who had driven her to madness, the baby she had never truly learned to love, and still there was a space between them, and Hope did not know if this was her doing or Melanie's. She was willing to take the blame. She saw how easily Melanie fit into Roy's lap in the evenings, what camaraderie there was between them, and she wondered what the trick was. How did Roy manage? He was rarely home, did not pay much attention to the children, and then suddenly he popped up, like a jack-in-the-box, and the children fell all over him, especially Melanie, who watched hockey with her father.

Hope couldn't stand hockey games. The sound drove her batty and she had to leave the room. Besides, television in any form was uninspiring. She allowed her children one hour of TV a day, and after that it was reading (no comics—who do we think we are, cavemen who require hieroglyphics?), games, playing outside, or just generally lying about and staring at the sky. She had a rule that applied to books, especially novels: if her children were reading, they didn't have to do chores. A book in the hand was of extraordinary value, which is certainly why Penny walked around the house holding an open book—her time of frantic cleaning had passed, and these days she did her best to avoid housework. Hope knew that her thinking regarding books went contrary to the general sentiment of the people of Eden. Books were seen as a waste of time. What was the point, unless you were reading for information? To lose oneself in a book was to be slightly wacky, a little greedy, and ultimately slothful. There was no value. You couldn't make money from reading a book. A book did not give you clean bathrooms and waxed floors. It did not put the garden in. You couldn't have a conversation while reading. It was arrogant and alienated others. In short, those who read

were wasteful and haughty and incapable of living in the
real world. They were dreamers.

* * *

When her mother, at the age of seventy-seven, fell and broke
her hip, Hope found herself spending afternoons at the hospital, reading to her at her request from William Blake or Robert
Frost. Poetry was her mother's first love, and with great ease
she would recite whole stanzas of, for example, Wordsworth.
The broken hip led to x-rays and the x-rays revealed inoper-
able cancer. Hope told Roy that she wanted to care for her
mother at home. "The hospital is so cold and unforgiving.
The nurses try their best, but Mother should be surrounded
by family."

And so the last months of her mother's life were spent in
the guest room on the main floor of Roy and Hope's home,
and Hope's life was changed. She couldn't just leave the house
and drive down to the grocery store, or take a day trip into
Winnipeg. And she didn't mind. The responsibility, the routine, grounded her and she found, unusually, that she looked
forward to the mornings, to feeding her mother and changing her bedding and talking softly to her. After school, the
children stuck their heads into Grandma's room to say hello.
Penny was the least squeamish of the children and would do
her homework at the desk beside Grandma's bed, pausing to
answer whispered requests for water or a bedpan.

The day came when Grandma was too ill to remain in the house and so she was moved by ambulance back to the hospital, where, within a week, she died. Hope was with her. One second her mother was breathing and then she wasn't. How easily she had slipped away. Hope touched her hands and kissed her forehead and sat and watched her. She wanted to say something but she could think of nothing profound, and besides, there was no one to hear, except Hope. Ever since her stay at the psychiatric hospital, Hope had been unable to cry, and even now, sitting with her dead mother, she found herself without tears. This did not dismay her, nor was she upset by the lack of dismay. Her mother had once told her (this was after the time, years before, when she had run away from home for a few days, leaving Roy to take care of the children) that one could run away from home, from husband, from children, from trouble, but it was impossible to run away from oneself. "You always have to take yourself with you," she said. And now, bending towards her mother, Hope wondered if in death you were finally able to run away from yourself. This might be death's gift. She knew that the thought wasn't terribly profound, but she was moved by the notion of completion and of escape.

She touched her mother's face and held her hand and said, "I miss you already, Mother." She reached for the pull switch beside her mother's bed and she tugged the cord and within a few minutes a nurse appeared. "My mother died," she told the nurse, and hearing these words, she felt their force and she closed her eyes and then opened them, only to find that her mother had not moved. The nurse bustled away and returned with the head nurse. Hope asked if her mother could lie like this, just until the children arrived. And her husband. "They would like to see her."

"Certainly, Mrs. Koop," the head nurse said, and she told the younger nurse to fetch Hope a glass of water.

She phoned Roy and told him that Mother had died. He asked immediately if she was okay, and she said, "Could you drive home and fetch the children? They will want to see her and say goodbye."

The children and Roy, when they arrived, gathered around Grandma's deathbed. Conner cried, as did Judith. Melanie was more curious than sad, and Penny coolly insisted that Grandma's teeth be put in. "Rigor mortis will set in and then it will be impossible." She went to the desk clerk and asked for permission to reinsert her grandmother's teeth. She returned and did it herself, sliding the teeth in with a slight snap.

"Ewww," Judith said, and turned away.

Roy seemed awfully pleased with Penny's bravado and smarts and squeezed her arm. "Atta girl," he said.

Penny simply shrugged.

Hope felt a tug of panic and tried to push it away. It settled in her lungs and in her back. She felt as if someone were crushing her chest. Roy looked at her and said, "Are you okay, Hope? You look pale."

She waved him away and said she was fine. "Don't worry."

She went down the hall to the bathroom and washed her face lightly and then studied herself in the mirror. She couldn't recall how many children she had, even though she had just been in the room with them. She thought maybe four, but she couldn't be sure. She called out their names—Judith, Conner, Penny—but she could not recall the fourth name. She walked slowly back to the deathbed and as she entered the room she saw Melanie, suddenly so tall and angular, like her father, and she said aloud, "Of course, Melanie."

Once again, as it had been with her father's, the funeral was simple and took place at the Holdeman church. The singing, uncomplicated and forceful and buoyant, fell onto her ears as she grasped Penny's and Judith's hands. Melanie, with her little monkey face, saw death and its arrival as a party to be attended, and she swung her bare legs and attempted to keep up with the singing. Roy's family attended the funeral. They were a remote presence, though Hope would recall later that Roy's brother, Harold, gave her a bear hug that lasted far too long. Their bodies pressed together intimately and she finally pushed Harold away, and in doing so she felt confused. Frida drove in for the funeral, as did Emily, and Hope took comfort from their presence. She felt surprisingly loved. The image of her mother on the funeral pamphlet came from years earlier, when she had been in her prime. She was leaning against a car, wearing a long skirt and high heels. Her hat was placed cockily to one side, she had a coy smile. She was beautiful. The Bible verse below her photo was from Psalm 116: "I love the Lord, because He hears my voice *and* my supplications."

She was so gentle. This was the main sentiment passed on to Hope by those who attended the funeral. A kind and gentle woman. Or as one man put it: she knew how to take care of herself. Hope understood that this was not meant to imply selfishness. Her mother had never shown selfishness. She had had a great capacity for others, perhaps because she knew how to take care of herself. Hope thought that she might learn something from this fact. It was never too late.

Several weeks after the funeral, Judith came to Hope and said that her friend Maxine was pregnant and wanted to get an abortion, except it was impossible in Winnipeg and so Maxine was planning to go to Minneapolis the following weekend, but they needed an adult to go with them.

This information was offered in one mad Judith-like gush, and Hope, who was working in the kitchen, cleaning up the Saturday lunch dishes, thought that she might have misheard. "What are you saying, Judith?"

"She's pregnant," Judith whispered.

"Maxine?"

"Yes."

"Who's the father?"

"It doesn't matter, Mom. She doesn't want the baby."

"It matters."

"If you don't want to help, forget it." And Judith turned to walk away.

"Hold on. Did I say that? That I don't want to help? I'm just trying to understand the facts."

"There are two facts, Mom. She's pregnant. She's going to have an abortion."

"Does her mother know?"

"Are you crazy? Why do you think I'm talking to you? I'm asking for your help."

Hope saw with absolute clarity what was happening, and she felt both very pleased to be trusted in this way and at the same time used. "Why me?"

"Who else, Mom? Every other person in this town would go nuts. They're all narrow-minded hypocrites."

"You don't have to use that language. Was this your idea?"

"What?"

"To talk to me."

Judith shrugged.

Hope experienced a shiver of pleasure that she could be trusted in this way. What was wrong with her? Perhaps the death of her mother, and the vacancy inside of her, had affected her thinking.

At that point Penny walked into the kitchen and stood, inspecting them. She was wearing hot pants and tall black vinyl boots. Her legs were so spindly and she was so awkward that Hope didn't have the heart to tell her that she looked like a daddy longlegs. She felt sorry for her. She lacked the flair and good looks of her sisters.

"This is private," Judith said. "Get lost."

"What's it about?" Penny sat down on a stool by the kitchen counter. Her knees were very sharp.

Hope too wished that Penny would disappear, and wishing this made her feel guilty. "Where did you get that outfit?"

"From Judith."

"That was yours?" Hope asked Judith.

"Yeah, and listen, Penny, if you don't leave, I'll take it back." She went to her sister and pulled her from the stool and gave her a push. Penny stumbled backwards on the high boots.

She straightened up. "Is it about sex?"

"Go away."

"Judith. We'll talk later. Okay? Give me time to think."

"But you don't know the facts. You'll jump to conclusions and make the wrong decision." Judith was now on the verge of wailing.

"Later."

And so, later that night, in the quiet of Judith's bedroom, she sat on the edge of her daughter's bed and said, "You're asking me to be complicit in something that is much too big. It's too big for Maxine, too big for you, and certainly beyond my responsibility. Maxine has to talk to her mother."

Judith shook her head. "It's going to happen. It'll take place in some dirty backroom where it's dangerous, or it can be safe. And you can help make it safe. You don't know the trouble she's gone to to find this place."

"What place? Are you sure it's safe?"

"No, I'm not sure. I'm not sure about anything, Mom."

"Has she talked to someone? To a counsellor?"

No response. Judith's face was resolute. Her hair was loose and long and fell to her shoulders and at that moment Hope saw the virtue and beauty and youth of a girl who believed she understood the world. She was suddenly and immensely grateful that it was Maxine and not Judith who was in trouble. A year earlier, in the middle of winter, Hope had attended the funeral of a sixteen-year-old girl who had been killed when hit by a car on Main Street. Haley Geddert. Hope had been weary from sadness and buoyed by the ecstasy of understanding that she had been spared such grief. She felt that way now. She said, "What do you need of me?"

Judith straightened, sensing victory. "Maxine needs a guardian, someone to sign the permission. She's seventeen."

"She understands the seriousness of this? The repercussions?"

"Mom, she understands everything. Especially the *repercussions* of having the baby."

"Oh, Judith, I don't know." Though she did know. She knew exactly what she would do, and it distressed her.

What amazed her, when the weekend was over, was how easily everything had been done, and she thought that in itself was just wrong. They drove, the three of them, to Minneapolis late Friday afternoon, arriving after dark, and they took a hotel room near the clinic. Everyone, Maxine's parents included, had been informed that this was a shopping trip. A weekend in the States. Penny had wanted to come as well, and had cried and thrown a tantrum when she was told that she wouldn't be allowed. Hope had considered telling Roy but realized that he would put a halt to the "adventure," and knowing this, she experienced guilt at her duplicity. She had never lied to Roy before, or deceived him. Maxine was the daughter of the local bank manager, the same man who had signed an enormous loan to Roy for the development of the new dealership. Hope saw herself as a confirmed criminal. Someone would have to pay.

Maxine was a short girl with curly dark hair and a round face and black pennies for eyes who talked non-stop as if she feared silence and deeper thoughts. Hope, as the chauffeur, had tried to talk about the abortion during the drive, but Judith had changed the topic and Maxine had been far too perky. She was impervious. That night they had pizza delivered and ate in front of the television. At some point, Hope turned off the TV and stood facing the girls. She announced that she had something to say and would say it once, and after that she would say no more. "Maxine, you can still choose not to have the abortion. Tomorrow, we can go shopping, buy some clothes, go out for a nice meal, and drive back home. You can have the baby, and if you still don't want to keep it, you can give it up for adoption. I know of several couples who would love a healthy baby. I worry that you girls will see the world as your candy store, where problems can be easily erased with a push of a button. Oops, there we go. Well, the world doesn't work that way. We all have souls."

It was a sloppy, sentimental speech and as the clichés spilled forth she cringed. In any case, her sentiments had no effect. The decision had been made, though Maxine now tried to comfort her.

"It's okay, Mrs. Koop. Everything's cool."

"Don't you think the father should know? Who is the father, Maxine?"

"You don't want to know, Mrs. Koop. Anyways, I told him, and he's all for it."

"For what?"

"This." She circled the room with her hand, taking in the small space and the larger world outside.

"The abortion?"

"Yeah. He thought it was for the best."

"Is he paying for it?"

Maxine laughed. "As if."

"Who is?"

"I have some money put aside for university. I'm using that."

It came out, without much cajoling, that the father was a married man of four, a stalwart community man, a church-goer, someone Roy had breakfast with every Saturday morning. Al Olfert. "But you can't tell," Maxine cried.

"Oh my," Hope said. She was amazed. "Lola, his daughter, isn't she your age?"

Judith rolled her eyes.

Hope was not naive. She knew that married men and women slept around and manoeuvred themselves into and out of difficult circumstances, and she knew that it was the manoeuvring itself that provided the thrill. "How did you manage this?" This was not exactly the question she wanted to ask. She really wanted to know where they had met, how Maxine had come to say, "Yes, Al, go ahead and put your penis inside me," how often this had happened, if Maxine loved him, if Al was willing to love Maxine, and why Al hadn't offered to pay for the abortion, stingy man. She felt sad for Al's wife. She said, "He needs to take responsibility."

Maxine lifted her eyebrows. "He ain't going to marry me." She laughed. "Nor me him. I have plans to travel, Mrs. Koop. I'm going to school."

"Let it be, Mom," Judith said. "Lola would go nuts."

"Lola should know what kind of a man her father is. All the children should know. Mrs. Olfert should know."

"Actually, he's kind of sweet. Very funny." This was Maxine speaking.

"Bah," Hope said, washing her hands of the girl's ignorance.

That night, she slept with Judith, and in hindsight she would think that the hours she lay beside her beautiful seventeen-year-old daughter, who slept in a T-shirt and underwear, were the trip's pinnacle of pleasure. How docile, how elastic the girl was while asleep. Hope woke early and studied Judith's face, slack and untroubled, strands of hair falling down over her cheek. One of Judith's legs, long and lean, had come to be thrown across Hope's own knee, and Hope lay there, barely breathing, waiting, waiting, waiting.

The clinic turned out to be a small two-storey house that had no sign on the front. Hope and Maxine were led through a kitchen to a room that resembled a hospital operating room, like the ones Hope had given birth in. She was dry-mouthed and worried, imagining with each step that she would be caught. She wanted to ask Maxine how she had ever managed to find this place, but then a nurse appeared and spoke to her as if she were the mother, and she went along with the charade and signed the consent forms. Maxine had given her the money earlier, to make it look as if she were paying, and she pulled out the envelope and thrust it at the nurse, who took it willingly. This surprised her. The whole scene smelled illicit. She left with Judith and they went for breakfast, returning two hours later to pick up Maxine, who was groggy and pale. They put her to bed in the hotel, and Judith stayed with her while Hope drove around the city aimlessly, imagining herself as a criminal. By the time they arrived home Sunday evening, Maxine was chipper, feeling quite well, and able to walk up the driveway to her parents' house and disappear inside. For two weeks, Hope waited for a phone call, for the world to crash down around her head, but it never happened. She saw Maxine one afternoon in the kitchen, eating grilled cheese with Judith, and Maxine called out, "Hello, Mrs. Koop," and for a moment Hope wondered if the whole trip had been dreamed. Was she the only person in the world who suffered dread?

Two weeks later she drove across the river and up Highway 75 and then west towards Winkler, where she checked herself in and confessed to her psychiatrist that she was an agent of death. She carried in her head a line of poetry: "There's Grief of Want / and Grief of Cold,— / A sort they call 'Despair.'" She thought that this might have come from her mother. Or perhaps Emily, because the words were cryptic and dark.

She stayed a month at Winkler, had one treatment of electric shock therapy, told her psychiatrist everything about herself—her actions, her thoughts, her fears—worked with him assiduously to find a balance regarding her medication, and returned to Eden only to find that the children were indifferent to her homecoming, as if they suspected that she might leave once again, without warning. At the age of forty-one, a stranger in her own home.

3

Age of Profit

Roy was now making a lot of money. The dealership, with its new location, was flourishing. And so, feeling flush and hopeful, Roy suggested that the family look for a cottage. Eventually, they found one on nearby Falcon Lake, close to the Ontario border, where many residents from Eden already had cottages and summer homes. A motorboat was acquired, and then a sailboat, a sixteen-foot catamaran that Hope attempted to learn to operate one summer and then gave up on in frustration. She preferred to sit on the dock and drink white wine and read while the children played around her. She had discovered John Fowles and Joan Didion. Both of these writers took her to places far from her life in Eden. In 1971, Judith graduated from high school and moved to the city to attend university. She had reattached herself to Angela Shroeder, with whom she would share an apartment. And Hope still saw Emily, who had dumped the restaurateur three years earlier, after, in her words, a glut of fine food and great sex. "The problem was he had no interest in monogamy," Emily explained. "I prefer a man whose wiener stays at home. If you get my drift."

Emily's vulgarity was refreshing. Hope wondered how she had managed to live in Eden all these years and survive the orderly discussions about linen tablecloths, the latest recipe for marshmallow salad, knitting, or trips south to Fargo. With Emily there might be some gossip, but within a few minutes the talk veered towards the conflict in Vietnam, sexual politics, psychoanalysis, and then, by the time Emily was finishing her third gin and tonic, to confessions and intimacies that made Hope feel she was part of a very small sisterhood.

Once a week during the winter months, they had lunch in the city. Hope motored there in her Caprice, Emily chose the restaurant, and Hope paid the bill because Emily had been running short in the last while. "The wolves are at the door," she said, laughing, though Hope knew it was no laughing matter. Emily was working part time at a community paper, going to school, and putting aside some money for Angela, who wanted to study theatre in Toronto the following year. During the summer, on the weekends when Hope was at the cottage, Emily would often drive out and spend two nights, and to Hope these were periods of high expectation, stimulation, and intelligent conversation. Emily was studying psychology, in particular the work of R.D. Laing, and on Friday evenings, at the lake, they sat in the screened-in porch and Emily talked to her about this brilliant man who, she said, believed that madness was the result of background more than an individual psychosis.

"What about me?" Hope asked, confused. "My mother was to blame for my sickness?"

"Families are connected. You don't live alone, Hope. Or maybe it's Eden. The place has locked you up and your mind is revolting."

Hope thought this was presumptuous. What did Emily know about the grey curtain of despair? She said, "I don't think it benefits anyone to point fingers or lay blame."

"But you do blame yourself. You've said so."

"Oh, I don't know. I was probably just shooting off my mouth. Or having a bad day. Let's not talk about the past. Not on such a beautiful evening."

Hope had finally learned to live in the present. Often, when she found herself in a space of tremendous comfort, usually out in nature, or when her children were all safe around her and on the verge of going to bed, she forced herself to take stock. Here you are, Hope, she told herself. What a beautiful moment. You may never again be here, at this spot, enjoying the calm. This habit of hers, to acknowledge the immediate and elusive joy of the present, kept her sane.

One Friday evening at the cottage, they were alone. Roy was planning on driving out from Eden on Saturday morning, and Conner had taken his sisters out in the motorboat across the lake to the marina. Emily and Hope sat on the dock, surrounded by mosquito coils. The light was dusty. A slight breeze was coming in off the lake. The neighbours to the east were out on their dock and were playing Bob Dylan on a small radio. Emily lit a cigarette and pointed it at Hope and said that Sam had been a great lover. "He did things that

Paul wouldn't have dreamed of. Went down on me, French kissed, just generally worshipped my body."

Hope was a little irritated. Emily was a stout woman, less lean than Hope, and with larger breasts. Hope was not generally given to comparing her own body to other women's. She accepted the variations of the female body and thought that she might be lucky in some ways and less lucky in others. Her breasts, for example, were fairly small, though Roy claimed to like them. Not that this mattered. Clearly, Emily had had too much to drink. The talk about Sam "going down" on her was fine—this was Emily—but it was the line that followed, about the French kiss, that set her on edge.

She didn't like to talk about her sex life with Roy. She had done this once before with Emily, years earlier, and afterwards she felt that she had betrayed Roy. But now here was Emily, with her thick ankles crossed and her red nails winking, extolling the prowess of a man she no longer slept with and claiming that her ex-husband, Paul, had had no interest in kissing, and all of this was too much and Hope blurted out, "Paul kissed me. He used his tongue."

At first Emily seemed not to hear. She leaned forward and put out the cigarette on the dock. Hope saw the crease of her breasts, heard the creak of the chair. She sat back. "What did you just say?"

"He kissed me." She had lost her courage and decided to be less specific.

"Paul did."

"Yes."

Emily was quiet for a moment. Then she said, "When was this?"

"Oh, you had been gone a number of years. I used to spend time with Paul in his woodshop, visiting, and one evening he tried to kiss me."

"Did you ask him to?"

"Of course not. I'm not attracted to him."

"Really? He's quite handsome in his way."

"I don't think so."

"Really?"

"Oh, don't be hurt, Em. You left him, didn't you?"

"But I still found him attractive. You must have done something to provoke him."

Hope laughed. She shouldn't have, she knew that, but the conversation had turned absurd and she felt the need to laugh. "Yeah," she said, "I was wearing overalls. Very attractive."

"Why were you wearing overalls?"

"It was dusty. To protect my clothes. Paul gave them to me."

Emily was unusually silent. She lit another cigarette and exhaled into the dusk.

Hope realized that the two of them were on the verge of an argument, something rare in their relationship. Always, she acquiesced to Emily, allowed her the upper hand, permitted her to be smarter, better read, more worldly, and now suddenly she had turned the tables and Emily was fumbling.

Hope said, "It was nothing. I pushed him away and told him to stop. I don't even know why I told you this."

"You had your reasons. Even if you don't know them. The subconscious, you know." She smiled briefly, but it wasn't a pleasant smile. "You know, Hope, your problem is that you let the world fall all over you. You're passive. You could choose to act, but you don't. You just sit there."

"That's just mean, Em. And it's not true. You're upset and you've had too much to drink and you should stop talking."

"I don't care, you know. You could sleep with Paul, for all I care."

"I don't want to sleep with Paul. What are you talking about? One time he tried to kiss me, and I said no."

"That's what I mean. You tell the story as if you weren't involved, as if Paul attacked you and you were just this inanimate object who happened to be in the way. You must have had conversations with him, moved in a certain way, perhaps even flirted."

"I didn't."

"How would you know?"

Across the lake a boat appeared, speeding towards them. The kids were returning. She was relieved. She stood and moved to the end of the dock as the boat slowed and stopped. Penny clambered out holding the rope. Her long legs, the green-and-white striped bikini. Judith and Melanie wore bikinis as well, even though Hope thought that Melanie was far too young. There was something so beautiful and healthy about them that Hope wanted to cry out, "Stop. Enjoy." When she turned, she saw Emily walking unsteadily up to the cottage with her drink, a towel tied around her thick waist. Hope sat on the dock with the children, who talked about teachers, specifically the phys. ed. teacher, Mr. Gattling, whom the students had named the Gun.

"What a creep," Judith said. "He stood over the girls when we did sit-ups. Looked down our tops."

"He still does," Penny said. "He was terribly mean to you, Conner."

"What do you mean? What did he do, Conner?" Hope asked.

Conner shrugged. He hated school and only did well in shop class. He never talked about what went on in school. Hope recalled one time, at a parent–teacher meeting, when she had challenged the math teacher, Mr. Brown. "Catering to the smart kids isn't teaching," she had said. "That's just lazy."

"It's your boy who is lazy, Mrs. Koop. And dull. He'd be better off working in the salt mines."

Only later, back home, had she come up with a good response—something to do with Mr. Brown's sagging lips, and how only a bully would feel good about picking on someone younger and smaller. But she was always too late and too slow with her responses. Now, as she watched Conner, she saw a healthy tanned boy who had an easy and forgiving smile. She felt a twinge of guilt and thought that Conner was like her. He let the world fall over him. He was passive.

Melanie went over and sat down beside Conner and laid her head on his shoulder. He patted her head. Eventually, the mosquitoes became too much, and they all ran for the screened-in porch of the cottage.

That night she lay in bed listening to the children in the main room, and at some point she fell asleep and woke much later and heard Conner and Judith down by the dock. She smelled cigarette smoke, though it was pungent, sharp, and only in the morning did she think that her two oldest children might have been smoking marijuana, but by then they were deep in their beds, sleeping the morning away, and at some basic level she was happy not to have to confront them. At night, unable to sleep, she had thought about her life and had created two lists. The headings for the lists were *Acting* and *Sitting There*. Under *Acting* she put marriage, having babies, Maxine's abortion, Penny's molestation, making love to Roy, baking, meeting Emily once a week, teaching Sunday school (she had taught for one year, when Judith was two, but hadn't really liked it), Harlin and the wedding dress (he had washed it in a machine and returned it two sizes smaller—she had given it to Goodwill), caring for her mother when she was sick, and finally, walking out into the field. She hesitated to include the last one but thought that it had been a decision of sorts, though it might just as easily fall under the heading *Sitting There*. And when she began to create the second list, *Sitting There*, she realized that everything in the first list could be switched over to the second. Choosing to do something resembled so closely Emily's notion of "letting the world fall all over you" that Hope became confused. In the end, the lists that she created in her head became a massive jumble of words that meant very little, in fact the whole notion of *choice* had been called into question. Exhausted by her thoughts, she fell asleep.

Roy appeared early in the morning, around 7 a.m., smelling of the interior of his brand-new Oldsmobile. He crawled into bed and quietly made love to her and then talked to her of work and how many units had been sold that week and his golf game the evening before.

She waited until he was finished talking and then said, "Emily and I fought last night. She finds me passive."

She knew Roy didn't know what to make of Emily. He put up with her only because she was Hope's best friend. Emily called herself a feminist, especially making this point in front of Roy, and this annoyed him.

"Am I?" she asked.

"Don't listen to her," Roy said. "She's an unhappy woman."

He kissed her neck. Her ear. And then he made love to her again. As she closed her eyes the second time she was not unhappy, but she was wondering if this was what Emily meant by the world falling all over you. It wasn't so bad, was it? At least she had someone who wanted her.

Mid-morning she fried bacon and made pancakes with blueberry sauce and she fed the children as they appeared, one by one. Roy left to play golf. Penny joined him. Emily eventually walked into the kitchen and sat down at the table. Hope poured her coffee and made her three pancakes. Emily ate silently and read the Saturday paper. Hope changed into her bathing suit and sat on the dock and read, and this is where Emily found her later, around lunch. Emily stood in her clothes on the dock and she said that she was going back to the city. She had things to do.

"Okay," Hope said. "Drive carefully."

"I was a little cruel last night," Emily said. She grimaced. "Too much to drink."

"That happens."

"I'm sorry."

Hope lifted her head. She was wearing sunglasses and her legs were crossed and her right foot moved up and down. "I forgive you," she said.

"It's just that I want the best for you, Hope. You're special, and I think you should know that, and sometimes I wonder if you do know that."

"I know that, Em. But thanks anyway. Drive carefully."

After Emily had gone, Hope closed her eyes and felt the sun warm her face and chest and thighs. Melanie, the child she had learned to love, came down to the dock carrying a small bag that held nail polish and clippers and an emery board. She sat cross-legged at Hope's feet.

"Would you like the full pedicure today, miss?" she asked.

"That would be perfect. Thank you."

* * *

Hope and Roy had never been diligent about taking photographs, and though there were a few family photos, black and white, from the sixties, and the odd photo of a child at play (one of Judith on horseback, wearing tall riding boots, her hair pulled into a ponytail), there had been little record keeping. Nor did Hope keep a diary, though Emily always urged her to. And so the past was like a vacant lot of the mind, a place where one might scrabble about looking for something of value, a remembrance of perhaps the trip to Disneyland or the family vacation in Portland, or of Christmas 1966. As the children grew—they now ranged from nineteen down to nine—she realized that if she did not begin to record the precious moments in their lives, she would eventually reach old age and have nothing to stir her memories. She decided to buy a camera, and purchased a Kodak Motormatic from a shop on Portage Avenue in Winnipeg. She was immediately baffled, what with all the bells and whistles, the depth of field, the flash, the shutter speed, the light meter, et cetera, et cetera. Roy, who should have been mechanically inclined, was even more stumped, or perhaps he just feigned uselessness because he didn't want the responsibility.

For a month after she had discovered the simplest manner of taking the most basic photos, she charged about the house snapping pictures of the children, who ultimately became impatient with the intrusions. The first roll of film was a dud because she had installed it incorrectly. The film never did advance. The second roll of thirty-six images, 100 ASA, turned out to be mostly blurry, though there was a lovely clear shot of Penny and Melanie standing by the front door, on their way to school. Penny looked distracted and impatient and Melanie was grinning madly. It turned out that Conner had taken that shot. Recognizing Conner's ability, Hope handed him the camera and several rolls of film and asked him to be in charge. Over the next month, fourteen rolls of film were used up and then stored in the fridge and at some point Hope carried them down to the drugstore to be developed. She picked up the photos a week later and went through them, only to discover that most of them were of Conner's friends and of various motorcycles standing in the street, or of cars, sometimes a grill, other times a dashboard showing a tachometer. There was a photo of Conner smoking, standing with his arm around a very beautiful girl whom Hope didn't recognize. She was disconcerted by this beautiful girl who was leaning so coyly against her son. She also didn't understand why he needed to smoke, though she didn't have the strength to confront him. There wasn't one photo of the family. Disheartened, she retrieved the camera and gave it to Judith, who was leaving for Europe.

After only a year of university, Judith had convinced her father that she would be getting a fuller education if she travelled in Europe. "I'd learn seven languages, be surrounded by real art rather than just looking at pictures of the *Mona Lisa*, meet Italians and Spaniards and French, eat fresh olives." The list went on and on and Hope marvelled at Judith's loquacity and Roy's gullibility. He agreed to one year of travel. She would be required to write a letter once a week, and to live for a time in one city and take a language course, preferably German, though French would be fine as well. The whole family drove her to the airport in Winnipeg. Judith was embarrassed by all the to-do, but she dutifully hugged everyone, and when it was Hope's turn to hold her eldest daughter, Judith whispered in her ear, "I'm so happy." She flew from Winnipeg to Toronto and then over to Amsterdam. They did not hear from her for three weeks and then a letter arrived, scratched-out words on thin blue paper that offered little solace to Hope, who read it twice while sitting at the dining room table.

On my first day, my first night actually, I couldn't sleep because of jet lag and I wandered the streets. There's a red light district where women sit in the windows, some on pillows, some on swings, and you can just hire them. It's all legal. Very bizarre. The bars and coffee shops are open very late and everyone is so friendly and most people speak perfect English, better than me. I met Rolf, a Dutch boy, who's very sweet. We hitchhiked to Paris together and then went to Salonika and we're planning to go to Crete next week. Or maybe to Venice. Don't worry Mom, everyone hitchhikes here. It's like the poor person's train, and very safe. I'm having so much fun. Tell Dad that I plan to go back to Paris to study at the Alliance Française. Though Rolf says I could live with his family and study Dutch, which is very close to German and I already know a few words. We met Marika, who's Swedish, and she's travelling with us for a while. That's how it works. Everything's cool, people come and go. I feel so stupid because everyone speaks at least three languages brilliantly. Though both Marika and Rolf like the way I think. Isn't that funny? The way I think? I'm not even sure what that means. You can send a letter to the American Express office in Athens. I'll be there next week for a few days. Or the Express office in Paris, where I'll be next month. I think, anyway. I'm so happy and love you all so much. Hugs and kisses to Penny and Conner and Melanie. Mom, you would love the small cobblestone streets of Amsterdam, and the bicycles everywhere. It's so gorgeous and romantic. I'm taking lots of photos and everyone says I have an eye for it.

All my love, Judith

Hope was pleased. Judith, the daughter who had so grudgingly offered love, was now dispensing all of it to her mother. She thought that she would indeed like the cobblestone streets and the bicycles. She had always had a hankering to see Anne Frank's house as well. Judith had made no mention of whether she had seen it. But then there was so much left out of this letter. What was she eating? Was she warm enough? Where did she sleep? With whom did she sleep? Rolf? Hope thought that this was entirely possible. Not because Judith was loose, but because this was the nature of the world in 1972. Hope, at the age of nineteen, had been studying nursing and had kissed only one boy, Jimmy Kaas, and the extent of her travelling had been the forty miles from Eden to Winnipeg. What wisdom did she have to offer to anyone?

When Emily heard that Judith was heading off to Europe, she had said that Hope should read *The Drifters,* a story about boys and girls Judith's age who travel through Europe in the late sixties. Hope ordered it through Book of the Month Club. It was eight hundred pages and she did immediately what she did with all big books. She cut it into three sections so as to make it more manageable and to save her wrists. A heavy book was hard on the joints, and in bed the weight lay on her chest. The problem with cutting the book up was that sometimes she misplaced the second or third section and so had to hunt through the house, trying to remember where the rest of the novel was stored. When she began to read *The Drifters* she immediately wondered if Emily was trying to poison her with dark and dangerous and desperate thoughts. Perhaps Emily knew something that she didn't. And then Judith's letter arrived and all she could think was that Judith had become one of the characters in *The Drifters*.

That night, Roy read the letter in bed. Hope kept glancing at him, anticipating his response. But he surprised her. He folded the letter, put it on the bedside table, removed his glasses, and said, "Well, she seems to be having a good time."

"You think so? Aren't you worried about the aimlessness and the drugs and the sex?" she asked.

"Did we read the same letter, Hope?"

"Well, the general picture of her activities, what she talks about. Prostitution, hitchhiking with a Dutch boy, maybe I'll go to Salonika, or perhaps Crete. All of that sounds aimless to me. She moved so fast through all those countries." She picked up the section of the book she had been reading. It was the middle section. The front few pages hung loose, and she tore those off and discarded them. "Listen, look, I'm in the middle of this novel and this is Judith's life as she's living it now." She flipped to a page and read a section where the young people are in Torremolinos, in the house of a rich man who organizes orgies. When she finished reading, she laid the book down, sighed, and looked over at Roy, who was sound asleep.

She wrote Judith regularly, sending the letters to American Express offices in various cities throughout Europe, often uncertain if she received them or not, though there would arrive the occasional letter in which Judith made reference to something Hope had written in one of her letters from Canada, and this was a relief—at least some of the mail was being picked up.

And then one day Roy came home late, sat down at the dinner table, unfolded his napkin over his lap, and announced that the dealership had won a trip to Barbados. "We'll be taking a little holiday," he said, looking at Hope. Melanie was overjoyed until she learned that only her parents would be going. "It's an adult trip," Roy said. "Sorry, sweetie."

Hope disliked leaving the children and worried that something might happen to Judith while they were gone. How would they be contacted? On the other hand, winter had been long that year, drawn out and cold, and as she shopped for a new bathing suit in Winnipeg, and a few lighter tops, and some shorts and several pairs of sandals, she found herself stirred by some sort of excitement, the anticipation of the exotic. Why should her children have all the fun?

Barbados turned out to be very poor, and during the drive from the airport to the resort, she observed the shanties and the barely clothed children playing in the streets and she wondered why the children weren't in school. She was depressed by the poverty, and became even more despairing upon arriving at the resort, where numerous swimming pools glistened like jewels and palm trees lined the twisting walking paths that led to their private villa. She saw herself eating up an overly large portion of the world. What gave her the right to this luxury and the wonderful food she would be eating, when that boy in torn shorts sitting by the shantytown got only gruel? Whose self was bigger? Who was more important? She sat on the edge of the king-size bed and told Roy that she felt sick.

"Did you see all those poor people? And look at us."

"We provide an income for those people. The economy is based on tourism, Hope. They need our money."

"That's just pure rationalization, Roy. A simplistic argument."

"Well, here then." Roy took out his wallet and removed the cash and laid it on the bed beside her. "Start with the chambermaids, and then head over to the restaurant and the waiters, and don't forget the bellhop, and when you're done here, head out into the streets and make sure everyone gets an equal share. Go on then."

"Oh, don't be ridiculous." She looked down at the cash as if it were poisonous. "You know that won't help. It's just that I feel so helpless."

"Well, get over it, Hope. Let's go for a swim."

She put on her black one-piece and tied her hair back with a pink scarf and she carried a wicker basket that held her books and suntan lotion and hat and sunglasses. She was aware of being noticed and took pleasure in the fact that she was still beautiful. She found a spot under an umbrella and ordered a margarita. Then another. Roy was beside her, laid out on his chair. He was wearing red trunks and black socks with brown shoes. She rarely saw him so naked in public and for a brief moment she suffered shame. His legs were alabaster. And those socks. The heat, even though she was under an umbrella, was astoundingly oppressive, and after her second drink was done, she rose and stepped carefully down into the pool, where she submerged herself up to her neck. She had had her hair done that morning, and she didn't want to ruin it for the evening dinner, at which the other couples from across North America who had also been invited on this trip would be meeting for the first time. The warm water of the pool and the alcohol had a soothing effect on her, and by the time she had recovered her spot beside Roy, she had come to accept her place in the world. To complain, something Roy thought she did too much of, was to be ungrateful, and she had made a decision to make the best of things, to be obliging.

There were nine other couples, owners of various dealerships throughout the States and Canada, who met for dinner that night and Hope sat beside Anita Stark, from Arizona, whose husband, Will, owned four dealerships in Phoenix. Anita was very gregarious. She kept touching Hope's right arm throughout the meal and she made Hope feel quite at ease. Anita was fit and she wore a tight top and a short skirt. She was a mother of three children very close in age to Hope's, and so they talked of children. Her eldest daughter was a classical pianist who was aiming for Juilliard. Anita said this so matter-of-factly that Hope became slightly despondent and replied that her eldest daughter was running with the bulls in Pamplona and hanging out with a Dutch teenager smoking hashish. "So you see," she said, and she let her sentence dangle, and Anita tilted her head, as if waiting for a profundity, but it never came. That was all Hope had to say. Her children would be failures.

Across the table from Hope that night sat a couple from Dallas. Flip and Denise. Denise was certainly Flip's mistress. She reminded Hope of Judith. Hope felt sorry for her because she saw immediately that five days with this older crowd might do this young girl in. Flip kept putting his arm around her in a possessive manner, as if Denise might suddenly try to run, or one of the other men might try to snatch her. Denise had little to say. She appeared bored and smoked Camels, tilting her head upwards in a disdainful way as she exhaled. The other couples hailed from Montreal, Vancouver, New York, California, and of all places, Fargo. Because Fargo was geographically close to Eden, Hope thought that she might have something in common with Cindy, the wife, but Cindy was incredibly shy and it was all Hope could do to tear several words from her small mouth. Her husband, Alistair, on the other hand, was a vociferous bore. He liked numbers, and he used those numbers when referring to his golf game or units sold at his dealership, or when assessing the bodies of women poolside. Cindy hovered and smiled bleakly, sipping a gin and tonic.

Five days with this group. She could not imagine what they would do. What they would talk about. It turned out that the men played golf and the women sat by the pool, or had pedicures, or went into town to shop for cheap clothes. Hope read. Interestingly, she found herself stuck by the pool with Denise, who said that she had no interest in snorkelling, or fishing, or having a massage, or shopping for trinkets in the market. She told Hope that if she had wanted to hang out with housewives, she would have stayed at home and phoned up Flip's wife. She lit a Camel. Called the waiter over and asked for a glass of white wine.

"I'm a housewife."

"Oh, no," Denise said. "Not like them. You're a little strange, Hope, but in a good way. You're not shrill. The other wives hate me. They're threatened, you see. They catch their husbands ogling me and they dissolve. Roy is so polite. I don't think he even knows I exist."

Hope laughed. "Oh, he knows."

"Well, he's very courteous."

"He's probably afraid of you. Anyway, his oldest daughter is your age."

"So is Flip's."

"How old *are* you, Denise?"

"Twenty-two."

"Judith is nineteen. She's in Spain, chasing matadors."

The glass of wine arrived. Hope indicated that she would like the same.

"I was the receptionist at Flip's dealership. I had big plans. I know, I know. I'm a cliché." She narrowed her eyes, perhaps expecting a rebuttal. Not getting any, she continued. "Flip's getting a divorce. And then we're marrying. He wants more kids." She shrugged.

They finished their wine and ordered more and they talked through lunch, which was served poolside. Fish and chips and coleslaw. They swam and then read and slept, and at some point Denise said that she wanted to go down to the hotel's private beach, she liked to sunbathe topless and she didn't think the hotel guests would appreciate that. Would Hope join her?

"Oh, I don't think so. I like to keep my body to myself."

Denise laughed. "No, I just wondered if you wanted to sit with me. I don't expect you to go topless."

Hope was slightly insulted, and then amused. Denise was so much like her eldest two daughters, patronizing and self-centred. On the beach Hope found an umbrella and a chair and sat beside Denise, who lay on a mat in just her bikini bottoms, face to the sun. She did not sneak any looks at Denise's perfect body—she felt it would be unseemly—though several times as they conversed she caught a glimpse of a breast or a nipple, and for some reason this made her want to cry out, "Leave him. Leave him."

Late in the afternoon, as the sun descended, Hope said directly and out of the blue that children could be depressing. Did Denise understand that?

"Oh, come on. You have four." Denise had turned over onto her stomach and this made it easier for Hope to address her directly.

"Exactly. Children will drive you insane. Literally."

"You're not insane."

Hope smiled. "A number of years ago I took a seventeen-year-old girl down to the States for an abortion. You mustn't tell my husband this. He doesn't know." This was a surprise, telling Denise this intimate secret. She wondered where this sudden need to confess had come from.

"One of your daughters?"

"A friend of my daughter's."

"That's so sweet. And brave."

"'Sweet' is a new twist. The father was an older man. He left her high and dry."

"Flip wouldn't leave me high and dry."

"Of course not."

"He wouldn't. I keep him very happy."

"Well."

On the second-last day at the resort Denise told her that the girls were planning a party for that night. She had taken to calling the other wives "the girls."

"Oh," Hope said. "I guess that's nice."

"Not just any party. A key party. I thought I should give you a heads-up. Anita Stark's idea, along with her husband. The men are gung-ho."

"Oh my. That's so embarrassing."

Denise hooted. "You're perfect, Hope. You might want to warn Roy."

"What about you? Are you? You know?"

Denise shook her head. "No way, Jose."

But she didn't warn Roy. She wasn't sure what words to use, and in any case he came back from golf quite tired and he had a nap and then they dressed for dinner, and by the time they were walking up the pathway to meet the group, she didn't want to get him all twisted up, and so she said nothing. As usual, there was a fair amount of drinking at dinner, and later there was a steel band that had to be tolerated, and then Louis, the car dealer from Montreal, took his wife Lila's hand and suggested they all gather at his villa. "*Ça va?*"

Alistair, who was sitting across from Hope, winked at her and said, "Absolutely." He had been flirting with her all week, and she had astutely and politely ignored him.

Anita raised her arm and cried out, "Let us go," as a few of the women giggled nervously. The men rose.

Roy took Hope's hand and announced that they would pass.

"Keeping that good-looking wife to yourself, eh, Roy?" Alistair said, and he hit Roy on the shoulder.

Walking back up to their villa, she realized that Roy had been many many steps ahead of her, and at first she was grateful and surprised, and then she wondered why they hadn't discussed this whole sexual escapade. It was as if Roy had decided for her. How did he know what she wanted? Well, of course she didn't want to have sex with Louis or Alistair, or any other Tom, Dick, or Harry—that was a given—but shouldn't she choose for herself? She removed her hand from his and stepped sideways so that there was a space between them. He allowed this.

Roy said, "Like rabbits."

She snorted. "Shenanigans."

And no more was said of it. They did not have sex that night, and she wondered why this was so. Perhaps Roy was in fact disappointed and, having held a fantasy in his heart all week, was bored by his wife's humdrum body. What pleasure could be taken from the same old pot when there were new and varied pots? Roy slept but she did not. The window was open, the smell of frangipani wafted in. The surf in the distance. The laughter over at Louis' villa. The noise of the party rose and fell.

She was awakened by a cry, a scream or perhaps a laugh. It pulled her from her sleep and up out of bed and to the window. Roy still slept. Her hearing was much better than his. She stood in the darkness, her hand parting the cotton curtain. A figure appeared. Anita Stark, stark naked. She was crying out in fear, or so it seemed, and then Flip, Denise's lover, ran down the path and caught Anita, who laughed and then whispered. All of this was too much for Hope and she turned away and climbed back into bed. Eventually, the human noises disappeared and were replaced by the croak of frogs, the breeze, and once again the surf. When Hope thought about Denise she felt sad. How did this happen? Poor thing.

In the morning, she and Roy ate breakfast on the patio café that faced the ocean. Roy read the local paper while Hope delicately ate fresh pineapple and stared at the sky and watched the other guests. They had just finished their last coffee and were rising to leave when Flip and Alistair appeared and took a table at the far end of the restaurant. Roy made his way over and talked to them. She was amazed, as always, by Roy's ability to push past discomfort and face the facts. She left, sliding down the path, hoping not to meet any of the group. Later, safe on the plane, she took Roy's hand and held it. "I had a good time," she said.

"Did you?" He seemed surprised.

"Yes. I did. Thank you."

"I'm glad."

"Denise was a lost little thing, wasn't she."

"I thought she held her own."

"It seemed so, and then it didn't seem so."

"Flip was crazy for her. But then, why wouldn't he be?"

"If I were to rank those people, I'd put Flip and Anita Stark at the bottom of the ladder," she said.

"Anita did have a high voice."

"Always at full volume."

"What's the ranking based on? Looks?"

"On goodness."

"Your problem, Hope, is that you think everyone is as full of effort as you are. They aren't."

She wondered what that meant. That she tried too hard? Trusted too much? That she was too forgiving? So be it. She wasn't going to change now.

Eight months later, Judith returned from Europe and announced that she had met a man in Paris, a collector and seller of art. Within the month, she planned to return to Paris, where she would be living with Jean-Philippe in his apartment in the 6th arrondissement. "It's gorgeous," Judith said. "You walk into his place and come face to face with a Monet. And there are books everywhere. He has parties and suddenly a famous movie director shows up, or an actress." Roman Polanski had been at Jean-Philippe's one evening for a late dinner. French dinners began around 11 and went till 2 a.m. It was marvellous. And the most marvellous thing was that Jean-Philippe saw possibilities for Judith's photos. "He thinks I should have a show."

Roy asked who this Mr. Polanski was.

"Oh, come on, Dad."

Later, in Judith's room, watching her pull dirty clothes out of her backpack, Hope sat at the edge of the bed and asked how she had met this Jean-Philippe.

"At a café. I was working as a server and he talked to me and then asked me for a drink and things took off from there."

This was bewildering, this notion that "things take off," as if there were numerous paths and one just chose a path willy-nilly and then, that having failed, chose again. Well, that wasn't how life worked, and Judith would have to discover the hard way that the world was an unforgiving place. Hope worried that her children did not adequately understand the ways of the world. Well, perhaps Penny did, but sometimes she could be too cynical.

"I wish we could meet him," she said.

"Oh, you'd love him, Mom. He's very sophisticated. And kind. And brilliant."

It turned out that he was forty years old. Judith managed to slip that in at some point, in an offhanded way, as if it were a minor detail.

"But, Judith, that's almost a twenty-year difference." Hope was breathless and felt panicky.

"He looks way younger. Like thirty. And his spirit, his mind, is very young."

"Has he been married before?"

"Once, for two years. To an actress. It ended badly."

"And does he have children?"

She shook her head, exasperated. "He loves me, Mom. And I love him."

Hope told Roy that he needed to have a talk with their daughter. "This man will break her heart, I can see it already. French men do that. They have a different code that they live by. He probably wears a scarf. And her photographs? It's terrible to say, but they don't seem especially original."

Judith had proudly shown a number of black-and-white photographs to her family, laying them out on the kitchen table. They were of people in the streets, but taken from above, from windows and fire escapes. Judith explained that the perspective was objective. "Jean-Philippe calls it god-like." She pointed at one photograph. "And then suddenly, there is a face, looking up, and it is intimate." Her voice, when she said this, sounded French, and Hope imagined that she was parroting someone, probably Jean-Philippe. At the table, studying the photographs, Melanie had exclaimed, Conner was indifferent, and Penny, skeptical like her mother, had shrugged and said, "Nice."

Roy said now, "She won't listen to us, Hope. That's Judith. So we can either take pleasure in her plans or fight her, and fighting her will only cause more friction." He paused, and then said, "And if this Jean-Philippe thinks she can make money from her art, good for her."

He was far too practical, Hope thought, though she knew he was right. Still, sometimes she wished he would be more emotional. Did he not care that their eldest daughter had a French lover who would eventually abandon her?

One day after supper she found Judith in her bedroom. She stood in the doorway and said, "May I come in?"

Judith was sitting on the bed, her knees drawn up towards her chest. She was writing a letter to Jean-Philippe. The thin airmail sheets crackled as she laid them aside, face down.

Hope took that as a yes and stepped forward. She stood in the middle of the room, aware at that moment of her daughter's hair colour and the shape of her face and the angle of her eyes, and she said, "Oh, you look so much like your father."

Judith wrinkled her nose, not exactly in distaste, but impatiently, and said, "What do you want? I'm busy."

"This man, is he trustworthy?"

"God, Mother. Of course I *trust* him. What's wrong with you? Are you jealous?"

"What do you mean?" She was standing in the middle of the room, wearing a housedress and slippers, and she saw herself as Judith must see her, and she was embarrassed. Certainly, any French woman her age, at this time in the evening, would be wearing a dress and high heels and makeup. "I haven't met him. All I have is your description. Do you have a photograph?"

"No. I don't. Anyways, what would that prove?"

"I love you, Judith. And your father loves you. If this is what you want, then we want it for you as well."

"I know, Mom. Thank you." And she went back to her letter writing.

That night Hope lay in bed, unable to sleep, and she thought about what she might be jealous of. Judith's freedom? Her youth? Her love life? When she was Judith's age there had been no room in her imagination for an older French lover who lived in the 6th arrondissement. Even now, there was so much that Hope could not imagine. It made her head ache. She wondered if jealousy was a form of desire. Sure it was. But the two were not necessarily attached. She desired Roy, and she wasn't jealous of him. Thinking in this manner, and resolving nothing, she fell asleep

* * *

The following year, travelling to Berlin for an automobile show, Roy and Hope stopped in Paris for three days to visit Judith and to meet Jean-Philippe. They stayed in a small hotel off boulevard Raspail. During the days, Judith took them to all the tourist spots—the Eiffel Tower, the Louvre—though she did this grudgingly. She had little interest in the traditional fare. One night they met Judith and Jean-Philippe near Les Halles and ate in a tiny French restaurant. "Isn't this place amazing?" Judith whispered. "It's three hundred years old." Jean-Philippe was a real gentleman. He greeted Hope by kissing her on the cheeks, once, twice, three times. He would not be distracted. He focused on Hope, and Hope was immediately besotted. His hair was long and slightly grey and he wore a purple silk scarf that he kept throwing backwards with one hand as the other held a ubiquitous yellow Gitane. He was short but well dressed. His shoes were exquisite. Hope had an eye for shoes. He spoke English with an up-and-down accent and Hope understood almost immediately why Judith would love this man. They ate short ribs and drank red wine and by the end of the evening Hope was quite drunk. As they walked through the narrow streets later, Jean-Philippe took her arm and guided her. Judith and Roy followed. Jean-Philippe whispered, "You have a most beautiful daughter, Hope." Her name, coming out of his mouth, was missing the "h." It went up in the air and floated away, as her heart was also floating away.

That night she dreamed that she was walking gaily down a Parisian street carrying a baguette under one arm, and suddenly the heel of one shoe snapped and she fell to the ground and skinned her knees. A crowd gathered around and pointed at her, jeering in a language that she did not recognize. She woke, confused, and heard the street washers outside the window. A grey morning light filtered in. She was losing Judith, and she was helpless to change that fact. Roy would have said, "Hope, you worry too much," and yet what a fine line there was between joy and sorrow. She had given her children every possible tool to survive, hadn't she? Or had she failed to instill in them the ability to judge others, and themselves? To raise a child was more than plopping down little clones of oneself. Who needed four more little Hopes romping through the world? What folly. The most difficult part of being a mother was to observe the mistakes of one's children: the foolish loves, the desperate solitude and alienation, the lack of will, the gullibility, the joyous and naive leaps into the unknown, the ignorance, the panicky choices, and the utter determination. In the light of the morning, she feared that Judith would be terribly hurt by this Frenchman with his suave flirtatious manner. Was he solid? Was he faithful?

In her more dire moments Hope saw how bleak the future was becoming. The world was spinning out of control and it was scooping up her children, one by one.

And so it was that she and Roy arrived home from Europe to discover that Penny had fallen in with a religious group that spent time handing out tracts warning people about the end of the world. It was a small group, based out of the Pentecostal church in Eden, and was run by a man named Garry Doerksen, who preferred to be called simply Eli. One night at the supper table, two days after her parents' return, Penny handed out a tract to each family member and proceeded to proselytize. She had become a robot, spouting nonsense. And yet Hope couldn't help but be impressed by her salesmanship, her knowledge of Armageddon. "Behold," she said, "a white horse, and he who sat on it had a bow; and a crown was given to him; and he went out conquering, and to conquer."

"What a load of shit," Conner said. He tossed aside the tract and helped himself to meatballs and potatoes.

"Your language," his father said.

"Well, it is."

Penny was very calm. "It's okay, Dad. For the cowardly and unbelieving and abominable and murderers and immoral persons and sorcerers and idolaters and all liars, their part will be in the lake that burns with fire and brimstone, which is the second death."

"Oh my," Hope said. "Isn't that a little harsh, sending your brother there?" She thought a little levity might be necessary.

"I didn't send him," Penny said. "He chooses."

Conner grinned. "Oops," he said. For two years now he had been dating that beautiful girl from the photo Hope had come across. Her name was Charlotte Means, and she floated in and out of the house, often appearing at the dinner table though rarely speaking. Hope wondered if she didn't like her own mother's cooking, or perhaps her mother didn't cook at all. Charlotte was present now, at Conner's right hand, her long hair framing her perfect face. She did not seem curious about the conversation, though she became more alert when Conner spoke. There was always a sense of disdain attached to her, as if she were too good for the Koops.

Conner said, "This Garry Doerksen was in prison. Just got out."

"Was not," Penny said. Her lips tightened and she sat up straighter.

"Was. For pederasty or something."

"What's pedasty?" This was Melanie, suddenly all ears. Up until now she had been picking at a single meatball, cutting it up into little bits and moving them glacially towards her mouth.

"Don't worry about it," Hope said. She looked at Roy, whose nonchalance affronted her. She told Penny that it was her turn to clear the table and do the dishes. "Even if the world is ending, we want to have a clean house."

Two weeks later, on a Saturday, Penny went out with the Pentecostal group in the pouring rain to a rock concert that was taking place in a nearby town. The intention was to blanket the large crowd with tracts and the message of the impending apocalypse. The rain descended and the farmer's field turned to soup. By the end of the day, the concert was cancelled, Penny had been spit at and cursed, and Conner showed up with his father's tow truck and made seven hundred dollars pulling cars out of the mud and back onto the highway, his golden girl beside him counting the bills. Penny came down with a cold and spent several days in bed.

The following Saturday, cleaning the bathroom, Hope found a stack of religious tracts in the garbage. When she asked Penny about them, she said something about Eli being a fraud. Hope was pleased. It was necessary for her children to have various experiences, to taste failure, to discover that not everyone was marching down the straight and narrow road, and it was also necessary to be able to pull back wisely from the precipice, as Penny had done.

And so Penny went back to studying biology and physics and chemistry with a vengeance. She was planning to go into medicine.

* * *

At the age of twenty-two, in 1977, Conner married Charlotte Means in the Eden United Church. It was an elaborate and large wedding, paid for by Eddie Means, Charlotte's father, who owned the lumberyard in town. Hope didn't believe that Conner should be marrying the girl he had dated since he was fifteen. He had become less and less the joyful and insatiable boy hungering after the world, and in his place there was a young man who seemed weak and soft. Hope anticipated that the security of marriage might free Conner once again.

The plan had been for Melanie to be the flower girl, but in the eight months leading up to the wedding, she grew half a foot, and by the time the wedding took place, she was taller than the bride and Charlotte asked her cousin Carly to take her place. Melanie was distraught and wept for a day, walking around the house in her nightgown. In the end, a compromise was reached, and Melanie lit the candles during the service, her long tremulous arms reaching up to touch the seven pink candles. She was incredibly skinny, as Penny had been once, and yet Hope saw only the beauty of her daughter, who, after completing her mission, reclaimed her seat beside her father. Really, children could break your heart.

Roy paid for the couple's honeymoon in San Francisco. Upon their return they settled into a house that Charlotte had insisted on, a few doors down from her parents' place. The whole situation was claustrophobic to Hope, but she kept her mouth shut. Charlotte was articling for a firm in Winnipeg, commuting back and forth, sometimes staying quite late, sometimes not coming home at night at all. Because Conner was Hope's only son, and because sons were more vulnerable than daughters, she worried that he would not be cared for. But what was there to be concerned about? The dealership was thriving. Roy was on top of the world and had begun to plan an expansion, perhaps Winnipeg, perhaps another town in southern Manitoba. Units were flying off the lot, he was well respected, and in 1979 his photo adorned the cover of a Winnipeg magazine as businessman of the year. Hope had the cover framed and presented it to him that Christmas, during the winter vacation in Hawaii. The family members were all present for the holiday. Judith had managed to fly out alone from France for a week. Hope was surrounded by her children. She was loved. Goodness and mercy. She even found a way to have a passable relationship with Charlotte, who for some reason, in Hawaii, seemed more generous.

One night Hope and Roy returned to their hotel room after a family dinner. The children had decided to head into town to find a disco. Hope said, "Have you noticed how Charlotte orders Conner around? He's a frightened lamb."

"They seem to have figured out how to be married."

"Was he always so passive? It's scary to watch. Where did he get that from? You're not like that. Do you think maybe I did something wrong? Or maybe it's being surrounded by girls. He needed a brother."

"He did. My older brother kept me tough."

"I wish he would stand up to her just one time. She'd be flabbergasted."

"She's incapable of being flabbergasted."

"Do you think she's pretty?"

"Yes, she is."

"I used to think so, but since I've got to know her, her beauty has worn thin. Listen to me. Running down my daughter-in-law."

"Well, you didn't marry her."

"Thank goodness." She paused, and then said, "Maybe Conner has my nature. Deluded."

"Melanie gets along with her."

"Melanie would get along with a rabid dog. I wonder sometimes what will happen to her."

"You wonder that about all your children."

"And so I should. They're my children."

"You're a good woman, Hope. A good mother."

"Do you think so?"

"I do."

"Did you notice, today, down by the pool? My legs are losing their shape."

"Never noticed."

"Well, look now. See? Gravity's doing weird things, Roy. You're gonna have to find someone younger."

"And train her? No way."

She hit him lightly across the head. She was standing by the bed. He was seated. She kissed the spot where her hand had landed. "There you go, Mr. Koop. What do you want to do? The kids are partying. We're all alone."

"We could lie down side by side. Right here." Roy patted the bed.

"You'd like that."

"I would."

"Okay." She walked across the room and turned off the lights. "Okay," she said again.

Not long after, when the thin years arrived, she would look back on the vacation to Hawaii as the last hurrah and wonder if she had appreciated the fullness of that time. She worried that she had taken it all for granted, the easy lassitude, the money, the pleasure of lovemaking, the pride she felt being surrounded by family. The world and the joys offered to her.

* * *

Four years after Conner's wedding, Penny was well into her third year of medicine and living in the city, coming home infrequently to do laundry or to eat, and sometimes deigning to share with her mother the odd detail from her life. She was an obsessed and hard-working student, and Hope wondered where her drive and vision had come from. Certainly not from Hope, who had studied French one year in order to be able to carry on a basic conversation with Jean-Philippe, but had given up when overwhelmed by the logic and simplicity of French verbs neatly aligned in her *Bescherelle*. It must have been Roy who passed down to Penny the genetic makeup to persevere, to memorize, and to press on like an implacable iceberg. And Hope was fine with that. She was maternal. Someone in the family had to dole out love.

Melanie graduated from high school that year. She was six feet two. Her height combined with her striking looks absolutely terrified boys her age, who consoled themselves by nicknaming her Giraffe. She had a scholarship to attend the University of Texas, where she would be joining the track team, her specialty being the high jump. At her graduation she took as her escort the phys. ed. teacher, Ollie Carlyle, who was single, twenty-eight, and known to be a bit of a playboy.

"Is that legal?" Hope asked one afternoon in June as she was fitting Melanie's grad dress. Hope was on her knees, stick pins in her mouth. She looked up at her daughter's chin.

"I don't give a shit," Melanie said.

"Well, Mr. Carlyle should maybe *give a shit*."

"Mom. It's not like we're dating."

"You're not?"

"No."

"Will he expect something in return?"

"He can expect whatever he wants. I'll do what I like."

"People will talk."

"You've never cared about what people think, Mom. Why start now?"

Was this true? Why didn't she know this? Perhaps she did know this at some deep level and was both ashamed and proud. Roy appeared to be indifferent to Melanie's choice of escorts. He was deeply preoccupied with the business. Interest rates had risen to 22 percent and he was having a difficult time simply paying the interest on the excess units on the lot. The bank was intractable, threatening foreclosure, and though Hope heard hints of the trouble, she was typically in the dark when it came to the business. One night she woke and found the bed empty beside her and she rose and went to seek out her husband, who was sitting in his leather chair in the living room.

She stood in her nightie and said, "What is it, Roy?"

"I couldn't sleep. It's okay, Hope. Go back to bed."

"Is it bad?" she asked.

"It could be better."

She sat on the couch across from him. He looked diminished, sitting in the blackness of the living room, the faint shadow of his head in profile, and she felt the despair trickle out into the room.

"Would you like some tea?" And she rose and boiled water and steeped a cup of tea for him and placed it in his hands, which were shaking.

"I'm sorry, Hope," Roy said. "You shouldn't have to suffer this."

"Don't worry about me, Roy. Take care of yourself."

"Forty years down the drain."

"Don't talk like that. Our children are healthy. We're healthy."

He did not answer.

She said, "We have friends. Couldn't they help?"

They did have friends and acquaintances with more than enough, but as one of these friends said when Roy went to ask for a loan, "Why throw good money after bad?" Another said, "You made your bed, you'll have to lie in it." And another, who owned the wealthiest business in Eden, said, "Roy, you know very well that we are not a generous family." His brother, Harold, who had left the business a number of years earlier to work as a manager with a new grocery chain in town, offered comforting words but had little advice and no money. At least Roy's father, who had started the business, was in a seniors' home and blissfully senile, unaware of the dealership's decline.

Over the month that followed, Roy attempted to save the business. He asked General Motors to take back one hundred new vehicles, thereby reducing his debt load, but GM wouldn't accept the returns. It was sink or swim. His debt grew and the bank panicked.

One Saturday morning, Roy went to the dealership early and returned half an hour later. He walked into the house and sat down at the kitchen table, looked right at Hope, who was standing by the stove, and said, "They shut me down."

"What do you mean?"

"They put chains on the doors. I can't even get into my own business."

"That's ridiculous. They can't do that."

"They did. I called Rollie at home and he said that his hands were tied. It wasn't his decision. It came from the head office." His face was pale.

"What will happen?" she asked.

"I don't know. Worst case, they'll take everything. The house, the cottage, the cars for sure. I'm sorry, Hope."

"Oh, Roy."

She knew that she should go to him, that she should hold him, but for a moment all she could manage was "Oh, Roy," and then she felt the falling away of everything physical around her.

"The furniture?" she whispered. "That too?"

He shook his head. He didn't know.

She stepped across the linoleum and took his head in her hands and pushed his face against her stomach. "It's all right," she said. "We'll manage."

And Roy began to cry. His tears wet her dress and she patted his back and thought that he sounded like a trapped animal. She worried that the children would wake.

"Shh, shh. Come."

And then he stopped crying and stood and went to the sink and splashed water over his face. He dried himself with a tea towel. His back was to her.

"We're not sick, Roy. We have our health. We have each other. The children."

He did not answer.

Over the next week, whenever she entered the living room she found him sitting in his chair, staring out the window that gave onto the large backyard. It was late summer. The begonias that he had planted alongside the house raged with high colour. The grass grew thick and green. One afternoon he mowed the lawn, carefully overlapping each previous cut. She stood by the kitchen window and watched him. He was wearing his suit pants, a dress shirt, a tie, and his good black leather shoes. As if he might step out of this picture at any moment and drive to his office. She studied his face for some sign of resignation, despair, hope, grief—but she saw only the intensity of a man who was cutting the lawn and doing the best job possible.

The final eight years in Eden had been the richest of her life. She took to calling them "the fat years," alluding in her biblical way to Joseph's interpretation of Pharaoh's dream in which the lean and ugly cows ate the fat cows. And the rich years disappeared with such stunning swiftness. Her house was yanked out from beneath her. She lost her vehicle and Roy lost his, and the cottage was sold at a ridiculously low price to a couple Roy and Hope had imagined were good and faithful friends.

* * *

Hope and Roy left Eden in the fall of 1981. They rented a small apartment in Winnipeg, in a building near the legislature. It had three stories, with no elevator, and they lived on the third floor in a one-bedroom. At midday, the sunlight poured into the south-facing windows and onto the few pieces of furniture that had been rescued from the house—a house that over the previous two years had been completely renovated. Hope's pride and joy. Gone now.

Walking across the bridge to Safeway to buy groceries, Hope remembered her youthful desire to be a nurse, and how the longing for Roy and children (she had slipped into motherhood so simply and naively) had conquered that early wish to be independent and employed and gainful. The pandemonium of the past month, the humiliation and loss, sat heavily on her. She saw herself carrying her grocery bags and imagined that others might see her as poor, which she now was.

She looked for what was familiar and found that the river was still dirty and flowed in the same direction, though there were now homeless young people with their dogs living under the bridges. These vagabonds did not frighten her. In fact she felt an affinity to their poverty and their destitute freedom. She thought that if she could be young again she might choose differently for herself. There were all manners of life to be lived. She did not need the limelight, but now, at her age, she felt hidden and undistinguished, a wisp of her former self. She had managed to pack several suitcases of clothes before leaving Eden, salvaging the best from her past, though now, on the street, she sensed that her clothes were out of fashion. It was early September, the days warm, the evenings cooler. She avoided the apartment during the day because she became overwhelmed by sadness, and so she walked, across the bridge and into a small park where children from the local daycare played. How lovely. Children.

When Judith heard about the bankruptcy she came back from Paris for several weeks. She slept on a cot in the living room and during the days she ranted about the smallness of the apartment and the narrow minds of the people of Eden. "You're damned lucky to be out of that horrible village," she cried out one day. She was sitting at the small kitchen table with Hope. Roy had left early in the morning, dressed in his suit. He did this every morning, seeking out work, and he returned every evening, worn out, claiming that a job was "just around the corner." Hope felt as if Judith's rage was aimed at her personally, as if Hope were to blame for the failure of Roy's business. And to counter that feeling, she told Judith that Roy had made mistakes of his own. He had got greedy. He had overextended his credit and planned to expand at the worst of times, and he hadn't paid attention to his family.

"Look at us," she said. "Is this how we end up? I did my job. I raised you children. Maybe I wasn't perfect, but I did my job and you children flew away and you're healthy and independent. Why couldn't Roy manage his side of the business? No, now we're stuck in this dirty little place and I barely have enough for food. Who are we?"

"That's so unfair, Mom, and you know it. Dad did everything for you. He still does, walking out of here every morning, pretending everything is fine. I feel sick when I see him. He always paid the bills, making sure you had your fur coats and your new dishes."

"Is that what you think? That I lay about like the Queen of Sheba? I raised you children. I fed you. I patched your clothes and your hearts. Don't you forget."

"Christ."

"You think I don't feel sick every time your father leaves this little hovel and then comes home all upbeat? Well, you're wrong. I'm full of sadness. Stop talking, Judith. You're just being mean right now, and I'm not sure why. Is it Jean-Philippe? Are you fighting? This isn't like you."

But it was exactly like her. She had always appreciated her father more than her mother. Only Penny seemed to understand Hope. She was the one child of four who did not always side with Roy.

When Judith finally returned to Paris, Hope was relieved. She no longer had the emotional energy to support both Judith and Roy. The other children were fine. They had lives to live, and yet this too felt like a betrayal of sorts. How was it that the sun still rose every day, that folks climbed out of bed and went to work, and that her own children, with apparent nonchalance, shrugged off the tragedy of their parents' life and carried on eating and drinking and making love?

Conner was the child most affected by the loss of the business, because he had worked as a salesman for Roy and it had been Roy's intention that he eventually take over the dealership. Conner found a job selling farm equipment. His wife, Charlotte, was a busy little beaver, making lots of money as a lawyer, and the few times that Hope and Roy were invited to their house for Sunday lunch, Hope felt that Charlotte, who had always been aloof, was even more disdainful. Invitations to Charlotte and Conner's house eventually petered out.

Penny was happily ensconced in medical school. She received the news of the bankruptcy in her typical cold and clinical manner. Shit happened. She wrote Roy a cheque for one thousand dollars and told him to use it for the down payment on a car. When he said he couldn't take money from a student, she said, "That's ridiculous. You paid for my schooling up till now. And besides, I've got some extra."

Roy went out the following week and, still faithful to General Motors, purchased a used Oldsmobile.

As for Melanie, she had a full scholarship to the University of Texas and was not in need of money. She had maintained contact with Mr. Carlyle, who spent the last two weeks of his summer vacation helping her settle into the house she would be sharing with four other athletes. That fall she wrote long letters to her father in which she described her rigorous schedule, the various classes, and the friends she was making. She was easily clearing six feet in her jumping, beating her personal record. She had broken off with Mr. Carlyle and taken up with a basketball player named Jane. "Yes," she wrote, "Jane is a girl." Roy was quite shaken by this revelation. He showed Hope the letter and wondered out loud if "taken up" didn't just mean that they were good friends. Hope read the letter and then put it down and said that she had had no inkling. None whatsoever. "She always liked boys. Though there weren't a lot of boyfriends."

Hope wondered if that was why Mr. Carlyle had entered Melanie's life. She might have chosen him because he was safer than boys her age. Or it might have been a statement on Melanie's part: Look at me, I'm not who you think I am. Roy had a much harder time with homosexuality than Hope did. Hope simply wanted her children to be happy and to live a good life. If that meant dating a girl named Jane, so be it. Roy, on the other hand, prayed for a change of heart. "Maybe it's just a stage," he said after another letter arrived, in which Melanie advised them that Jane had been replaced by a girl named Marion.

"That's such an old-fashioned name, don't you think?" Roy asked, as if trying to convince himself that "old-fashioned" and "lesbian" were two words that could not walk down the same road.

Her letters were addressed "Dear Dad (and Mother)," and this was disturbing to Hope, who imagined that was a signal of some sort, that her own life was parenthetical— Hope apparently existed outside of the complex motion of Melanie's life. She had always hoped that her power and influence over her children would extend beyond the vital years of child-rearing. Her fear was that her little girl had been damaged in some way by her mother's illness, by her absence, by her inability to love Melanie. Hadn't she made up for that? Nobody could accuse her of being indifferent now.

Before the bank foreclosed on the business, Hope had visited the bank manager, Rollie Tiessen, who was the father to Maxine, the girl she had driven to Minneapolis for an abortion ten years earlier. So long ago now. Hope had dressed up for the meeting, had put on one of her finest dresses and had her hair done, and then driven to the bank and announced herself. She was made to wait two hours for Mr. Tiessen. When he finally saw her and allowed her into his office, he didn't apologize or appear to want to take any responsibility. He was a successful man. His stomach stretched his starched shirt and hung over his belt. She wondered, oddly and quietly, how he managed to see his penis. Did he find it without a mirror? His daughter had certainly known how to find penises.

He was a man in great demand, and he applied haste to the meeting. He did not look at her, but looked instead at his smallish hands, as if they were coated in precious metal.

"Is there something you can do?" she asked.

"There is nothing, Hope. My hands are tied. Businesses are falling like rotten trees in a forest."

"I would think that would be exactly your responsibility. To save those trees."

"One must help oneself, Hope." He smiled thinly. His head was perfectly round, like that man on the Monopoly board.

"There is nothing?"

"Nothing."

"Is this about Maxine?"

"What do you mean?"

She saw that he had no idea of the abortion. She paused, held her breath, then said, "I'm sorry. I was thinking about something else. It's very hard."

"I understand. I'm also sorry."

"Everything will be lost."

"You are alive and healthy, Hope. As is Roy."

She felt incredible rage and hoped that this bald man with his red nose and fat paunch would die of a heart attack. Soon. "We are not mere things, Rollie. Do you have a job for Roy? Or me? Perhaps I could be your personal secretary. I could run errands for your younger daughter. Take her on trips to Minneapolis." She stood and walked out of the bank.

Roy would hear of this meeting, and he would then blame her for making matters worse. But how could they be worse?

She drove to Gertrude's Inn and ordered a Denver sandwich and salad, and when she was finished eating she asked Grace, the waitress, to put it on Roy's bill. Grace nodded and walked away and Hope saw her conferring with the manager. Eventually Grace returned and said, leaning forward as if a secret were to be shared, "I'm sorry, Mrs. Koop, but you will have to pay for the meal."

"Of course, Grace. I understand." And she pulled from her wallet a fifty-dollar bill and laid it on the counter. "Keep the change."

It had pleased her enormously, that encounter: the tepid attempt to shame her and then her aggressive response. She had walked out of Gertrude's Inn with her back straight, looking at each customer who would meet her eye, never wavering, waiting till their gaze fell away in embarrassment and sheepishness. She had nothing to be ashamed of. These people did. Profit, profit, profit. Wealth as a sign of God's blessing, of having lived a pure life. Nonsense.

Now, back in her little apartment, alone, waiting for Roy to come home in the late afternoon, she wished she had that fifty-dollar bill back. She could have used it. For the first time in her married life she found herself counting money and worrying over the balance in the bank account. In the cabinet above the stove she kept envelopes of cash, usually in twenty-dollar denominations, for laundry, groceries, car repairs, clothing, medication, utilities, and entertainment, though the only amusement they could afford was the occasional movie. Gone were the days when Roy bought expensive seats at football games, or Hope met Emily at the theatre centre downtown. If there was money left over in the envelopes at the end of the month, she and Roy dressed up and went to Hy's Steakhouse, but even this felt like play-acting, as if they were trying to recover a life they had once known.

At the grocery store she had purchased two round steaks, mushrooms, a bag of carrots, a loaf of bread, a quart of heavy cream. And with this she would create dark gravy from the drippings, mixing in a tablespoon of flour and then the heavy cream. She would cook the carrots and sprinkle brown sugar over them, melt butter in the pot. She had pasta to boil as well, over which she would pour a ready-made sauce. Ice water and coffee, which Roy liked to drink with his meal. A Kit Kat for dessert: three pieces for Roy, one for her, though she knew that Roy would slide his third piece back her way. She had a sweet tooth.

He had found work with an old acquaintance, Murray Fineworth. Murray installed drywall and he had said he could use someone tall like Roy, though Roy suspected Murray was doing him a favour.

"Let him," Hope had said.

Roy returned at 6 p.m. every evening, his hair, face and arms dusted with a fine white powder. He showered, dressed in a suit and shirt and tie and dark socks and shoes, and sat down to the meal she had prepared. He talked enthusiastically about his day. He would get a raise next month, from ten to eleven dollars an hour. The eight-foot sheets, three-eighths, were manageable, but the ten-footers were a back-breaker. His fingers were cracked and bloody. He developed an allergy to the powder and took to wearing a mask and gloves. Still, his hands bled. In the evenings, after supper, she cleaned up while he settled in front of the TV. Later, she would inevitably find him sleeping, his head lolling sideways onto his shoulder. She would then guide him to bed and help him undress. Hang up his jacket, his pants, his shirt.

One night she found in his right pocket the money clip he carried. It held ten one-hundred-dollar bills. She slipped it back into his pocket and felt there a piece of paper, and this she removed. The paper was folded. She opened it. Roy's handwriting. "Whatever is true, whatever is honorable, whatever is right, whatever is pure, whatever is lovely, whatever is of good repute, if there is any excellence and if anything worthy of praise, let your mind dwell on these things. Phil. 4:8."

She folded the paper and put it back in Roy's pocket, next to the money clip. She went into the living room and sat down and looked out the window at the night sky, which was threatening rain.

4

Age of Longing

Hope's first grandchild, Rudi Koop, was born on Christmas Day in 1982. She and Roy drove out to Eden to see the newborn the following day. A winter storm had left the roads icy, and as usual, driving in those conditions she suffered a sense of dread and impending doom, though she did not mention any of this to Roy, who would have called her ridiculous. She should be celebrating.

Charlotte was propped up in her hospital bed, breast-feeding little Rudi, when Roy and Hope entered her room. Charlotte saw them and reached for a blanket and covered Rudi's furry head and her swollen breast. Conner was ecstatic. He described the birth in great detail, the crowning, the afterbirth, the colour of the baby, the length of labour down to the minute. He had filmed the whole birth and said Hope and Roy should come over and they could watch it together.

"I don't think so," Charlotte said. "I don't want your parents ogling my bottom."

Conner chuckled nervously and Hope changed the subject, asking Charlotte if her milk had come in yet. This too seemed an intrusion, and so Hope shut her mouth and focused on the child. She was allowed to take him for a short time while Charlotte closed her eyes and slept. Roy, Hope, and Conner spoke in whispers, and when Charlotte woke, she snatched Rudi back.

"He's got your mouth," Hope told Conner, and she reached out and brushed Rudi's lips.

Charlotte seemed understandably tired and irritable, though when her own mother arrived, she was immediately revitalized. Hope realized that some daughters and mothers had a special bond, and she wondered, without any great expectation, when her own daughters would have children.

Hope had found an adorable cotton sleeper at a Boxing Day sale and she handed it to Charlotte. "It's a little feminine," she said, "but he won't know the difference."

Charlotte took the sleeper and placed it on the side table by the bed. On subsequent visits Hope hoped Rudi might be wearing it, but she never saw it again.

Ever since the loss of the business, Charlotte had been cooler towards Roy and Hope. When they dropped by the house to see Rudi and marvel, Charlotte usually excused herself and disappeared upstairs with the baby. Driving home one day, Hope said, "I guess now that she isn't getting an inheritance, we've lost our value."

"I don't think that's how she operates," Roy said.

"She hates me. Every time I go near Rudi, she recoils. She just takes him away, as if I were going to strangle my own grandson."

Roy was quiet. Hope was being hysterical. She knew that was what he was thinking. But then men didn't have that sixth sense about other women. They imagined that magnanimity was everywhere.

When her first granddaughter, Ilke, was born two years later (a spitting image of Hope when she was a baby), Charlotte was even stingier with time and visits. It broke Hope's heart not to be able to see the children regularly. Distraught, she called Conner.

"Have I done something? Have I been too aggressive?"

"Char's overwhelmed, Mom. It's not about you."

"Her own mother sees the children every day. All I want is once a week. Or every two weeks. A few hours, that's it."

"Her mom lives here. Right next door. She's been a big help."

"Well, I'd be a help if you'd let me. Are you two okay?"

"We're fine. It's busy. We didn't realize how much work a second child would be."

"Tell me about it. When you were born it was madness. And you were full of beans. How about Rudi? Does he explore like you?"

"He's actually quite calm. He likes to draw. The sight of paper gets him very excited."

The next visit, a month later, Hope presented Rudi with a watercolour set—forty different tubes of paint, five brushes, and a thick spiral-bound book of watercolour paper. Charlotte said immediately that Rudi already had a set, given to him by Charlotte's sister.

"Well, I'm sure it'll last for years," Hope said. She looked at Charlotte's sour mouth and hated her. And was immediately sorry. This would not do, not if she was to keep seeing her grandchildren.

The fact was, both Roy and Hope were now bound by the demands of their jobs and so they couldn't just willy-nilly drive out to Eden to see the grandchildren. And come weekends, they were both tired out, though Hope went to great efforts to invite Conner and his family for spaghetti dinner or ribs. Over the past year, Hope had been working for Merry Maid, a domestic cleaning company. At first the ugly yellow uniform and the foul demands of the job had humiliated her and she whispered a little thank-you that her mother didn't have to see her changing the sheets on a stranger's bed. Cleaning like this was so intimate and familiar, and whenever she encountered the woman of the house, she would think: Don't think you're so special, I know all about your dirt and your crap and your garbage. She had always imagined that a tragic shift in fortune was something that happened to other people, but look at her now. And, oh my, her hands, how they had aged.

Miss Ling, one of her co-workers, was a Chinese woman with the thinnest ankles Hope had ever seen. She had worked for Merry Maid for ten years. Her husband, Jian, worked in a factory that built windows and doors. They had one son, who was seven years old and brilliant with the piano, and hearing this, Hope imagined that the boy was a prodigy of sorts. Ling was optimistic and she was tireless, and when Hope flagged, usually in the late afternoon, Ling stepped in and helped her on the second floor, cleaning the toilet and the tub, or perhaps finishing up with the vacuuming. "Hope," she would say, "sit down for a bit, rest your feet." Ling saw herself as Hope's daughter and protector. When Hope talked about her hot flashes, Ling had just the remedy and produced little packages of Chinese pills, tiny black balls that she was to take twice a day. "Good for the kidney," she said. "It will make you want to have sex as well." She didn't smile as she spoke, merely nodded as if sexual desire were something looming and necessary.

They were a crew of three, the third worker being a Polish woman named Katerina, who was forty-eight and a single mother of three children all in their teens. Hope didn't get along with Katerina. The three women usually ate lunch in the bright yellow Merry Maid car, and it was here that Hope and Katerina set to arguing, often about politics, for Katerina called herself a socialist and Hope thought this was ridiculous and unfortunate. Katerina, in fact, was itching to start a union, and she tried to sway both Ling and Hope. She had forty signatures so far, women at Merry Maid who, upon reflecting on their bleak situation, saw the possibility of a meagre salvation. Roy didn't believe in unions, and so neither did Hope. She believed that hard work and fidelity would be reciprocated by management. Katerina guffawed and called Hope naive. "Don't you want a pension? Benefits? Sick time? Overtime? Some sort of security? You're what, Hope? Fifty-five? Who's going to care for you when you're sixty?"

Ling, perpetually sanguine, tried to change the subject. She passed Hope part of her lunch. "Hope, here, please try the ginger noodles."

When Hope and Roy were still living in Eden, Hope had had a woman come in once a week to clean the house and do laundry and ironing. She had always imagined that Erna Loewen, her cleaner, had been quite happy. Hope set out sandwiches and cookies for her, offered her tea, and at the end of the day, laid out a two-dollar tip on the counter. Erna had never complained, had seemed quite contented, and had always been very polite and grateful.

Well, now here she was, a cleaner like Erna Loewen, stooping to scrub toilets in a monstrous house out in Birds Hill, where horses grazed in paddocks and the three-car garages harboured expensive toys such as snowmobiles and boats and ATVs. She had once let it slip to Ling and Katerina that she too had lived this life, and the confession had not elicited pity as she had expected. Katerina had merely said that the pockets of the rich were full because her own pocket, and others like hers, was empty. "It can be no other way." When Hope told Roy this, he smiled vaguely, but surprisingly he offered no argument.

One day, Katerina did not show up for work. Again, the next day she did not appear, and so Hope and Ling completed the work of three people, and by the end of the day Hope was worn out. That afternoon, the coordinator, Bertie, arrived. She wanted to talk to both Hope and Ling privately.

Hope sat in Bertie's car. It was a cold January day and Bertie kept the car running. The heater was blowing warm air onto Hope's tan shoes and her sore ankles, and for a brief moment she saw the space she was in as luxurious and safe.

Bertie held a clipboard and a pen. She said, "On Tuesday, you cleaned a house in River Heights." She said the address. "The owner claims a watch was stolen. An heirloom that had been in the family for many years. It was in the master bedroom. Was it Katerina who cleaned the master bedroom that day?"

Hope's mind was a muddle. She recalled the house, and she remembered having washed the kitchen floor and the stove, but she was thinking too that this was not right. "Katerina doesn't steal. She's not that stupid."

"We're not saying she did. A watch went missing. It went missing after you and Ling and Katerina cleaned the house. Naturally, there are questions."

"Maybe the family misplaced it."

"No. The watch was kept on the dresser, in a box, and it had been there for the last year. The owner said it went missing after the house was cleaned."

Hope was quiet. Then she said, "What do you want me to say? Yes, I stole it? What would I want with an old watch?"

"Just tell the truth."

"I didn't take it."

"Did you see Katerina that afternoon? Anything suspicious?"

"No."

"Did you ever feel that Katerina was an instigator?"

"Good grief."

"You have an excellent record with Merry Maid, Hope. Five years, not a complaint. We believe that Katerina is collecting signatures. Is that true?"

"Is that a crime?"

"No, but management is concerned that the staff might be unhappy."

"Are you happy, Bertie?"

"This isn't about me, Hope. Please. Understand that I have a job to do. If I don't do it, I'll get fired."

"Where *is* Katerina? Did you throw her under a bus?"

"Let's just say that she won't be working with you and Ling anymore."

"Oh my." Then she said, "I quit."

"What do you mean?"

"I'm done. Finished."

"Hope, you can't do that."

"Yes, I can. Just watch me." And she got out of the car and shut the door. It was very cold and she had no ride back to town, unless she waited for Ling to finish work. She walked back into the house, found Ling, and told her the news.

All Ling said was "Oh, Hope. I'm sorry." And she returned to work.

Hope sat on a chair in the foyer, still wearing her coat. She knew that Roy would be disappointed. Two years earlier he had left his job as a drywaller, taken the real estate test, and become an agent. He had just recently begun to make a little money selling houses, though it was her income that kept them afloat. But not anymore. In a moment of self-pity, she saw herself as selfish and egotistical. She did not know the value of things. She thought money grew like potatoes, just reproduced. She spent too much on cosmetics, on haircuts and colour, on shoes, though she hadn't bought a new pair for three years. She had a touch of the maniacal. She could not bake. She didn't like to make love often enough. She ate too much, had a sweet tooth that would lead to diabetes. Demanded her own bank account when there wasn't enough for one account. Was needy. Careless. Did not think.

She was extremely tired. She thought that she would have to call a cab and take the thirty-dollar ride back into town— half a day's pay. She stood and went into the kitchen and picked up the phone, which was completely forbidden—they were not allowed to use clients' phones. Well, she no longer worked for Merry Maid. After she had called the cab company, she stepped over to the fridge and took an apple and she sat at the kitchen table and ate it slowly, watching out the window for her ride.

She did not want to return to the apartment just yet—she was not ready to admit to her poor behaviour, a sure result of her pride—and so she asked her driver to drop her off at a hotel downtown, at the corner of Portage and Main. She carried her kit of cleaning supplies, was still wearing her yellow Merry Maid outfit beneath her coat, and to all intents and purposes, she looked like a bag lady. She went directly through the lobby of the hotel to the bathroom and washed up, smoothed her hair back. From her purse she took her makeup and applied it carefully, studying herself in the mirror. She wrapped her scarf around her neck, allowing it to drape and fall so that it covered her name, Hope, which was stitched to the yellow uniform. Her kit, with the brushes and cleaners and rags, she left in the bathroom. She carried her coat over her arm and went into the lounge and sat in a dark corner. She laid her coat over the chair beside her. She drank a Tom Collins and then ordered a glass of red house wine. It was getting late, past the supper hour, and by now Roy would be fretting. Perhaps he would phone Ling, though Hope believed that he would not stoop to such theatrics. He was very careful not to show his anxiety.

She ordered a hot roast beef sandwich and a coffee and another glass of wine. She began to relax. The ebb and flow of guests in the lounge kept her interest. Men in suits and young women in high heels and short skirts and jackets with wide shoulders. She tried to remember when she had last walked into a lounge on Roy's arm, wearing heels, feeling the warm stir of desire at her core. She finished and paid the bill and then, quite spontaneously, she approached the desk, took out her credit card, and asked for a room. "High up, please, with a view of the river." She took the elevator to the twenty-first floor and stood by the window overlooking the railroad tracks, and beyond that the frozen river, and she thought how easily one could pretend that all was fine. She showered and put on a robe and then sat down and phoned Roy.

"Roy, Roy, I'm okay. Don't worry. I have a surprise for you." She told him which hotel to come to, and she said that he should use the house phone in the lobby and call room 2130. "Okay? And ask for Charity. Can you do that?"

"What are you talking about, Hope? What are you doing?"

"Just come. Okay?"

She hung up and went to the bathroom and looked at herself. She applied makeup once again, and found herself wishing that she had some proper underwear or nice lingerie. All she had was the Merry Maid outfit. She removed the housecoat and wrapped herself in a towel. Her knees looked tired. And so she put on the housecoat once again and ascertained that her calves still had some life in them. She did not know, would never know, if her body would have disintegrated to this extent if Roy had managed to keep the business. The fact was, if she still lived in Eden, she wouldn't have had to work at that backbreaking job, and she would be taking better care of her face and her nails and her hair. Worry and manual work had worn her out. Still, rich women got old as well. The skin dried out, the breasts disappeared, the arms gathered flesh. Watching Roy undress in the evenings sometimes, she was amazed at how his body seemed to stay younger than hers. Though the skin on his neck was looser, and his ankles had lost their hair, up to the edge where the socks rested.

She sat on the bed and she waited.

When the phone rang she answered and said, "Charity speaking."

"Is that you, Hope? Who's Charity?"

"Is this Roy? Please, Roy, come up to room 2130." She hung up. She was a little breathless and dry-mouthed. Roy needed to work on his imagination. She'd always known that.

She answered the door to his knock and she could see the relief on his face. "I thought that there was an actual woman named Charity, though I knew it was you. Everything's very confusing, Hope. Where have you been?"

She placed a finger on his mouth and shook her head. "Shh." She pulled him towards the bed.

At night, in a Winnipeg winter, the lights reflect off the snow and the effect is one of brilliance, as if a heavenly

spotlight is lighting up the whole city. There is no darkness to speak of. This was the light that fell into the room
where Hope and Roy lay, covered by a down quilt, their
hands touching.

Roy, who did not usually like surprises, said that this had
been a fine surprise. "Where did this come from, Hope? Or
should I call you Charity?"

She made a small noise, which might have been a snicker
or a moan. "Oh, I've been saving it," she said. "I quit my job
today. I was completely beaten up. I couldn't do it anymore.
And on my way home I thought that we have no time for
pleasure anymore, and so I decided to change that. You're
not upset?"

"No. I saw that. That you were exhausted. I'm glad for
you."

"What will we do?"

"It'll be fine. I'll make a few more sales, and it'll be fine."

She didn't believe him, but she turned to him and kissed
his forehead and said, "You're a good man, Roy Koop."

* * *

Did she have friends? This was a question that sometimes arrived in the middle of the night when insomnia set in, which
happened more and more and, she supposed, was also the result of aging. She drove out to Eden once a week and saw
friends with whom she had maintained a relationship after the

bankruptcy. She visited Irene Wall, wife to one of the wealth-
ier men in Eden, a woman who was now in a wheelchair and
collected folding chairs. Her garage and attic and basement
were replete with chairs, some simple metal "church basement" chairs and other finely crafted turn-of-the-century
wooden chairs that cost hundreds of dollars. Tea times with
Irene usually concluded with a tour of the chair museum.

She also met Emily once a week for coffee at a small café
in downtown Winnipeg, and it was here that Emily introduced her to several women her own age. The women were
retired, or their husbands were retired and had settled into
golf. All of them appeared to take winter vacations in Florida,
something she and Roy could not afford. These women, with
names like Vi and Arlene and Pat, were part of a book club,
and at some point, with great generosity she would realize in
hindsight, they asked her to participate. She had always read
but had never truly talked to anyone about what she was reading. She had merely formed her own opinions and then forgotten them. For over a year she met with six other women,
dutifully read the books—many of which she would not have
chosen to read on her own—and offered the occasional opinion, which was usually out of sync with the opinions of the
rest of the group. She suffered a sense of smallness. These
women were so clear about what was true and intended and
wrong about a novel that Hope was dumbfounded. Vi, especially, was a real talker who seemed to know exactly what the
author was attempting, and who based her opinions of a book
on whether she could identify with the main character.

Hope attended the monthly meetings not because she

enjoyed the discussions, but because she was lonely. There appeared to be a consensus among the women that men were completely different creatures from them, even (or especially) those men to whom they were married, or the men they had taken on as lovers and partners. Vi used the term "partner." She was recently divorced and was dating a man her own age who was a birder. When Hope heard Vi speak of this man, this birder, she came away thinking that there was very little passion in Vi's life. Everything appeared to be set out as a series of building blocks, with Vi as the builder. She was organized, if nothing else. One evening, after a brief discussion about the book they had all read, they moved on to other subjects. Pat laughingly told a story about a couple who were joined at the hip. They couldn't let each other out of their sight. "In each other's pocket," she said.

Hope was immediately worried that Pat might be referring to her and Roy.

Arlene said, "Well, I believe that this group here, you lovely women, give me pretty much everything I need."

"What about sex?" Hope asked. She hadn't meant to speak but she was offended for some reason, and her emotions overwhelmed her.

"Hope, you're talking like a man," Vi said. "Women are different. We don't need sex like men do."

"But what about romance?" she asked.

Arlene laughed. "Men have a singular vision of romance as well."

Hope said that she knew a woman who, in order to put spice back into her marriage, had rented a hotel room and, using a different name, invited her husband to join her. She paused.

"To please whom? Her husband or herself?"

"Oh, I don't know," Hope said. "Both, I guess." She had lost her bravado and was no longer sure what she believed or wanted. Perhaps she had never known what she wanted, had merely followed Roy's whims and wishes and desires. These women might be right in thinking that more could be had from a relationship with women than one with a husband.

What had Roy truly given her? Kindness and bravery and affection and, in the early years of marriage, a home and safety and stability. But then, after the loss of the business, she had had to find her way once more, standing by Roy's side. What other choice was there? She was so inured to the dance of marriage that she could not imagine anything else but marriage. Just last month, when Roy was sick with a urinary tract infection, she had spent the nights lying on the floor beside the couch where he slept, holding his hand, waking to check his breathing, fetching him glasses of cool water, feeding him his pills. What else to do? Run away? Join a coven? Leave Roy high and dry? In any case, she had no means of supporting herself. Since she had quit working for Merry Maid, she swore she would not stoop to slavery ever again. And Roy had told her she did not have to. What he made as a real estate agent would carry them through.

That night, in bed, she asked Roy if it was a terrible thing that they were in each other's pocket.

"What a curious thing to say."

"Shouldn't we have other friends? Confidants? Is it possible that we are too close, that we depend on each other too much?"

Roy was perplexed. "Where'd you get that idea? Are you wanting to find someone else? Do you have another man?"

"No. Where would I find another man?"

"Oh, they're out there. Truckloads of them."

"Oh my." She had a sudden image of all these wagging demanding penises. "I don't think so."

"You don't like being in my pocket?"

"Am I then? Look at Emily. She's free, isn't she?"

"I would think she has her own set of troubles."

"Yes, but she chooses exactly what she wants. If she decides to go to New York to visit Angela, she buys a plane ticket and goes. If she wants to eat grapefruit for breakfast, she does so."

"You can have grapefruit for breakfast."

"I think I will. Tomorrow I will go to Safeway and buy some grapefruit. Even if you don't like it."

"Good. Can we go to sleep now?" He turned and kissed her cheek in the dark. "Good night, stranger."

"Good night, Roy."

But she could not sleep. She was now worried about Rudi and Ilke, her two grandchildren. They were four and two and it was a month since she had last seen them. Charlotte kept them on such a busy schedule that when Hope called to say she was driving out to Eden and would like to drop off a gift for the children, inevitably both were busy.

"Really, Hope," Charlotte said, "Conner will let you know when they have time to see you."

"Is he there?"

"No, he isn't. Goodbye, Hope."

That had been one of the more pleasant phone conversations. Usually, Charlotte didn't talk to Hope, just avoided her. Let Rudi answer the phone, find out who it was, and pass on the message in his sweet voice that Charlotte was busy. Her children called her Charlotte rather than Mother or Mom, and Hope thought this was a symbol of some deep disorder on Charlotte's part. She probably resented being a mother.

And still Hope phoned, because then she got to speak to Rudi, and sometimes Rudi would lay the receiver on Ilke's ear and Hope would babble and listen to Ilke babble back. Amazing children. She loved them. Perhaps more than she had loved her own. They were so precious and easy-going and sweet-smelling and their chubby limbs were perfectly smooth. Hot breath on her face. "Grandma Ope." Her heart ached.

Whenever she drove out to Eden in the '78 Caprice that Roy had purchased for her, she found herself driving past Charlotte and Conner's house, imagining that Rudi and Ilke might be playing outside, or that she might catch a glimpse of them in a window. Neither Hope nor Roy was allowed to just "drop by." It created too much chaos for the children. When Conner told Hope about this new rule, she looked at him and said, "This is what *you* want?"

He looked defeated. He shook his head and said that he was sorry. "Charlotte says that you spoil Rudi and Ilke."

"That's my job," Hope cried. "I'm the grandma. Does she hate me?"

"She doesn't hate you, Mom." His voice was so uncertain that Hope saw it might be true. She was disliked.

"It makes me so sad, Conner. How did this happen? How about I stop spoiling them? I won't bring any more gifts."

He shook his head.

What a weakling, she thought. Was this her son? The child who used to scamper off wildly on his own, who explored the world at breakneck speed? He was broken. The last time they'd had this discussion, he'd looked at her and said, "Don't force me to choose, Mom. Because I'll choose my marriage over you and Dad."

"Well, it's only right," she said. "But why do you have to choose? Am I a leper?"

And so, once a month, usually on a Saturday afternoon, Conner drove into the city with Rudi and Ilke and dropped by the apartment. What wonderful times they had. Hope pulled out a few toys she had saved from when her own children were young, and against Conner's wishes, she usually had a small present for each child, often just a chocolate bar or perhaps a yo-yo, or one time a Barbie for Ilke, which turned out to be a disaster because Ilke loved the doll and insisted through tears and tantrums on taking it back home. And of course Charlotte discovered the Barbie and phoned Hope and told her that never again was she to buy a "slut" doll for Ilke. In fact, there would be no more gifts. She hadn't approved of these visits, and the whole thing smelled of a conspiracy. "Do you love your son, Hope?" she asked. "Because if you do, you won't pit him against me." And she hung up.

Slut? Well. To Hope's way of thinking, the Barbie bore a strong resemblance to Charlotte.

A few years earlier, at a Thanksgiving dinner held at Charlotte and Conner's house (this was when their presence was still endured by her daughter-in-law), Hope had entered the kitchen to offer her help and had come upon Charlotte and her mother standing at the kitchen sink. Their backs were to Hope, and Charlotte was talking. "She deliberately sets the children on edge. Puts thoughts in their heads. And her clothes. She always wears the same old blue skirt and spills on it constantly when she eats. She's fat. She's sloppy." Hope had believed for a moment that Charlotte was talking about someone else, until she realized, upon looking away and then looking down at herself, that she herself was wearing that same old blue skirt, and that Charlotte was talking about her. She stepped backwards from the kitchen and slipped away to the upstairs bathroom and stayed there a long while, studying herself in the mirror. Was she really that fat? She *had* put on some weight in the past few years, but she had never considered herself fat. Eventually, she composed herself and returned to the dining room, where the family was seated, already eating, and she took her place, marvelling that no one had come to find her, not even Roy. What had amazed her the rest of that evening was her self-control, her ability to pretend that she was simply Grandma Ope sitting down to eat a pleasant meal with her grandchildren.

After Charlotte's phone call the ties were quickly broken, and the visits with Rudi and Ilke became secretive. One Saturday, a month after the Barbie incident, while Rudi and Ilke were watching TV and Conner was sitting and having coffee with Roy, Charlotte phoned again.

"Are they there?" she asked.

Hope innocently asked, "Who?"

"Rudi and Ilke. Has Conner brought them to you?"

She lied. She said that she had not seen the children. But if they showed up, she would tell Conner that Charlotte was looking for them. When she hung up her hands were shaking and her shoulders as well, because she knew she had been deceitful. She had taken the call in the bedroom, and she walked out through the living room to the kitchen, and on her way she touched her grandchildren's heads, and then she went and sat next to Roy and took his hand.

When she looked lovingly at her grandchildren, Hope had always imagined that she saw parts of her or Roy in them. Certainly she saw Conner in their eyes, the shape of their feet, even the way they walked. She often noted that Rudi had Grandpa K's hairline. And so when she learned to her horror that Rudi and Ilke were not Conner's children, and therefore not Hope or Roy's grandchildren, she did not know what to do with this information. She at first tried denial. Conner was on the phone, and he had broken the news to her in a quiet steady voice, though she sensed that he might be on the verge of crying, and she said, "That's nonsense. Rudi's the spitting image of you."

"It's true, Mom. Charlotte wouldn't say this if it weren't true."

"How long has she known this?" And having asked this question, she saw how foolish it was. Charlotte had known from the exact moment of conception. Rudi was four, and so for five years she had known. And said nothing. "Who are the fathers?" she asked.

"A man she met on a business trip. And one of the lawyers from her firm. That was Ilke."

She was quiet. Then she said, "Oh, Conner."

"Why didn't she just leave me after Rudi was born?"

It turned out that *now* she would be leaving Conner. She wanted a divorce. She would keep the children, who were hers, though she would allow him the occasional visit. She didn't want the children to be too confused and upset. She planned, after the divorce, to marry Ilke's father, the man who had had no contact with his daughter up till now, save for the infrequent weekend visit, during which he had been introduced to Rudi and Ilke as a friend. A friend.

And what about the grandparents? Would this duplicitous man's parents just jump in and become the new grandparents? Hope felt rage and bewilderment and jealousy and terrible grief. Over the next months, as the court system decided in its cold-hearted way the path her son must walk, she wondered if she was ultimately to blame, if she had spoiled Conner as a child, if he had gathered up her own propensity for failure (though she had never really attempted anything other than motherhood) and was now paying the price. Might there be some sin in her past, some flaw that had trickled down like a poison into Conner's life? She should have stopped the marriage from the get-go. The girl had been haughty and puffed-up. And highly anxious. Her blue eyes had darted here and there fearfully, like those of a snared rabbit. And then she had taken up cycling, long treks down the California coast with a bevy of other cyclists, leaving Conner with the children for a week at a time. She had always been overly fond of her body, wearing short skirts in summer, prancing about on the dock of the cottage (when they still had the cottage) in her bikini, commanding Conner to fetch her another drink. "Okay, sweetie?" The marriage had been doomed from the start, and Hope had done nothing, said nothing.

One night, eating dinner with Roy, she declared Charlotte evil.

Roy raised his eyebrows. "She doesn't know what she's doing," he said. "Like Conner, she's spoiled and selfish. When I look at the two of them I think they deserve each other."

"Oh, Roy. Don't."

"The thing is, Hope, it takes two to tangle."

"She was the one doing the tangling," Hope cried. She missed the little children. She had not felt such helplessness since the failure of Roy's business, and she found herself for the first time criticizing her husband, who seemed to her now as powerless and ineffectual as their son.

A good lawyer was needed, but it turned out that Charlotte, being a lawyer herself, had access to the best counsel, and Conner was stranded with a mousy family lawyer in ill-fitted suits who mumbled his way through the proceedings. In the end, the court, wise and detached, ruled that Conner had acted in good faith and was, in every definition save the biological, the father, and so would be allowed time with the children every other weekend. Hope despaired. It was a pittance.

And too, there was the unexpected shame she felt. During the court case, Ilke's father had been present, flanked by his own parents. They had made quite the trio, finely dressed, smelling of money, and against her will, Hope had found herself sneaking glances at them, even admiring the new grandmother's clothes, her hair, the cashmere wrap around her shoulders. She realized that Rudi and Ilke would be very fortunate. They would want for nothing.

Penny had taken time off work at the hospital to join her parents in the courtroom. She sat beside Hope and took notes in a little beige book. Hope wondered what the point was. What would she do with all this useless information? Penny, it turned out, had little empathy for Conner, who she felt had always been sloppy in life and probably knew subconsciously what mischief Charlotte had been up to. And if he hadn't? Well, that was idiocy in itself. Penny felt sorry for the children. Adults, she liked to say, tended towards greed and disorder. Children were inclined towards health. Somewhere, perhaps at the age of nineteen or twenty, the curiosity and life force of the child was tossed aside for a mind-numbing existence of acquisition and complacency. She knew this because she herself was an adult.

Penny would not have children. She had married a man named Ted, a biophysicist who claimed that the world was nearing a sixth extinction. He announced this with perverse glee. Well, thought Hope, of course he didn't mind that the world was ending. He had no progeny. He was fifteen years older than Penny, which made him almost closer in age to mother than to daughter. He was solid and faithful and boring. This was Penny's description, and she took great delight in it. She found no significance in beauty or wealth or age. The opinions of others carried little weight. She liked Ted because he had no expectations of her.

Hope felt that she was disappearing. Rudi and Ilke represented her lineage. And now, how would she be remembered? This was not a new feeling. Her whole life had been one of disappearance, of slipping silently through the world, unnoticed. She told this to Penny one afternoon in the middle of the winter, after they had left the courtroom and stopped for coffee at a nearby café on Broadway. They were alone. Penny, on that day, appeared to be quite curious about her mother's feelings. She had her beige notebook, and her pen, and she opened it occasionally and jotted something down. Hope said, "When you were little, we had to tear your notebooks away from you. Otherwise, you would have forgotten to eat and sleep. What are you doing?"

"Oh, just keeping track."

"Of what?"

"Of you."

"Oh, why ever?"

The previous summer Penny had taken a month off to fly to a writers' colony in Italy, where she worked at a collection of short stories that, she explained to her mother later, were quite bad. Full of artifice and dead ends and characters who spoke in paragraphs. Paragraphs. She had worked with an older American writer who one night after a late dinner said that he would like to sleep with Penny. He found her very attractive.

"Is it my breasts you like then? Or perhaps my ass? Or is it my crooked bicuspid? Put a bag over my head and the bicuspid would no longer exist. And would you still want to sleep with me? I prefer older men."

"But I *am* older."

"Not old enough." And she kissed the writer on the cheek and said good night.

She called Ted that night in Canada and told him about the writer, and together they had a good laugh. She came away from the conversation thinking that Ted wouldn't have minded if she had slept with the writer.

She told Hope that the following day she sat in the shade of a lemon tree, and all in a three-hour rush, she wrote a story about a plastic surgeon who attaches the heads of horses to young female bodies and keeps the women in a stable. The American writer loved it. "You can publish this," he announced, and she did.

When Hope read the story, printed in a small magazine out of Boston, she was mystified. Why didn't her daughter just stick to ears and noses and throats? She was a doctor, not a writer.

The routine was for Conner to drop by on the Saturdays when he had the children, and the family would go out to the planetarium or the zoo and then return to the apartment for dinner. Hope would cook hot dogs or Kraft Dinner or she might make French toast. One Saturday, the family sat around the table and Rudi announced that he had two fathers. He said this in a matter-of-fact manner, his small mouth working around the word "fathers." Conner lifted his head sharply and asked, "Who's your favourite father?"

"Oh, Conner, don't," Hope said. Her son seemed tired and worn out. He was losing his hair, which surprised her.

She didn't recognize him at times. She wondered if this happened to other mothers—that they arrived at a point in their
lives where their children had become strangers.

"Don't," Ilke repeated. She had discovered imitation as
the route to learning a language.

Later, alone in the kitchen, Conner told Hope that Charlotte
was thinking of moving to Toronto. The kids would go along.

"Can she do that?" she asked.

Conner shrugged. "I'm not sure I care anymore."

"Yes, you do."

And it appeared he did, because two weeks later, Conner
took the children and ran, driving west through the mountains to Vancouver. Hope learned of this on Sunday night
when Charlotte called to ask if she'd seen him. The children
had been dropped off at a friend's house and Conner had
picked them up without telling her. She was frantic, on the
verge of hysteria.

"I hope you're not colluding with him, Hope."

"How or why would I collude? I haven't seen them. You
should know, Charlotte, that he was terrified you were going
to take the children to another city."

"I'm not moving. Anyway, they're my children, not his.
Your son has gone crazy, Hope. He threatened to kill me. And
the other day someone burned down my shed. I'm sure it was
him."

"I don't think so. That's not Conner."

"Then you don't know your own son, Hope."

Conner phoned Hope and Roy on Monday evening
and said that he was staying in a motel on Vancouver

Island. His voice was muted, the sound of the television in the background.

"The police are looking for you, Conner. And the children. You won't hurt them, will you? This is what Charlotte thinks. And everyone else."

"The only person I want to hurt is Charlotte. I could kill her."

"Yes, well. She said you threatened her. And burned her shed. Surely you didn't."

When he did not answer Hope said, "That won't do. You must go to the police there on the island and give your name and explain the situation. Perhaps they will be lenient."

"I doubt that."

"Think of Rudi and Ilke. They must be terrified."

"Not at all. They think it's great. Out of the clutches of their dragon mother."

"You're angry, Conner. Tell me where you are."

"Why, Mom? You're not going to call the police."

"No. Give me your address. I'm going to come and get you. You stay put. I don't want you to move. Wait for me, do you promise?"

Years later, when she thought back on her trip to Victoria, she recalled the sushi she ate on the flight from Calgary to Vancouver, something she had never touched before. And the young mother with a baby who sat beside her on the short hop over to Victoria—the baby was a squalling fat thing who repulsed Hope, even though she smiled and cooed and said, "Watchanamelittlefella?" as she chucked its ugly chin. And the light scattering across the snow of the Rockies, which reflected the shadow far below of her own airplane, a fleeting indication of her own existence.

She found Conner and the children huddled before a small television in a questionable motel at the edge of Victoria. The children clung to her and she thought, These are frightened things. That night she took everyone out for pizza. She had brought the children gifts—a puzzle for Ilke and Duplo for Rudi—and as they played she told Conner that she planned to phone Charlotte that night. He did not argue. He was out of money, had not shaved, and his clothes were dirty. "You foolish boy," she said, and she turned back to the children.

Driving back alone with Conner's car through the Rockies and across the Prairies, she imagined herself as a migrating animal that, while emancipated for the moment, was actually guided by some homing instinct that overpowered any notion of free will. She played Conner's music, much of which she did not like, and then found under the seat a cassette of Kris Kristofferson, and she grew very fond of it. She dawdled. She drank coffee in truck stops where the drivers sat alone and ate beef. She took rooms along the highway, in motels with names such as The Flamingo and Hark Back Inn. She talked to Roy every night and gave him an update on her progress. She napped by the roadside and woke with a start and drove on, along a thin black ribbon. She wondered how she had never managed to do this before, to drive alone and with complete freedom on the Number One Highway that crossed Canada.

Charlotte had flown out to the coast and then flown with the children back to Winnipeg. The police had arrested Conner, and Hope had made sure that Rudi and Ilke did not witness this. After the mayhem had subsided, Hope sat in Conner's car and cried briefly, and this had surprised her, because ever since her time in Winkler, she had lost her ability to cry. But now she cried. And then stopped.

One evening, as the light fell away, she took a room on the outskirts of Regina in one of those chain hotels. She sat in a chair by a window that looked out onto the parking lot and nibbled at a takeout salad. A memory had arrived that day, during the last hour on the road, of Conner at the age of twelve. He had been caught shoplifting a hockey stick from the local hardware store. The strange thing was that Conner didn't like hockey, had never been interested, and yet there he was, stealing a stick. She had driven over to talk to the store owner, Ben Fehr, in his office while Conner sat on a chair beside her. Ben said that he wouldn't press charges. He trusted that Hope and Roy would set the boy straight. He looked at Conner. "You've got good parents, son, and you shouldn't be humiliating them in this way." Then he addressed Hope. "This isn't the first time, Mrs. Koop. It so happens that two months ago Conner and I ended up in this same room. He was to tell you, and it disappoints me that he didn't."

"I'm disappointed as well, Ben." She turned to address Conner, who appeared to believe that the conversation the adults were having was not about him at all. He seemed uninterested. "Why didn't you tell me, Conner?"

He shrugged.

Hope felt that she was failing in every way.

"Your boy is spoiled," Mr. Fehr said. He shook his head and said the word "shiftless."

She nodded. She did not defend Conner. The hardest part was that Conner had witnessed her lack of fortitude. She had been devastated then, and she felt the residue of shame now.

Approaching the lights of Winnipeg the following April evening, she wished that she might have the courage to just keep driving. She did not miss Roy. Or her children. Or the small apartment. But she went home. First, she stopped and picked up some hot food for Roy, and then she brushed her teeth in the restaurant bathroom, tidied her hair, and inspected her makeup. She was sixty. Still young enough to care how she looked as she returned to her husband of forty years.

For two months Hope did not visit her son in prison. She sent cigarettes and biscuits and cakes along with Roy, but she herself stayed away in protest. She was still angry. When Roy came home from his weekly prison visits, she sat down across from him and asked after her son. The details he offered her were so bare that her imagination filled in the blank spots and she pictured Conner overwhelmed by the chaos and darkness of prison life. She visited him only once. Sat in the large room where visitors were allowed and folded her hands in her lap and studied her boy, who was thinner, with even less hair. She was aware of the other families gathered in bunches, of conspiratorial whispers, of children playing. She and Roy were the oldest people in the room. This fact was sobering.

"How's the food?" she asked. When all other topics were off limits, focus on eating.

Conner shrugged. "Not French cuisine," he said.

She laughed, a quick short yelp. "You never liked fancy food in the first place."

Conner leaned forward, twisting his hands together. "Have you heard from Charlotte? The kids?"

"Not a peep."

"I write them letters, but I don't know if Charlotte lets the kids know. Could you call on them, Mom? See them?"

"Oh, Conner. I don't think so. There's a restraining order. You know that. Fact is, you aren't supposed to even write letters."

And so it was. Not only was Conner denied access to the children, but so were Hope and Roy. It was a shame, she thought. As if Rudi and Ilke would choose not to see their grandparents. Upon hearing of the restraining order she had fallen into a depression, and then lifted herself up through anger and rage, and then tumbled again, and finally settled upon resignation, which was a difficult and hard-earned emotion, according to Emily Shroeder.

"People see resignation as giving up," Emily said. "It isn't. It's acceptance of a situation that is beyond your control. You have accepted the loss of your grandchildren. Which doesn't mean you can't picture them moving through the world, playing piano, going to school, making friends, thinking of Grandma and Grandpa Koop. Who knows, when they are older, they may come back to you."

Penny turned up her nose at what she called Emily's fatalism. The other children might also have disagreed, but they weren't around. Judith still called regularly from Paris, especially now that Conner was in prison. And Melanie was progressing in the world of high jump, train- ing for the upcoming Olympics. One Saturday afternoon, Hope watched a track and field competition beamed out of Sydney, and there Melanie was, all limbs, mostly naked except for little bottoms and a tiny tank top, a twinkling stud in her belly button, no breasts to speak of. What did the girl eat? How elastic she was, so focused, rocking on her heels before beginning her approach, and then the colt-like steps, the bounce, and the takeoff into the Fosbury flop. Hope knew of the flop only because Melanie had explained it to her during a rare visit. She saw two of Melanie's attempts, one successful, one not, before the camera switched to the steeplechase, and even then, as the runners moved around the track, there was the occasional glimpse of the high jump pit and the girls, perhaps Melanie, warming up.

Hope believed that Melanie would not have been as harsh as Penny in judging Hope's notion of resignation. Melanie had always been more easy-going, forgiving, like-this like-that. She made few demands, except the singular demand she made upon herself to jump as high as possible. Penny was more rigorous and less sympathetic. In fact, there were moments when Hope believed that her middle daughter was simply too cold and cal- culating, that her expectations were too high. As a mother, it was much easier to love a child who had failed, because that was the child who came back home and said, "Hold me."

Resignation, quite simply, brought peace. It was as if by saying "I am incapable," she became capable once again. The sweetness of existence could be discovered only by forgetting herself. She now preferred to live without any thought of the future. She scampered, like a fox, between bliss and oblivion.

* * *

Roy died at night, in bed beside Hope. She woke, as usual, around 6 a.m. and knew immediately that he had left her. He was lying on his back, looking up at the ceiling.

"Roy?" she whispered. "Are you there?"

Nothing.

She lay still, staring at the tiny grey hairs in his left ear. His lips were parted slightly, his eyes open.

"Oh," she whispered, and she lifted a hand and touched his face. And pulled it away. She slid sideways, away from him. She sat up and studied him. In death he was still Roy, or so she wanted to believe.

She got out of bed and tiptoed to the door, opened it, stepped down to the bathroom and peed. She didn't know what to do. She walked back to the bedroom, paused, and then gently knocked. "Roy?" she called out. She stepped back into the room. He lay as before. She sat on the edge of the bed and reached under the blanket and took his hand. This was not his hand. Still, she held it and waited. Then she lifted the hand to her mouth and kissed it. "I'm sorry," she said. "I'm so sorry."

For the next hour she sat with him and patted his leg through the blanket, and she tried to will herself to rise and go to the phone, but what was the point? There was no rush. Roy wasn't going anywhere. Neither was she. She talked to him softly. "Here I am and there you are and who knew? Did you? I'm sorry to have slept through your passing. How lonely it must have been, me lying asleep beside you while you just floated away. In a bit, not yet, but in a bit, I'm going to call Penny, who will know exactly what to do. She's always so efficient and competent, not like me, who seemed to hold you back with my needs. There were times, though I've never told you this, when I thought, He should have married a different woman, a woman who understood money, a woman with more love, more forgiveness. A bigger heart. But you got me, didn't you. And now you'll never know better." She stopped talking. Waited. Then started again. "Funny thing, how one evening you're eating fish and go to bed and kiss Hope good night, and the next morning you find yourself like this, in this state, and your wife sits and holds your hand and talks to you in a manner that she never talked to you before. With no expectations, no repercussions, just little old me throwing words down into a deep dark well. Can you hear? I think you can. I'm sorry I wasn't better and I'm sorry I wasn't the best. Not for trying, you know. My repo man. My sweet car dealer. You with the most beautiful hair. Tall and big-hearted and gorgeous. Goodbye."

She waited. Placed his hand back inside the blanket. Closed his mouth and his eyes. That was better. She realized that she would have to begin making up her own life, by herself, working it out minute by minute. Starting now.

She went to the phone in the kitchen and picked it up. When Penny answered, Hope said, "Your father passed away during the night. You should come."

For Hope, tossed about by Roy's death, the funeral was like a shelter from the storm. Penny, who had written the eulogy, ordered the flowers, and, over the last three days, spoken in soft tones with the funeral director, was constantly at her side. Nothing was required of her. She wore a charcoal-coloured dress that Roy had always favoured, and she clutched a small handbag throughout the service. The handbag held her lip gloss and Roy's money clip, now empty. The funeral took place at a small north-end Mennonite church. Hope, who had always enjoyed singing, was surprisingly put off by the hymns and the choice of music. It was all so gloomy, and she wished, during the service, that she had asked for chamber music to be piped in, rather than the stolid thumping coming from a piano played by a very tall thin woman she had never seen before. She told herself to remind Penny that when she died she wanted a pine box, a single violin playing, and a minor speech prepared by one of her children. She certainly didn't want this preacher, a youngish man who was far too evangelical. Roy wouldn't have liked his tone or his fervour for salvation.

Emily sat with the family, as did Berta and her husband. Roy's brother Harold kept leaning forward to blow his nose. He was a solid man whose wife of forty years had recently died of cancer. He had hugged Hope in the church foyer, next to the casket, as if they were now more connected. Hope's cousin, Frida, and her husband, George, sat next to Conner at the far end of the pew. Hope, looking at Conner at one point, thought that as Roy's son he would suffer the most. She feared for him. He sometimes appeared with a certain woman on his arm and the next month there would be a different one. His love life was a blur. And would he ever work again?

To Hope's delight, and she imagined to Conner's as well, Rudi and Ilke were at the funeral. They came for the whole day, brought by Penny, who had made the arrangements, and Hope caught herself experiencing too much joy as she clutched their sweaty hands. When she lost sight of them—at the burial for instance, the cold air sweeping across the bare ground—she called out their names several times in a high desperate tone, until she saw them and beckoned wildly to come. Come here. Ilke was a little princess. In fact, she was a miniature version of her mother. Gorgeous, with long wavy hair and a button nose and perfect skin. She even walked like her mother and, to Hope's horror, had already acquired her mother's haughty assertiveness. Rudi was a rounder smaller version of Conner, or this is how Hope saw him. He was ten now, and had gained some pounds. He seemed to be only interested in the food. She tried to get him to sit beside her and though he did this briefly, he soon disappeared. That was Conner way back, she thought.

Ling, from Merry Maid, was at the service and Hope was surprised by her strength when they hugged and the ferocity of feeling in her face. "I remembered all the stories you told about Roy," Ling said. "He was a funny man.

And kind. And I never met him." She laughed and squeezed Hope's hands.

Hope introduced her to her children. She was proud to be seen with Ling, who represented a world separate from Eden and Mennonites. It gave her some worldly purchase. Her life had become bigger after the bankruptcy. Though this might not be true, she imagined others might think it was.

At the reception, which took place in the church basement, a man in a yellow suit stood at the microphone and praised Roy. What are you doing? Hope thought. It's too late. Where were you when he needed you? This was during the *freiwilliges,* the Mennonite term for "open mike." Hope hadn't wanted to have an open mike, but everyone insisted. She knew what they wanted: redemption. No one would speak ill of the dead, and all reports would be glowing, and Roy would be remembered as a quality man. Well, she'd always known who Roy was, and she didn't have to have some stranger going on and on about how *he* had known Roy. In fact, when Rollie Tiessen, the bank manager from Eden, approached the mike, she sat up straight and clutched her coffee cup. She smiled carefully and looked off into the distance and heard not a word Rollie said. Later, when someone told her that Rollie's acknowledgment of Roy's tenacity had been wonderful, she smiled and said, "Yes, he was tenacious, wasn't he."

Her children surrounded her. Melanie, unfortunately, wore a very short black dress, and it seemed that whenever Hope looked this way or that she saw Melanie's long legs flashing, and she wished it weren't so. The girl had every physical charm imaginable, but she lacked a certain social sensibility. Hope wondered if her sexual leanings made her more flamboyant, less aware of what was acceptable. She knew that she couldn't ask Melanie that, but as she had discovered long ago, private thoughts were private and therefore safe, though her children might be surprised by *her* private thoughts. Judith had flown in from Paris alone. Jean-Philippe was busy with meetings he couldn't postpone and this seemed fine with Judith, who spent her time complaining about Jean-Philippe, who was predictably French.

"Well, what else should he be?" Penny had asked.

"Mature. Kind. Thoughtful. Like Ted."

Judith thought that Ted was dreary, but then so did Penny. She was quite vocal about the fact that she preferred a predictable dreary man to some French playboy who was probably bedding a young Catalan girl right at that moment. It was known that Judith and Jean-Philippe's relationship was somewhat "open," and that Judith suffered jealousy in a larger way than Jean-Philippe. Hope had talked to Judith only once about this, about a year earlier, and all Hope had said was "Do you think that's smart, to share yourself in that way?"

Hope thought that Judith was far too thin. She wore a dark blue wool sleeveless dress that showed off her ropy arms and legs. She had pulled up her hair and this accented her sharp jaw and forehead. She now worked alongside Jean-Philippe in his gallery. She was looking more and more French, Hope thought. Emily, who sat beside Judith at the reception, felt the same way. She said, "You look like you've stepped right off the Champs-Élysées."

Emily and Judith talked about Angela, who was now living in New York. Hope watched them lean into each other and recalled that time, long ago, when Emily had smoked marijuana in her new apartment while Hope breastfed Melanie.

She brought that up. She described the scene and asked if either of them remembered that day.

Judith shook her head and said, "You were smoking a joint, Emily? I had no idea. When was that?"

"You kids," Emily said. "You think we didn't have a life. Fact is, we blazed the trail so everything would be easier for you."

"It was 1964," Hope said. "You had just left Paul."

"I don't think you ever blazed a trail for me," Judith said.

"Well, that's what you *would* think," Emily said. "You can't imagine that your mother and I had big lives, that we courted danger, that we had to tolerate chauvinism."

"Dad wasn't a chauvinist, was he?"

Hope lifted her shoulders helplessly. It didn't matter anymore.

"You take your freedom for granted," Emily said.

Judith shrugged. It appeared that she couldn't imagine it all going wrong, or perhaps she didn't want to consider it.

After the funeral, and after Rudi and Ilke had been picked up by Charlotte (Penny had walked the children out to the street so that Charlotte and Conner wouldn't have to face each other), Hope's children sat at the dining room table in her small apartment and talked about her future as if she were not present. In fact, she felt so left out of the conversation that she stood at one point and walked to the bedroom. She left the door ajar and listened to her children plan her life.

Melanie was concerned that she would get lonely now that Dad was gone.

"She might," Penny said. "But she'd feel the same even if she was surrounded by people."

"Have you seen the kitchen?" Judith asked. "It's filthy."

Was this true? She cleaned quite studiously, perhaps missing a corner here and there, though it was true that since Roy died, she'd let the dishes lie dirty.

Penny, always one for a solid plan, said, "There're some retirement homes I could look into."

"I could live with her," Conner said.

"Oh God, no," Penny said.

"That's ugly." This was Judith, who was actually agreeing for once with Penny.

"There's nothing more clichéd than an older son living with his mother."

Melanie laughed, cheerfully. She said, "Find a woman your age, Con. You're still young."

Lying on the bed, listening to her children talk, she realized that they had no clue about death and loss and grief. She wished they would leave so she could be alone with her thoughts and her loneliness and her sadness. Now that the funeral was done, she felt overwhelmed by sadness.

After Judith returned to Europe and Melanie left for Vancouver, where she was training, and Conner and Penny settled back into their local routines, she spent a desultory few days going through Roy's things, trying to match socks, throwing out his underwear, stacking sweaters, and finding among his books and files the novel *The Drifters,* all three sections taped together, a bookmark stuck in the middle. Roy must have had a go at reading it, so many years ago. Perhaps he had been attracted to the adventure. Had he ever longed for something he didn't have? She smelled the book and set it aside. She picked at scraps of paper in the bottom of Roy's drawer: grocery lists (*bacon, milk, dental floss*) written in his slanted style, and a note to Hope that read, *Hope, I will be meeting Elma at Art's to discuss. See you tonight.* She remembered Elma as the new accountant Roy had hired at the dealership five years before the business went under, a frightening blonde with a gash for a mouth and hands that fluttered and landed around her neck and clavicle. Hope hadn't liked Elma from the get-go. She was the kind of woman who walked into a room as if she were on a manhunt. You could smell danger. Hope had no clue what Roy would have been discussing with Elma. It was perplexing. Though the note was fifteen years old, it held some import. Perhaps Roy had had secrets. This happened. Wife, suddenly orphaned, discovers mistress in the closet. For some time, though not excessively, she considered the possibility, and then dismissed it and tore up the note.

She wondered if she might be trying to sort out the disappointment she felt in herself. That she had never experienced much passion, that she had been too careful, that the brilliant expectations she had had for her life had come to very little. At this point, in this meagre assessment, the children didn't count. They were entities unto themselves. Her own life, a span of seventy, maybe eighty years, she judged as scanty, incomplete, lacking. But in what? Love? Safety? Success? Peace and understanding?

These were her dark thoughts as she piled Roy's clothes and shoes into green garbage bags and called the Diabetes Society for a pickup. She considered briefly that Conner might want some of his clothes, and in the end set aside a purple cardigan. She kept a shirt for herself, and for a while she wore it to bed, until Roy's smell was erased and then she hung it in the closet.

She found herself looking and waiting for Roy. She would walk from one room to the next and expect to find him there. Well, not really. She knew he was dead, and yet for a brief moment as she entered the kitchen, she expected to see him sitting at the table reading the paper. Or when she exited the bathroom at night and made her way back to bed, she was always slightly surprised to see his side empty, the blanket flat, the pillow unused. Or at night, she woke and reached for him and he wasn't there, and she experienced outrage that he should just up and leave her. And then a sadness that made her hands and face numb. Several times, while puttering in the kitchen, she heard him call her name, and she said, "Coming," only to discover as she walked from room to room that she could not find him. She was indeed alone.

She realized, one spring evening, as she sat in her chair and looked out over the parking lot below, that she had been abandoned. And there was nothing to do about it.

5

Age of Hope

She became contented with her life, and being contented, she felt guilty. More and more she found herself revelling in the present moment, simply accepting that what she was enjoying might never pass her way again. She wondered at times, as she drifted down the street to meet her daughter Penny for a late-afternoon tea, if she had ever been as happy. Over the past number of years she had discovered baroque music, playing it loudly on the compact stereo Penny had bought for her. Roy had never appreciated classical music, and now here she was, floating through her new condo, ecstatic about Bach. The condo was another pleasure. Purchased with the money gained through Roy's life insurance plan, and with some extra help from Penny, it was clean and modern, eight floors up, with a balcony that offered a leafy summer view of the brown river below and in winter a glimpse of the skaters as they glided down the path created by the city.

She had become selfish. Or perhaps simply self-contained and self-satisfied, as Penny would have put it. She rose in the morning at the hour of her choosing, dressing or remaining in a housecoat. She drove out to Eden for coffee with Irene Wall, returning when she liked. She gave up large meals for snacks of crackers and cheese, or perhaps a fried egg and toast. Roy had provided amply for her through the insurance, and she felt guilty that she was better off financially with him dead—she ate out at will, she spent money without having to account for it. She talked with Judith on the phone in the middle of the night, without having to worry about waking anyone else. There was no one else. Only Hope Koop.

It astounded her sometimes how she had managed to stay married for so long, given the freedom she now felt. But she hadn't known, had she. She still got very lonely, but she managed the solitude by watching television, talking to her children, and riding the elevator in hopes of meeting other residents in the building. This method of lessening loneliness just fell into her lap one day when she missed her floor and continued to ride up in the presence of a young man who engaged her in the most civil manner. They had a brilliant conversation about movies and she let it slip that her daughter had had dinner with Roman Polanski, and this impressed the young man to no end. She did not tell him that the dinner had happened years ago, nor did she tell him that she knew very little about Mr. Polanski and had seen only the one film that Judith, during a visit home, insisted she watch. A film based on Thomas Hardy's novel. A sad story.

The young man in the elevator had long black hair and he reminded Hope of her son, Conner, back when Conner had hair, and as she said goodbye to this young man, whose name turned out to be Alexander, she experienced pity both for this Alexander and for her son. A strange and unexpected emotion. Once upon a time, during a discussion with Emily, the notion of pity had cropped up, and Emily, perpetually well-informed, had said that pity was a product of one's own insecurity and was directly related to jealousy and failure. Well. She decided not to dwell on this.

The lobby was also a fine place to meet people, even if on a one-time basis, and it was here too that Hope sometimes fell to talking with Ibram, the doorman. Ibram was originally from Lebanon. He still had family back there, and every five years he returned for several months. Ibram and Hope spoke of travel and food, and at Christmas they exchanged a little care package. She gave Ibram cookies and homemade chocolate, and he gave her sweet desserts made of honey and sesame oil and coconut, along with fresh almonds.

The condo she purchased had cost a fair bundle and so had cut into her plans to travel. She mostly made do with looking at maps from various countries and reading travel guides, but she had enough money put away for one trip. She thought that a Russian Mennonite study tour might give her a sense of Roy's history, but when she spoke with the woman organizing the tour, she found herself disagreeing with her, not with what she said about history, or the Mennonites, or even Russia, but with the manner in which she said it, haughtily, as if Hope were a child. And so she chose not to go to Russia.

Instead, she travelled to France and lived for several weeks with Judith and Jean-Philippe, who spent most of their time hissing at each other or descending into outright arguments. Judith was no longer working at the gallery and had found a part-time job in a clothing store, very upscale, that catered to wealthy Parisians. She hated the job, and this, along with other financial demands, weighed heavily on the relationship. She often came home late. Because the apartment was small, Hope was constantly in the way, and so she found herself going out alone into the city, seeking shade from the brilliant sun, spending far too much on coffee served in little cups, nibbling at croissants. The heat wave that summer had taken the lives of numerous elderly folks, and for a time Hope believed that she too could easily be a victim of the heat.

Perhaps because she was usually alone, with few distractions, and perhaps because her own daughter seemed to be avoiding her, she found herself thinking about her parents. Passing by a patisserie, she smelled the fresh pastries and baguettes, and she was reminded of her childhood when she would visit her father in the early morning at the bakery and sit on a stool and eat fresh cinnamon buns as he worked. His view was simple: there was nothing better than serving people bread. He had told her this only once, but she recalled it now with utter clarity. Memories of her mother, on the other hand, were less precise but more emotional. A scene, a song, an image from a movie could stir a recollection of her mother's hands or her voice calling out softly, or of her crossing the backyard in Eden long ago during those months when Hope was ill. She felt a deep longing.

One day on the sidewalk at the edge of the Seine, thumbing through some modernist prints, she came upon a replica of the Degas print that Emily had given her so long ago. At first she felt faint and out of sorts. She was taken back to a time in her life when everything had been topsy-turvy. She had been crazy, and then she was healed. The little open suitcase, the bent back of the small woman, the dark room. But the suitcase. How strange, she thought, but then realized that it was much more logical to find Degas here in Paris than in an insane asylum in southern Manitoba. Her confusion and wonder was a testament to her unsophisticated life. Later, she found a small café and sat for several hours watching the people pass by. She drank an espresso, and then ordered a toasted ham sandwich and drank some sparkling water. The shade of the umbrella protected her. Her mother, who had always wanted to visit Paris but never had, would have loved this scene.

The next afternoon she set out again and found herself in the Louvre, wandering through the great halls, overwhelmed by the tourists and inundated by the numerous works of art that at some point all bled into one great indistinguishable master painting. She panted and padded in circles. She had to find a bathroom. She approached a security guard and asked in French where the toilets found themselves. The guard pointed and gave the directions and so she set off on a complete goose chase that ended in a dark corner near the rendition of the Opera House, done to perfect scale, and it was there, unbeknownst to the swarm around her, that she gave in and peed on the floor. She stood there and looked off into the distance, purse clutched to her chest, as the urine rolled down her leg and formed a puddle at her feet. When she was finished, she slipped away and hastily sought the nearest exit, passing by the sign for the women's washroom. Too late. Out through the large courtyard to the street, where she hailed a taxi, got in, and sat, her bottom wet, humiliated, on the verge of tears.

She wasn't sure later why she told Judith the story of the unfortunate incident at the Louvre. Perhaps she believed it would be an amusing anecdote. Perhaps she was trying to say: take care of me. Judith was horrified and related the tale to Jean-Philippe, who was apoplectic. Over the next hour there was, or so it appeared to Hope, who understood little French, a teaming-up on the part of the two of them against her. She had unwittingly united them. For two days Jean-Philippe would not speak to her, and when he finally did speak, he said, "It is necessary that you realize, Hope, that to piss at the feet of the master painters, it is a sacrilege and a travesty."

"Oh," she said, "I was lost. It was impossible to find a bathroom. Don't the French have to pee like normal people?"

"They control their bladders," Judith said. "And they're not fat."

At that moment, Hope was eating a peach pastry that she had picked up at the patisserie. She held her fork in the air, paused thoughtfully, and then deliberately ate another mouthful. Judith had always had a taste for cruelty, especially towards her mother. She seemed to reinforce what Hope knew in her own mind regarding her physical appearance. That she was overweight. Hope was aware of the French women her own age who strolled along the wide boulevards in Paris, perfectly coiffed, in high-heeled shoes, wearing expensive clothes. They were like aliens. She said, "French women eat like birds. I'm not a bird."

"*C'est vrai,*" Jean-Philippe said.

Hope turned red. She felt helpless. She said, "Perhaps I will take a train and visit the south."

Judith did not argue. In fact, she made the arrangements, buying her a return train ticket and booking a hotel in Marseille. Two days later she rode in the taxi with Hope to the Gare de Lyon. Ever since the plan had been set in motion, Judith had been softer, more forgiving. "You'll have a wonderful time, Mom. The Mediterranean is gorgeous."

"I worry," Hope said. "Won't it be even hotter there? And will the hotel have air-conditioning? Will I get by with English?"

Judith took her hand and patted it. "You'll be fine. It's an adventure. Phone me when you arrive."

"I wish your father were here."

"I know you do."

"You shouldn't fight so much with Jean-Philippe. You don't know what you have."

Judith smiled. "It's the heat. It makes us all crazy."

"*Je suis fou,*" Hope said.

"*Folle.* You're a woman. *Hope est folle.*"

"In fact, I worry that she is."

"Oh, Mom, you're not."

"I feel like it sometimes. The other day, in a café, watching the people, I felt terribly alone. As if every other person knew exactly who they were, but I didn't. For a moment I even forgot my name."

Judith looked concerned. "Does that happen often?"

Hope shook her head. "I'm not senile. I meant in a philosophical and moral way. Who is Hope Koop?" She sighed. "This city has made me into a romantic."

"It can. It did me."

"And then?"

"I don't know."

"Are you having an affair, Judith?"

There was a pause, and Hope knew she was right. She didn't really want to know the details and so she squeezed her daughter's hand and said, "Thank you for making the arrangements."

She thought later, on the train, after she was settled in her window seat and facing the direction the train would be travelling, so as to see the approaching villages and the cows and sheep in the fields, that ever since Roy's death she had become a coward. Especially when it came to her children. Or perhaps she had become weary of confrontation. Fighting with and caring for her needy children wore her out. They were still so demanding. Hope did not recall that she had given her own mother any grief when she was Judith's age. She married, had children, raised them, helped her mother die, buried her, and never once had she called on her for help or counsel. There was something to be said for independence and for not revealing the sauces in your kitchen, as Jean-Philippe would say. It did not surprise her that Judith was having an affair.

And it should not surprise Jean-Philippe either, though it certainly would, because men seemed to think that they were immune to emotional pain, that "fucking around," if she could use that term, was the domain of men. Well, it wasn't. Women could be as cruel and foolish and selfish as men.

She was glad that Judith did not have children. She could not bear another catastrophic breakup like Conner's, where the grandchildren were torn from her bosom. She had not seen Rudi or Ilke for several years now, not since the funeral, though Conner did give her the annual school photographs, which Hope taped to the fridge door. The children were stretching out. Their faces had changed. If she were to pass them on the street she might not recognize them. A year ago, while at the Bay shopping for a bra, she had seen Charlotte pass by the lingerie section. She was wearing a red coat with a faux fur collar and at first Hope had not recognized her, and then she heard her speak (she was with another woman, equally handsome) and she knew that it was Charlotte. Hope followed her, past the underwear and over into the women's jacket and blazer section where, she presumed, a lawyer might buy a suit. She stood very near the two women, rocking on her feet. It was the other woman who noticed Hope. She looked at first confused because Hope was standing so near and was staring with such great intent. "Yes?" the woman asked, and Charlotte turned.

"Hope," she said. "What do you want?"

"You whore," Hope said, and she turned and walked away.

Roy would have been appalled. But Roy was dead, and so he could not be appalled. Or perhaps he had been appalled up there in heaven. She, on the other hand, was here on earth, and she felt no remorse, no guilt. She wondered if she would have been so flagrant if Charlotte had not been wearing the red coat, or if her legs weren't so shapely and long. If she had had an axe in her purse, she would have brought it down on her head.

Upon arriving in Marseille, she was immediately struck by the filth and heat. It was a port town and appeared to attract all kinds. She had consulted her map and discovered that her hotel was a five-minute walk from the train station. Feeling adventurous, and thinking she might stretch her legs, she decided, unfortunately, to walk. She found herself wandering down narrow streets with shops that sold piping and toilets and copper wire. Men sat in circles at the edge of the sidewalk, smoking water pipes. She meandered here and there, dragging her heavy suitcase. Her ankles were sore, she was thirsty, and she despaired of ever finding an exit from this hellish maze. Near a shop that sold cigarettes and newspapers, she sat on her suitcase in the shade and fanned herself with the folded map, keeping an eye out for a passing taxi. None appeared. She wondered what Judith had been thinking, pushing her out the door and sending her down to this polluted city where vagrants held out filthy hands and asked for sous. She longed for the cool clean comfort of her condominium on Wellington Crescent in Winnipeg.

A voice spoke. "Madame, you require assistance?"

She looked up and saw a middle-aged man in a brown

suit. He carried an umbrella, which was opened. The man's face was clean and kind. His eyes were deep blue, rather like Roy's when he had felt deeply satisfied with himself and the world, which often occurred after they had made love.

"Oh, yes," she said. "I am lost." She wiped her forehead with a small white cloth that she kept in her purse.

The man in the brown suit said, "Please, which hotel?" She handed him the map and pointed at the spot where the hotel was supposed to be. He studied it and then he took her elbow and helped her stand. He asked for her suitcase. "With your permission?"

"Yes. You may." He might be a thief or a con man, but she did not care. Let him steal her belongings—they were mere things. As long as she found her way to the hotel, where she could draw a bath and clean herself and drink coffee and then sleep. She followed him up the sidewalk, the suitcase clattering at his heels. He had handed her the umbrella, and she now held it and immediately felt relief from the sun. The man in the brown suit stopped at a small restaurant that sold noodles. He offered her a chair, asked her to wait please, and disappeared into the rear of the shop. He came out five minutes later, just as a car pulled up to the curb. He opened the rear door of the car and indicated that she should get in.

She shook her head.

"I apologize," he said. "You will be safe. The driver will take you to your hotel. No need to pay."

"And my luggage?"

He raised a hand and a young boy appeared and picked up her suitcase and placed it in the trunk.

"Please," the man said, and he took her elbow and helped her get into the rear seat. His touch was deft and kind. The door closed. She looked up at him from behind the glass of the closed window. He opened the front door and spoke to the driver in a language she did not understand. Then he turned to her and said, "*Bon voyage*." And he was gone.

Later, soaking in the bathtub of the hotel room, staring at the high, finely detailed ceiling, she considered the man in the brown suit. The comfort of strangers was not foreign to her, but the fact was that in her life she had not had access to very many strangers until this day, when the man in the brown suit arrived like a celestial traveller, unbeckoned and nameless.

Unwittingly, she had kept the man's umbrella, and over the next week, as she struck out to explore the city, to go to restaurants, or to walk in the parks, she carried it with her, expecting at any moment to see the man in the brown suit and thereby return it to him. But she never saw him again, and so she returned home with the umbrella and hung it on her coat rack by the front door, where it sat for a time, until she lent it out to a friend—she forgot which friend—who required protection walking home during a summer squall that descended with a black ferocity, and then dissipated as quickly as it had arrived.

* * *

Hope had always been less adamant than Roy about attending church, in fact she had often stayed home Sunday mornings when he attended, saying that she'd rather feed the children a hearty breakfast than sing old hymns. In hindsight, she wondered if her children might have benefited from a more rigorous religious education. Perhaps Conner would have married more wisely and had children who were actually his, or Judith would have found someone who was faithful, or Melanie would have been less confused about her sexual orientation. This second-guessing usually came upon her when she heard other women, old friends from Eden, speak of how successful their children were, or how beautifully their grandchildren were coasting through the world. Doubts assailed her and she imagined that she had failed to give her children a solid foundation. Though she had given them love, hadn't she?

In the latter years of her seventh decade, she began to drop by an Anglican church that she had discovered quite by accident one Sunday morning when, walking by, she heard music coming from the open doors. She entered, sat down near the back, and heard a man in white vestments speak in a manner that was both familiar and lofty. She knew immediately that he was lofty because he sprinkled his sermons with Greek and Latin phrases, read parables by Kierkegaard, and quoted philosophers, dropping their names like raisins into a rice pudding, and though she did not recognize many of these writers, she took pleasure in hearing their names.

The pastor, a Reverend Wenders, one day quoted Aristotle: "One who throws a stone has power over it until he has thrown it, but not afterwards." She was so moved by this passage that she approached Reverend Wenders after the service. She had to wait for a long time because there were numerous parishioners, more genuine than she was, who also had important things to say to him. When she finally caught him, they were alone, and she introduced herself as Hope Koop, as if this might have some meaning for him. He seemed impatient. He said, "Yes?" and he waited.

She was disconcerted. She had imagined that Reverend Wenders would be as personable in person as he was behind the pulpit, but this seemed not to be the case. Perhaps he was tired. All these needy people.

"Oh," she said, "I just wanted to thank you. For the sermon." She paused, waited, saw that he would not prompt her further, and so said thank you again.

"You're welcome, Hope," he said, and he turned from her.

She was pleased that he had remembered her name, even though she had just told him not one minute earlier. This was a sign of someone who listened and cared and took note. But she had wished for more. She had imagined she would lean towards him and whisper confidentially that the passage about the stone throwing had moved her greatly. And then she would shift gears slightly and explain why it had moved her, confide that a number of years earlier she had wanted to kill the woman who had been her daughter-in-law, but instead had called her a vulgar name. To her face. And in doing so she had released the stone from her hand and no longer had power over it. More than that, she wondered if it might be possible to write a letter to this woman, asking forgiveness. But what concerned her was that the letter was also a stone of sorts—wasn't it?—and once sent she would have lost all power over the letter as well, and was that a wise thing to do? Or should she let sleeping dogs lie? Or was the dog even sleeping? She thought not, because she still did not have access to her grandchildren, and the stone that had been thrown—the vulgar word, that is—and the throwing of that stone had guaranteed that she would not see the grandchildren until they were much older and could decide for themselves if they even wanted to see Grandma Koop. They might not, though she couldn't imagine why not. And in conclusion, she wondered if her desire to write the letter, to take back power over the stone, was ultimately a selfish act, one that indicated the simplest desire to hold Rudi and Ilke, whom she still loved dearly.

All of this went unsaid, because Reverend Wenders had said a simple thank-you, and disappeared. But Hope did not despair. She was grateful that what had been stated, that line about the stone, had allowed her to even think these thoughts—surprising thoughts indeed, thoughts that would not have even jumped into her head if Reverend Wenders hadn't helped them arrive. And so she was grateful to him.

She went home and pondered on these things for several days and then she sat down one morning and wrote a letter to Ms. Charlotte Means, her ex-daughter-in-law.

Dear Charlotte,
It is me, Hope. I imagine this is not a letter you want to receive, or even read, but please bear with me. I have been thinking much about relationships these days

(I have time to think), and I want to say that I am no longer angry with you. I am too old for bitterness and anger. I have discovered a new country, a place where brooks babble and birds flit from tree to tree. I find myself in the midst of that bucolic setting and I feel peace. And feeling that peace, which has arrived completely unbidden, unwilled, I want to say that I am sorry for whatever grief I have caused you. I cannot speak for my son, Conner, who has his own road to walk, but in my case, please know that I am sorry. I have tried, over these past years, to hold the memory of Rudi and Ilke, but I find lately that my recollection is failing. I hope they are well, and thriving. Please, if you can, tell them that I still love them and that I think of them constantly. That day, when I saw you in the Bay and I was so rude, I simply lost it. I threw a stone that I could not take back, and that stone, I am sure, hurt you. I am sorry. About my life, I am well. As well as I can be for a woman who is turning seventy. I pray for your family. I pray for Rudi and Ilke. Thank you for listening.

Hope Koop

She kept the letter for a week, and then finally mailed it, walking up to the post office in Osborne Village, where she stood in line behind a girl with pink hair and tattered black stockings. She had imagined she had no expectations regarding the letter. It was an act of bravery and clemency, for herself only.

And she was correct to believe that nothing would come of it. Even though she waited with faint anticipation for a response, it never came.

And then Emily's Paul died. In fact, killed himself. Hope was sure of it, because Emily was so sure of it. Paul had driven his car, a Belair sold to him by Roy when he still had the business, into the back of a parked tractor-trailer on the Trans-Canada Highway. He had had no business driving on the shoulder at a hundred kilometres an hour. Broad daylight, perfect weather, warning triangles posted, and still Paul had hit the tanker and the car had spun into the ditch, engine smoking, leaving Paul himself a tattered mess of flesh and irretrievable organs. Emily and Paul, after all the years of living apart, were still married. At the funeral, held in Eden, Emily was held in suspicion by those, many of them mere acquaintances, who saw her as a betrayer and a wayward woman. She had lived a selfish life.

Hope helped Emily clear out the house. Emily had recently had double knee replacements and was just barely becoming mobile, and so she sat in the middle of the house while Hope trotted about, noting the contents. Pieces of furniture that Paul had built were everywhere, stacked on end in the basement, the living room, overflowing the workshop. There was hardly room to walk. In total, there were fifty-five end tables, all made of cherry. Hope did not take any of the pieces, even though she was offered whatever she liked. She had gone modern, she said, glass and steel, and this was true. She had bought a new dining set at Design Manitoba. Leather and steel chairs, glass-topped dining table—something Roy would have found pretentious. Later in the day, drinking wine and sitting in the backyard on oak folding chairs that Paul had built, Emily surveyed the house and said, "It might be best to simply make a bonfire and burn everything."

Alone and driving back to the city, Hope wondered if that wasn't the difference between her and Emily. Emily's answer to trouble was to set fire to the strife, and in doing so, to make it disappear, whereas Hope held trouble close to her chest, as if she might suffocate the difficulty or worry it into submission. Emily, after several glasses of wine, said that she should have been more vigilant. She had spoken with Paul once a month, and their last conversation had been disjointed. "He kept repeating the word 'disarray.' He was trying a different medication, and it wasn't working. Without me he was desolate and lonely."

"But Emily, he was desolate and lonely when you were still living with him," Hope said.

"Was he?"

"Yes. You told me that. I remember when you left him, you told me that you would die if you stayed."

"I was young. And desperate. I felt hemmed in. Funny thing, I still feel hemmed in. Maybe more so."

"When Roy died, I was terribly lonely. Inconsolable. Still, there was suddenly all this space around me and though at first it was overwhelming, I grew to like it. Quite quickly. Shamefully."

"You're too hard on yourself. I envy you."

"Don't be ridiculous. There is nothing to envy."

"See? This is exactly what I mean."

But Hope hadn't seen. What did Emily mean?

She recalled the lilac bush in Eden, beyond the kitchen window, which bloomed briefly for one week every spring, and then became just another shrub with green leaves, indistinguishable from every other shrub. What was the point? She had told Penny one afternoon, as they drank tea on Penny's front porch, that she believed in heaven, though she wasn't sure about hell. "Actually, I don't believe in hell. And truth be told, I'm no longer sure about heaven either." She said this with a certain amount of glee, as if tasting rebellion for the first time.

It was on this same day that Penny announced it was time to move beyond the short story and write a novel. She was going to take a leave from the hospital. The novel would be about a woman born in 1930 whose existence was both minor and major.

Hope was wary. She smelled a rat. "What do you mean, 'major'?"

"She is a woman. And what is there about the life of a woman that is worth exploring? A woman does not fight in wars, does not invent, does not make something out of nothing, except for the exceptional woman, like Madame Curie or Jane Austen. Most women your age had children and raised them, and then what did the children do? They took the mother for granted." Penny sighed. "I don't know. I haven't figured out the major part yet, though it has to be there. Doesn't it?"

"I was born in 1930."

"You were."

"Oh, why write such nonsense?" And then, pleased, she said, "Leave out the unfortunate parts." And then, "If you must tell the truth, be kind."

"It's not about *you*, Mom. You might recognize bits and pieces, but it *is* a novel."

"I was not perfect. Never perfect. I was the furthest from perfect. But then that was not my intent."

She was amazed that her middle daughter showed any interest in her. All of a sudden. And then she realized one day that the interest was ultimately selfish. Penny needed a story, was incapable of making something out of nothing. She called her up one day and said, "It will be too episodic. You'll need some backbone to the story. A plot. My life was plotless." And she pictured her existence printed out on several hundred pages, formless and wilting in a drawer somewhere. "No one will want . . ." She struggled to conclude the sentence.

Another time she called Penny and said, "You might think twice about using my life. But if you go ahead, please leave out certain things I have told you. Paul's kiss, the abortion, I don't believe it would benefit anyone to know that, the bankruptcy, my work for Merry Maid, humiliating, the hotel room scene, whatever sex talk I have let slip, my weakness for sweets. You could wait till I am dead. And failing that, try to lie a little. Also, at all costs, avoid sentimentality."

Penny laughed. "Mom, this is fiction. If you want the facts, write a memoir."

"Don't. I'm not even sure this is working, so you can forget about it, okay? Probably nothing will come of it."

"Oh." This was disappointing. For a month now Hope had discovered that the space she occupied had grown slightly. She imagined herself a minor player in a drama that was self-contained. Somewhere out there a box was being built for her, and the box itself would not allow for spillage or chaos, or if chaos did present itself, the moment of disorder would be brief. The narrative of her life would be clean and unsuspecting, with tiny bumps like potholes on the road. She had, in a self-deprecating though ultimately hubristic manner, told Emily about Penny's novel. She had sensed that Emily might have been slightly miffed, and it made sense. What was so important about Hope Koop? Emily, in every way, had lived a more *interesting* life.

The next time Hope saw Penny, she said, "You know, Emily Shroeder is a fascinating person. She's incredibly well read and has lived a bustling, dare I say, almost dangerous life. For a time she had a lover who was a chef. Her daughter lives in New York, where Emily lives for months at a time as well. Even Paul, her husband, died in a tragic way, from a suicide." She heard herself, and paused. Waved her hands in the air and said, "I would think the voice is most important. Don't you?"

Within a few months, perhaps because Penny stopped mentioning her novel, the subject was shunted off to the side, and in every way this was a relief to Hope, who was finding it difficult to live both her real life and the projected other life. She settled down and gradually let go the idea of immortality. Who did she think she was?

Over the past year Hope had been taking day trips out to Altona to visit her cousin Frida. George, her husband, disliked Frida having too much fun, and so their coffee times usually took place in Frida's kitchen while George hovered nearby. Frida had no access to money, wasn't allowed to answer the phone, rarely saw anyone, save Hope, and was beginning to talk of death, as if she had some premonition of her own demise. Hope was worried.

Over the last while, when they had moments of privacy, talk had turned to escape. At first, because it was a touchy subject and Frida was a fearful woman, the word "escape" was not used. Instead, Hope talked about what was normal and abnormal. She told Frida that it was not normal that she did not have money. And it was not normal to be disallowed use of the telephone. "It's a basic right, Frida. You should be able to pick up the phone and call your friends. You should be able to answer the phone and not have George screen your calls."

"He doesn't like you, Hope. He thinks you're putting thoughts in my head."

"The thoughts are already there, Frida. I could be anyone." She did not tell Frida that the feeling was mutual. She did not like George. He was a sweet talker in public, a man with two faces.

"Well, he doesn't think you're a positive influence."

"That makes sense, doesn't it? That he would think that? He's afraid."

"He is?"

"Oh yes, and fear can make a person do crazy things." Hope thought this was true, simply because she had been afraid at certain points in her own life and had acted in an unwell manner. "He's afraid that you will leave him."

"Oh, no, I'm not planning to leave him. Where would I go?"

"Well, there is Irmie."

Frida had a daughter, Irmie, living in Ottawa who refused to speak to her father. Irmie made it known that Frida lived in a prison, but she did little to help her mother. She didn't come home for visits, and she talked with Frida by phone only once a month, though she had told her one time that if she needed a place to live, she could come to Ottawa.

Hope was a patient woman, and for a year, as Frida flip-flopped between leaving George and staying, she neither encouraged her, nor tried to dissuade her. She merely asked questions. Sometimes, on Sunday afternoons, as George napped in the bedroom, she and Frida talked in whispers about various scenarios and images of freedom. These were other women, nameless and faceless, who had lived in situations that were very similar to Frida's.

"Penny told me just last week of a friend, let's call her Jane, who took her three young children and moved into an apartment. The husband had gambled away the mortgage, the car, the cottage. Nothing was left. Jane didn't even write a note. She just packed up the kids and left."

"George doesn't gamble. And our house is paid for. He insists on doing the grocery shopping. I can make lists, but he doesn't always follow them."

"Has he hurt you? Physically?"

"Oh, no. Never."

"He doesn't touch you, then?"

"Only when we lie together. Once a week."

"Do you want that?"

She shook her head. Nodded. "It doesn't hurt." Then she said that she was embarrassed. Sex talk made her nervous.

"It's okay. Don't worry."

"What about Roy?" Frida asked one time. "Did you ever want to leave him?"

"There were moments," Hope said. "And to give Roy credit, he would have said, 'You can go.' A marriage is a balancing act of giving and taking."

"But you didn't have to leave. Roy died." And as she said this, Frida put a hand over her mouth as if she had overstepped some moral boundary. "I'm sorry."

"And it might be that you wish George were dead."

"Oh, no. I don't. Do I?"

And then, one afternoon after an especially difficult week, Frida said, "I want to leave." Immediately she looked horrified. Her hands shook.

Hope touched her elbow and said, "Are you sure?"

Frida nodded.

"Okay," Hope said, all business. "This is what we will do."

She had, in preparation, called a women's shelter and they had been very specific about protection and having a plan and making sure that Frida had a safe place to stay. One time the word "violence" was used and Hope had been adamant that George was not violent. He had never been violent.

Over the next weeks, whenever Hope visited, she collected some of Frida's clothes and her personal effects, taking them home with her, preparing a suitcase for the trip. She purchased a flight to Ottawa, using her own money. She called Irmie in Ottawa and said that Frida was planning to leave George. The date was set. Frida would be arriving in Ottawa on an afternoon flight.

"Are you sure this is what she wants?" Irmie asked. "I mean, it's about time, but I can't quite believe it. My mother has never chosen for herself. It's always about Dad."

"She's decided." No wonder Frida had been stuck for forty-five years. Even her child had no faith in her. Where was the agency?

Hope was not afraid of George. Whenever she arrived at the house and George answered the door and said, "Oh, you again," Hope simply said, "Yes, it's me, George," and walked past him and went to find Frida. George didn't know what to do with a woman like Hope. She was like that innocent-looking cloud on the horizon that becomes a tornado.

The day of the great escape, as Hope would refer to it later, in a rendition devoid of irony and pathos, she drove to Altona in the middle of the night and parked her car on the street outside Frida's house. Frida planned to leave the bed and walk out with her winter coat over her nightgown and climb into the car, and Hope would whisk her away. She had prepared a Thermos of coffee and a tuna sandwich for Frida. Food and a hot drink could calm an uneasy soul.

The street was quiet. A soft snow fell through the light of the streetlamps. A cat crossed in front of Hope's car, jumped on the hood, padded about for bit, and then disappeared. Frida's house was dark. And then the door opened and Frida stepped out in slippers and an ankle-length down parka. She closed the door and stood on the porch, not moving.

"Come, Frida," Hope whispered.

And then she came, an old woman, shoulders slightly bent, hair in a tight perm, looking back now and then at her house.

She climbed in and shut the door.

"Is everything okay?" Hope asked.

"I forgot my key. I've locked myself out," Frida said. She looked at the house one last time, and then said, "You can go."

Hope drove through the quiet streets, and it was only when they had passed the town limits and were on the highway that Frida began to cry. Hope handed her the Kleenex box. Frida whispered, "Poor George, he will be so worried. I should have told him. What will he have for breakfast?"

"Toast. Cereal. He's very capable."

"The coffee maker has been finicky lately, and he won't know about the broken switch. It needs to be wiggled to make it work. I should have left him a note."

"Do you want me to turn around, Frida? I can do that. Absolutely." According to the woman at the shelter, this was not the thing to say. *Stay calm, don't give in to her panic, talk her through the doubts. Carry on.* As if Frida were a mere animal with no free will. Why shouldn't she choose, either way? Hope had found that the counsellor in the shelter, probably late thirties, was unfeeling about Frida's quandary. It had seemed such a simple matter to her. Just leave. "But she's close to eighty," Hope explained. "She's leaving the place she's lived in for sixty years." The counsellor had made a face, one of impatience, and Hope thought then that she was incompetent.

Frida was steadfast. She said, "No, keep going," and she began to put on the clothes that Hope had brought along. Hope talked to her, mostly nonsense about her own children, about a movie she had seen the previous week, a comedy of sorts that hadn't been particularly funny, but she liked movies no matter the subject. "Give me a movie star on a big screen and I'm happy," she said. "I would think that in Ottawa you'll have the chance to see some movies with Irmie. It'll be very comfortable. Irmie has a bedroom ready for you."

"I forgot my glasses," Frida said. "They're on the bedside table."

"You can get a pair in Ottawa. They're very cheap these days. Maybe you can even get two for one."

"I don't know." Frida worried her hands. She had managed to change into her clothes, awkwardly, fighting her way out of her down coat and her nightgown, baring herself briefly as Hope kept her eyes on the road. Her face was pale, a round puddle of flesh that could no longer countenance her own perfidy. She began to cry again.

Hope took the Thermos and unscrewed the lid, managing this poorly as she drove. Some coffee spilled on her lap, scalding her.

"Shit," she said.

Frida laughed through her tears. Reached for the Thermos and poured a little. Handed the mug to Hope, who took it and drank.

"This was for you," Hope said. "I was going to give it to you at the airport." She pointed to the tuna sandwich.

"I'm sorry," Frida said.

"Why? You're very brave."

"Oh, I'm not. I'm not. Please take me home."

"It'll be fine, Frida. You're afraid. But Irmie is waiting for you, and I will check you in at the airport. You've been fearless."

"Not anymore. This is all wrong. Take me home."

Hope pulled the car over on the shoulder. Touched Frida's knee. "You've come this far. A long way."

Frida was suddenly and irrevocably clear-headed. "I can't."

Neither of them spoke during the return trip, except once when Frida whispered, "I'm sorry," and Hope said, "You have nothing to apologize for." To the east was the grey ghost of a late-rising sun. Hope pulled up in front of Frida's house. The lights were on.

"He's awake," Frida said.

"I think I should come in with you," Hope said.

Frida shook her head. "That'll only make it worse. I can manage." She climbed from the car and opened the rear door and pulled out the suitcase.

"You phone me, okay? Frida? Call me today."

"Yes. Yes, okay." And she turned and walked back up the sidewalk, the little suitcase banging against her coat.

Hope watched as Frida rang the doorbell. The door opened, George stepped back, and Frida entered her home. George looked to the car where Hope sat, and then he shut the door.

She sat and waited and watched. The car ran and the heat blew over her ankles and calves. There was nothing to report. Only silence.

The next day George phoned, and when she answered he said, "You bitch," and he hung up. He called again the next day, exactly at three, and as soon as she heard his voice, she interrupted him and said, "Do not phone here, George, and swear at me."

"You stay away from her, Hope, and I'll have no reason to call. You've embarrassed her and yourself."

"How is that, George? There are only three of us who know of Frida's wish to leave. Four if you count Irmie. And so how is that an embarrassment?" She was arguing with George, an impossible thing, but she could not help herself.

"Oh, I'm sure you've told people about me, Hope. George is cruel. George doesn't let Frida do anything. Well, let me tell you this, Hope. Frida has a weakness for drama and storytelling. She makes things up."

"I've known Frida for all my years, George. There's nothing weak about her."

"You're not welcome in our home, Hope."

"Frida agrees?"

"We both agree. We've talked about you, about you and Roy, and we agree that you like to encourage other women to leave their husbands because you didn't have the same courage. Those are not my words. Those are Frida's words. She said that."

Hope set the receiver down. Her hands shook. She realized she was gasping for air.

A month later, she phoned Frida's house and Frida answered. She sounded so soft. So careful. "George has changed, Hope. It's much better now. You see, I answered the phone. It feels like when we were young and first married." She giggled.

"I'm happy for you, Frida," she said. They had little to say to cach other, as if both ashamed in some way by what had come to pass.

She wondered if the shame she felt was for herself or for Frida, or for women in general. For a week she found herself disliking her own kind, the frailties and weakness of her sex. And then, the following week, she felt tremendous strength and was proud of all women, especially Frida. Why had she expected Frida, who had been married forty-five years, to simply walk away from her house, her linens, her towel sets, her silverware, her recently renovated kitchen, the solidity and comfort and scent of everything she had wished for, fought for, acquired, and accrued? Who was Frida, if not all that?

She knew that she had fallen short in some way with Frida. The sense of failure was like the smell of a mouse rotting in the ceiling tiles—faintly sweet and occasionally overpowering and then sometimes not there at all. And then the stink eventually dissipated and all that was left was the carcass, hidden and dried out, the infinitesimal skeleton of a rodent that once scampered through the house.

The problem, she came to see, was that she had tried to liberate Frida even though Frida hadn't felt the need to be liberated. Over the course of time, she had convinced Frida that she lived in a prison. But who was to say that Hope was any less manipulative than George? They both wished to control her. Hope thought that she might have misplaced her righteousness. Her virtuous act was, from Frida's point of view, not so virtuous. And so she forgave her.

* * *

Hope was discovering that she was most in need of forgiveness. Because she was living with a sense of sin herself. Six months before Roy died, Hope had told him that she was no longer interested in sex. She had been working up to this announcement for a while, and then one evening, during an argument about something completely unrelated to sex, she had declared that she was done with the act. She no longer had the desire. "You can go elsewhere. Hire someone or find a lover, but I'm finished."

"Hope, that's ridiculous," Roy said. "I'm not going to go elsewhere. You know that."

"Well, I've made up my mind."

Roy did not speak to her for several days. And then one evening he presented her with twelve roses in a cut-glass vase. There was a card attached that read, "To Hope, with love from your husband, Roy." She suspected that this was a trick of some sort, and so she was muted in her response, though she did thank him and kiss him on the forehead. She knew that men, even as they grew older and were less inclined, believed sex was a necessity. It was a performance, a testament to their potency. It was as if men were employed by a circus that demanded a nightly trapeze trick. Even old age should not be an impediment. Emily's brother, now in his eighties, had remarried, and in order to have sex he required a penis pump. Why? Why not just accept the frailty and weakness of old age and simply cuddle? Why such a need to stay youthful?

In some closeted corner of her mind she wondered if Roy had died of rejection and heartbreak. She had kept her word, no sex, though there had been a minor setback one night after they had watched a movie together and she had drunk too much wine and she had *entwined* with him. This was the word she used, but only with herself. To "entwine." He had been so grateful that night, so effusive and soft, that she wondered if she should reverse her decision. And then, after he died, she found herself in bed wanting him. She was bereft, and she thought that she might have sinned.

She hadn't confessed this sin to anyone, not until Judith came for a visit. It was Hope's seventieth birthday, and Melanie would be arriving from Vancouver the next day, but on this evening, sitting with Judith on the balcony of her condo, she began to speak in broad terms about love and marriage and children. Earlier that day, Penny had told Judith of Hope's attempt to free Frida. Hope had listened to the story as well, trying to interject once or twice, but failing, because it appeared that Penny knew the story better than she did.

"No shit, Mom," Judith had said. "You did that? Where did that come from?"

Hope was insulted. Who did her children think she was? Some weak nondescript seventy-year-old who no longer had any purchase in the world? The cult of youth had inflamed even her daughters, who were themselves practically too old for that. And now, in the evening, Judith was confessing that she was sorry she hadn't had children. "I'm forty-six. I know there are women who have babies at forty-six, but think of the poor kids, stuck with such old parents."

"Does Jean-Philippe want children?"

"He would. But he's sixty-six. I look at him sometimes and imagine that I will be his nurse. We still have sex though."

"Oh," Hope said. She wondered what had happened with Judith's affair. And then, for whatever reason, perhaps guilt wedded with opportunity, she confessed that she had deprived Judith's father of pleasure late in the marriage. "Only for a bit. He died not long after, but I see now that I was wrong. And selfish. Why couldn't I have just given in? I guess I'm saying this for your sake, Judith. Take my advice."

"Jesus, Mom, I'm not a kid anymore. I can decide for myself what I want. Anyways, I don't think you killed him."

"Don't say 'Jesus.' And I didn't say I killed him. I disappointed him. And that's a terrible thing."

She was sorry she had told Judith this little tale, as if forgiveness could be had through public confession. She knew better. She knew that by talking intimately with her children she was making herself into a comic figure. Her children, kind as they were, had no inkling about her inner life, her dark and wayward thoughts, her need for independence, even her lack of affection for them. There were times when Penny was overbearingly self-righteous, and Judith mean, and Conner a disappointment, and Melanie simply unreliable. Emily would have understood. With Emily, Hope could say just one word and immediately there was a mutual vibration, even when they fought or disagreed. They understood each other.

When Melanie arrived for the birthday party, she brought with her the young woman who was her partner and lover. Hope had not yet met Ariel, and so was slightly nervous, though she needn't have been, because Ariel was very much like Melanie: young and immature and easy-going. When Melanie had told her mother that she was in love with Ariel, Hope had said, "Are you sure? You might want to be sure." Melanie had laughed and said that she was as sure as she needed to be.

Hope was very happy for her youngest daughter. She was even happier when she heard that Melanie was trying to get pregnant. The sperm was donated by a rower on the Olympic team. Allan Forsythe, six foot six, and a man who, Melanie claimed, if she had been attracted to men, would have made a fine husband. Hope imagined a granddaughter becoming an adult in a world in which she no longer lived. This was her melancholy bent, and it did not sadden her as much as amaze her. There was so much that she would miss. A toast was proposed and white wine was found in the fridge, a half bottle that had been opened two weeks earlier when Hope had entertained Emily. "Where's Judith?" Penny asked, looking about, and Conner made a face and said that she was crying in the bedroom.

"Oh, shit," Penny said, and she raised her glass, drank with the others, and then went to console Judith. They returned later, arm in arm, and Judith approached Melanie and hugged her and said, "I'm so happy, and so jealous, but mostly I'm happy." And then she hugged Ariel as well, and Hope was aware of how muscular Ariel's forearms were, and how short she was.

There was some discussion among the children that weekend about Hope, and she was pleased to be the centre of attention, even though much of the conversation focused on her reckless driving and the need for a maid. Well, the truth was, she was a bit of a menace on the road, but then she had always been a reckless driver. The Belair she had inherited upon Roy's death had gradually acquired various nicks and dents, testaments to a corner cut too close or an attempt at parallel parking gone awry. When she hit a parked car, she immediately left the scene of the crime and moved on down the street to find a different parking spot.

However, she was offended by the idea of a maid. "What are you thinking? I can still cook and clean. And I'll be driving when I'm ninety. Mrs. Kraus, in Eden, she's ninety-five and still drives a standard."

"That's wonderful for her," Penny said, "until she kills some kid on a bicycle."

One evening after dinner, Hope said, apropos of nothing, "I refuse to be a burden on you kids."

"Oh, Mom," Penny said, "you're not dying."

"Of course I'm dying. We're all dying." She turned to her other three children. "Your sister's writing a book. About me."

"What?" This was Judith.

"I am not, Mother. It's a novel. And it's sliding all over the place. It lacks structure."

"Like my life," Hope said.

"That's not true," Judith said. "Do you feel that, Mom? Your life has been full."

Hope sensed that Judith wanted her life to be full because if it wasn't, then she was an embarrassment and a failure, and perhaps this meant that Judith's life was not full either. It was a selfish statement, completely without empathy.

"I know that it's been full," Hope said. "Look at my children."

Conner had stepped outside to the balcony for a cigarette, and he returned now and studied Penny. "Are you? Writing a book about Mom?"

"No."

"Well," Hope said, "it's about a woman born in 1930 and it follows her life. That's what you told me, isn't it?"

"Does she have children?" Melanie asked.

"Three," Penny said. "Maybe." She made a face.

"Where's it set?" Judith asked.

"Oh, here and there. Eden. Winnipeg."

"You're actually using the name Eden?"

"For the rough draft. It feels more authentic."

"If I'm in it, I'll sue you," Conner said. He looked quite serious, and then he grinned.

"She won't publish it till I'm dead," Hope said. She was enjoying herself. Her heart was full. She loved all of her children. She was going to be a grandmother. Immortality beckoned after all. "I wish we had more wine."

Mr. Arthur Templeton. What a debonair and aristocratic name compared to hers. She'd always felt, deep down, that her name belonged on a farm, that one might easily conjure up the image of a long row of cages filled with hens, poor girls, losing track of their eggs as they rolled down into wire gutters. In her early days, during the age of her despair, she had opened the *Concise Oxford Dictionary* and discovered to her chagrin that the word "coop" came from Middle Low German and was, variously: *1 A basket. Only in ME. 2 A wickerwork basket used in catching fish. ME. 3 A cage or pen for confining poultry etc. ME. 4 A narrow place of confinement; slang, a prison.* She imagined a dirty little shanty in which a family of sixteen lived, though she wasn't sure where this idea came from. Over time, though, she managed to sublimate all these images and definitions, and had come to see her acquired name as positive. She construed associations. A coop represented a safe place. It provided food. Wickerwork baskets, freshly dipped in the Sea of Galilee, full of fishes. Various other baskets, replete with loaves. The Sermon on the Mount. Jesus come to walk among the poor, freeing prisoners. Eventually, she came to accept her name, and to appreciate the sharpness of the singular syllables, the symmetry in the number of letters: Hope Koop.

She first introduced herself to Arthur Templeton in the lobby of her condominium. She had just returned from a shopping trip at Safeway and was standing near the elevator when the bag that she was holding broke and five potatoes, Yukon Gold bought in bulk, spilled out and bounced along the tiles, coming to rest in various corners. She was alone in the lobby—Ibram was outside talking to a tenant—and so she set about gathering up her potatoes. She had retrieved four of them and was down on her knees, peering under the couch in the middle of the lobby, trying to find her last one, when the elevator doors opened and out stepped an older man dressed in a dark suit, wearing a fedora, and wielding a cane. The man paused in the middle of the lobby and said, "You lost something?"

Hope looked up. She was aware of the man's polished shoes, the fine cut of his suit, and his sharp jaw, above which played a slight smile. She felt foolish, caught in this humiliating position. She stood. Brushed off her slacks. "Oh, no," she said. "Well, yes. I lost a potato."

"Under there?" The man pointed at the couch.

"Yes, it escaped."

"Indeed," the man said, and he lowered himself with great care to the floor and peered into the dark space where the potato had disappeared. "Aha." He swung his cane under the couch and the potato rolled out. He picked it up, stood, and handed it to her.

"Thank you," she said.

He held out his hand. "Arthur Templeton."

She took his hand and said, "Hope Koop."

"Ah, yes," Arthur said, as if he recognized her, or had been waiting a long time to discover her. He said, "Spuds for dinner, then?"

She was surprised to hear him use the word "spud." It seemed so out of place with his dress and demeanour.

"I like to bake a potato every night. It's easy, I find."

"It is." He studied her. "I've not seen you before. You live here?"

"For four years."

"Well, I'm a blind man then not to have noticed such a beauty."

"Oh," she said. "Thank you for your help. It was nice to meet you." And she passed through the open elevator door and did not look back at him.

How odd, she thought as she rose to her floor. There was mirror in the elevator, and she saw herself and was grateful that she had worn her finer dark blue slacks and a cream-coloured jacket to walk to Safeway. After her trip to Paris she had become more careful about what she was eating, or perhaps she was just less interested in food since Roy died. In any case, she had lost a little weight and had acquired a new wardrobe. Even her daughters had remarked, at the time of her birthday party, on her new outfits. She had her hair coloured with highlights every four weeks at a small salon down the street, and now, aware of her appearance, she thought that while she might no longer be a beauty, she wasn't bad looking. "Oh, look at you, Hope," she said. She felt light-headed.

Over the past few years, Hope had begun to feel invisible. She belonged to a whole herd of grey-haired women in running shoes who apparently did not exist. She felt it when she came face to face with the young girl who served her at Starbucks and she had to navigate the silly debit machine. All those buttons. The younger girls were often kind and helpful, certainly because they must have grandmothers her age. The disdain she felt came from women in their forties who were desperately trying to stay young. It was as if these women saw a reflection of their future selves and were frightened. Hope was slightly offended and slightly amused by this.

So now, to experience the flutter of being seen was special indeed. Indeed. Hadn't Arthur just used that word? What a confident word. As if there were nothing to be doubted, complete certainty. This was something else she had noticed about Arthur during that brief encounter. He seemed so sure of himself.

She kept an eye out for him, subtly, but she did not see him. And then, two weeks later, on her way to meet Conner for lunch, she ran into him just outside the lobby doors. She thought later that he might have been lying in wait for her— the encounter was too coincidental—but at the time she put it down to chance. He raised a hand and bowed slightly and said, "Hope Koop."

"Mr. Templeton."

"Arthur, please." He said that he had just been thinking of her. He had an extra ticket for the symphony the following night. Would she like to join him? "I hope this isn't too forward, but my daughter, who was supposed to be joining me, had to postpone her trip. She lives in Kansas City."

"Oh, but I don't know you."

"I'm not dangerous. In any case, you can outrun me." He lifted his cane and smiled.

He was quite brazen and she wondered if Arthur Templeton was *fast*. A playboy. However, he had a daughter, which made him, in Hope's mind, a family man and therefore safer, and so she said, "Yes, I would like that." She was immediately sorry because she felt that she was betraying Roy, and she couldn't imagine what she would wear.

"Good. Then I will call on you at 6 p.m." He nodded, said goodbye, and slipped away.

She wore a dark dress with a matching belt and a necklace of pearls. She was dressed and ready to go by 3 p.m. and spent the remaining hours alternately studying herself in the mirror and sitting at the dining room table staring out the balcony windows. She had not eaten since lunch, and by the time they were seated, her stomach was grumbling and all she could feel was embarrassment. She needn't have worried. Arthur was hard of hearing. It felt very intimate sitting side by side with this strange man who, during the concert, leaned towards her and whispered little details about Shostakovich and the various movements. Arthur, she realized, was erudite and well informed.

He insisted on taking her out for a late-night snack— highly unusual, he admitted, as he was usually in bed by 10 p.m. They ended up in a French café not far from the condominium, where she finally ate. Creamy pasta with legumes and shrimp. They shared a litre of wine. She learned that his wife had died six years earlier, and he had been an economics professor at the university. He had one daughter, Cheryl. He was eighty-two. He did most of the talking, though she did manage to tell him a little about herself and her children. And Roy. She felt that Roy should be sitting at the table with them.

Two days later a single rose arrived in a cut-glass vase. A note came with it that read, "Hope, thank you for the won-

derful evening. With affection, Arthur." She was startled by
the word "affection," and then pleased.

The following week, they took a taxi out to Assiniboine
Park and walked slowly through the Leo Mol Sculpture
Garden, talking the whole time. Arthur was a conversational-
ist, much more so than Roy had ever been, and he was a very
good listener as well. A week after that, in what she felt was
their most intimate time together, she drove him out to Eden
and showed him the house where she had lived with Roy and
raised their children, the dealership that Roy had owned and
then lost, the church she had been married in, the site where
her first boyfriend had died in a plane crash, her parents'
grave. He was curious about Mennonites and she gave him
a cook's tour of her own experiences, of Roy's background,
of the enclave of Eden, making it clear that she herself no
longer adhered to the Mennonite faith, though she still considered herself a Christian. "Absolutely," she said. He told
her that he was an atheist, the first she'd heard of this, and
she refused to believe him. "It's such an arrogant statement,"
she said.

He laughed and suggested they find a bite to eat in town.
"Take me to your hangout."

"I don't think so. Tongues will wag."

"What fun," he said. "Hope has a lover."

She flushed and said nothing in response, aware that words
were forceful and full of temptation. That afternoon, before
they said goodbye, she told him that she didn't like the word
"lover." "It sounds silly. We're too old for that kind of talk.
And the truth is, it wouldn't work. You don't believe in God."

"I'm sorry, Hope. I didn't mean to frighten you."

"I'm not frightened, I'm just being practical. I have had one *lover*. His name was Roy."

"This is what I like about you, Hope. Your obstinacy."

She lifted her head, suddenly alert. "And you? You have had others?"

"Bernice, my wife."

She didn't believe him. He was constantly flirting, with waitresses, with young women at the grocery store, with her. This was not so disturbing as it was amusing, and somewhat awkward, as if he still imagined himself as a young man. She was suddenly tired. She said goodbye.

And yet, she had, just the other morning, woken with a warm heart and an image of lying beside Arthur. Of course, she hadn't been naked or anything so risqué, but she had pictured touching him, and he her, and this is what had produced the warmth and the confusion of feeling. Her imagination was passionate and full. "Stop it, Hope," she said. But she didn't stop, because these thoughts made her happy. Arthur made her happy. She went out and bought muted rose-coloured underwear with lace trim and a camisole with a tiny satin bow perched where her cleavage was supposed to be.

She had not mentioned Arthur to either Penny or Conner, though they might have suspected something. The last time Penny visited she'd noted how vibrant Hope seemed. "It's like you've gotten younger, Mom. What's going on?"

"Oh, nothing."

Arthur cooked a meal of curry and chickpeas and chicken, laid over a bed of rice, and he served her in his dining room, where the lights were turned down and candles flickered. He'd put on some music—Henry Purcell, he said, and Hope nodded, as if Purcell made perfect sense, though she'd never heard of him. She asked where he lived.

"He's dead," Arthur said. "Many years."

That evening, she was very aware of Arthur's mouth, of the sensuality of his lips, and though she tried to calm herself, she realized that she was growing quite fond of the man sitting across from her. She had come to realize that a relationship needn't be symbiotic, that two people didn't have to see eye to eye on everything. Arthur was more political than she was. Unlike Roy, he believed that unions were a good thing. He walked in marches. He served at a soup kitchen on Christmas Day. He taught her to play chess. He took her to hear chamber music. He had plans to travel to Egypt and the Middle East. About this plan he was rather wry, saying, "If I don't die first."

In September of that year, the day the towers fell, he knocked on her door in the morning, and when she answered he walked straight to the TV, turned it on, and sat down. She lowered herself beside him. At some point, she did not know when, they were holding hands. The images were truly horrific and if she had been alone she would have turned off the television. Yet she knew that as long as the television was on and Arthur remained sitting beside her, they would continue to hold hands, and this is what she wanted. A wall had come down—a wall that she had erected and fought so hard to maintain—but now that it had crumbled, she was awash in the wonder of the man beside her. His texture, the soft hand in hers, the bluish veins, the beautiful thin hair tucked back behind his ear, the neck, the shirt collar and the tie.

"Kiss me, Arthur," she whispered.

He had not heard. She leaned forward and kissed his cheek. He turned. She kissed his mouth, lightly, and then pulled back and smiled and said, "There."

She had uncovered a small miracle within the larger catastrophe that was taking place out there in the world. Here you are, Hope, she told herself.

Autumn was glorious and they took to walking arm-in-arm through the fallen leaves up Wellington and through Munson Park and then back again towards Hope's place, where she prepared a light lunch of salad and sandwiches while Arthur napped on the couch. They ate their noon meal out on the balcony, overlooking the river, and when the weather turned they sat at the dining room table, eating and talking. Arthur was fond of ideas, and Hope, not so happily sometimes, felt like his student. About his feelings, he said little, and this was disappointing, and so she tried to balance the conversation by talking about her own emotions. She did not know, for instance, if he loved her, and one day she asked him this directly.

"Do you love me, Arthur?"

"What a silly question, Hope. What do you think?"

"You've never told me."

"Well. I love you."

"But you might just be saying that because I asked you."

"Can't you tell?"

"I'm not sure. I wonder sometimes."

"Do you love me, Hope?"

"I think so. I do. I think so, yes."

"So you see. You've never said the words. And yet I believe you."

"Even though I'm not sure?"

"But your actions are sure."

"Are you happy?" she asked.

"Very." He smiled and reached for her hand.

She had been teetering on the edge of a cliff the past few days, and so now, taking a deep breath, she jumped. "Do you ever imagine getting married? Again?"

Arthur laughed briefly and looked down at his plate. He looked up. "My goodness. That's a thought, isn't it? Never."

Hope did not speak. She felt great shame and, oddly, some anger. She put down her fork and knife and she stood and walked to her bedroom and closed the door. She sat on the bed and said, "Oh my."

When Arthur phoned the next day, she hung up on him. When he knocked at her door three days later, she stood on the inside, observed him through the peephole, and did not answer. He sent her flowers, cards, a letter. In the letter he tried to explain himself: she had asked if he "imagined" getting married again. He had not meant "never" as de facto never again getting married. He was quite able and willing to think about marriage, though he considered the institution flawed. He concluded by saying that he was old and used up, and that she was still sprightly and young and deserved a man who would be around for a while. She folded the letter carefully and placed it in the china cabinet. "De facto," she muttered. "What bunkum." When she had finally settled down, she parsed her thoughts and wondered if she had in fact mentioned marriage because she knew exactly what Arthur would say. He had, in past conversations, been rather cynical. Never about love. Just marriage.

She had acted childishly. She was too old for childish things. On Thursday afternoon, two weeks after their disagreement as she had come to call it, she baked an apple crisp and carried it, along with a tub of ice cream, down to Arthur's apartment. She knocked. And waited. Knocked again. She returned to her place and put the ice cream in the freezer, and then wrote a note to Arthur saying that she had a little dessert she would like to share with him. She descended to his floor and slipped the note under his door.

He did not call. She phoned the next day, but all she got was his voice mail. She left a message. "Hi, Arthur. It's Hope Koop. I hope you got my note. Give me a call when you have a chance."

Still no call. On the weekend, pretending simply to be curious and affable, she asked Ibram if he had seen Arthur Templeton.

"Well, Mrs. Koop, he's gone to Kansas City to stay with his daughter."

"For a visit?"

"Longer, I think. His condo's up for sale."

She was bereft. She had not felt this abandoned when Roy died, and she wondered how this could be. She was also very angry: with herself, but more so with Arthur, who had simply up and run away. Thank goodness she hadn't married him. She called up Emily and spilled the whole story, taking the blame. "He was debonair and sweet and intelligent. When I think of it now, Emily, you would have been better suited for him. He was a Communist."

"Hope, Hope. You're funny. Take some credit. I think it's wonderful. That you felt love. At our age."

"Do you think so?"

"Oh, yes. To be a trout gasping on the chopping block and then suddenly you are back in the water."

"I pushed him away," Hope said. "Intentionally. I gave myself a mammoth scare and then blamed him. I have always suffered from what Roy used to call a dangerous independence. You would think that by now I would have learned. Arthur winked. I've never trusted men who wink."

She moped about, and in order to settle herself, she frequented a café where she read and drank coffee and nibbled at a warm cinnamon bun, all the while aware of the comings and goings of other customers. She felt less lonely in a public setting, even though she was alone. At Emily's suggestion, she was reading *Madame Bovary*, and though the story was compelling, she found Emma to be insipid and weak and wanting. All this desire for things and love, running off with young men, ignoring her child.

Hope had settled on a version of her own affair that she felt comfortable with. She had been slightly overreaching, too aggressive, and she had taken everything too seriously. Were she to do it again—and she wouldn't—she would be more lighthearted.

One evening over dinner, she told Penny of her travails with Arthur, portraying it as a comedy. Ted was present as well, but in his typical manner, he had little to say. Hope wondered if Ted had heard her tale of woe, or even believed in woe. Penny said, "Oh, Mom, we should have met him."

"You would have, if he hadn't run away."

"Write to him."

"Oh, I don't know. That would be like begging."

"Not at all. Until you settle this, you'll fret and stew. A letter would be an olive branch."

"I don't want to marry him."

"It's not a proposal." It was Ted who said this. He looked at Hope and lifted his shoulders. "Just a letter."

And so she wrote him. She managed to acquire his forwarding address from Ibram and she wrote a short, light note in which she described the weather in Winnipeg, which had turned terrifically cold, though there was as of yet no snow, and that made the cold seem even harsher. She spoke briefly of their relationship, though she did not call it a relationship. It had been a friendship. She wrote, "I was a pickerel gasping on the kitchen table, and for a time you put me back in the water." She signed off: "With affection and gratitude, Hope."

Arthur's daughter, Cheryl, wrote back. She said that her father was in the hospital. He was dying. "Perhaps Dad never told you he had cancer. He was very private about these things. He did speak of you fondly. I read him your letter, and I am sure he caught most of it. The pickerel made me chuckle. What a lovely image of late love. I'm sorry that we never met."

Hope called Penny and left a message on her phone. "Penny? I got a letter. Arthur's dying. I know you're busy at work, so no need to call me back."

Half an hour later, Penny phoned. "Are you okay, Mom? Do you want me to come over?"

"Don't be ridiculous. You're working. I should have seen it. He was quite thin."

"Oh, Mom, I'm so sorry."

"I am too. He's in the hospital. Just like that."

"Are you sure you don't need someone there? I could call Ted."

"I'm fine. I was just going to make tea."

"I'll drop by tonight."

"Only if it's convenient. You have a life."

She made tea and sat and looked out the balcony doors at the blowing snow. Rereading the letter, she marvelled that Cheryl should think Hope had been talking about late love. She tried to conjure up images of Roy, but she kept finding Arthur: his face, his long fingers, the manner in which he shuffled lightly away from the stereo after slipping Henry Purcell in the player. She had known him only six months and yet there he was, usurping her husband. For a time, she was quite hurt that Arthur hadn't ever mentioned his sickness. And then she thought that perhaps he had been sparing her, he had been more selfless, less fearful.

She wrote Cheryl a brief note. She said she was very sorry to hear that Arthur was dying. "We did love each other. Such a surprise. And such great luck."

She found, over the next while, that her thoughts flitted here and there. From rice pudding to the first car she had owned—a Fleetmaster, to Melanie at the age of five learning to tie her shoes, to Emily's first apartment in Winnipeg, which had smelled of sausage and smoke. She wasn't losing her mind, she just had difficulty holding a singular hard fact for any specific time. She recalled that this had also happened when Roy died.

This may have been why she rear-ended the young man in his Porsche, an accident that happened at the corner of Osborne and Pembina on a very cold November day. Clouds billowed from the exhausts, the roads were icy. She was trying to make it across the intersection on an amber, and she had gunned the engine slightly when a tiny black car cut in front of her. She had no time to find her brake pedal, and she rear-ended the black car, drove up the corner of its small back and crossed the sidewalk and ran directly into a hydro pole. Her airbags deployed, though she wouldn't have been able to say that she noticed. All she felt was a crushing of her chest and for a time the world disappeared, and when she opened her eyes, a swarthy man with dark hair and big lips was screaming at her and hitting the driver's-side window with his cellphone. Fortunately her doors were locked. The man, whose car she must have hit, reminded her of a boyfriend she had had long ago, before she met Roy, and this boy had wanted to touch her in the darkness of his car. She had not let him, thank goodness. And then, a fireman in a fireman's hat replaced the swarthy man. She tried to lift her arms in gratitude, but they were useless. Her throat bubbled. "Be careful," she said. "And thank you."

She had three broken ribs and a bruised heart. The firemen, she learned later, had used the Jaws of Life to extract her from her car. It all seemed so grand and unnecessary. She had been placed in a private room in the Health Sciences Centre, where Penny, as a physician, had some clout. Hope noticed that the nurses treated her with special care. Perhaps this was typical. In any case, she was both chagrined and grateful. She didn't want to be a bother. She loved the attention.

Other than her two stays in Winkler, which had been all about her *mind,* and the birth of her children, Hope had not spent much time in a hospital before. She had never been sick. In fact her own GP, a younger woman with a very sweet face and a fresh spirit, marvelled every year at Hope's vigour. "Mrs. Koop," she would announce, "you're a wonder. I wish all my patients were so healthy." But now, here she was, with cracked bones and a battered heart. Visitors arrived. Frida, of all people, motored in from Altona. George had driven her. He was waiting in the car. Frida held her hand while Hope regaled her with the story of the mad swarthy man, the Porsche, and the Jaws of Life. When she was done, she said, "How are you, Frida?"

"I'm happy, Hope. What I did, almost leaving George? Well, it was like a shot across the bow."

Hope wondered where Frida had discovered that expression. She didn't usually speak in metaphors and certainly not military metaphors. Frida had coloured her hair and it was pulled back behind her small ears with two gold clips. She was wearing lipstick. She carried a nifty purse. She seemed well, though she still had the habit of turning her head to look behind her, like a small wary animal.

Penny dropped in three or four times a day. In the early mornings, before she prepped for surgery, she arrived breathless, carrying a cup of coffee. She bent to kiss her mother and asked about her night. And then she asked about pain and she inevitably found Hope's chart and checked on her medication. She returned at lunch, whistled through wearing a slim-fitting dress underneath her white lab coat, and again in the evening she appeared, less peppy, perhaps a little short with Hope, who might simply have asked for a glass of water.

Melanie sent flowers. She was not yet pregnant, and there had been talk of perhaps Ariel having the baby, and for some reason this did not disappoint Hope or even surprise her. She might have been more surprised if everything had worked out as planned. Would she ever have grandchildren?

And then Judith flew in alone from Paris. When Hope heard of her imminent arrival, she said, "I'm not dead yet." It turned out that Judith had been planning a trip. She was considering staying in Canada for a time, to give herself a break from Jean-Philippe. There were murmurings of Judith perhaps living with Hope until she could get back on her feet. Hope was wary about this, especially when Judith entered the hospital ward wearing her old fur coat. Her face was red from the cold and her long hair flowed down over the collar, and all Hope could think was "What a beautiful daughter," and "I did not look that good at forty-nine," and "Where did she find that coat?" In the end, Judith, unpredictable as usual, quickly grew tired of the hospital, and the cold climate, and she returned to France to sort out her affairs.

Emily visited her every second day and she always arrived with a fresh collection of poetry that she read, leaning forward and reciting in a low voice. Once it was Pablo Neruda, another time Emily Dickinson. And though Hope didn't often understand the point of the poems, the language was arresting and she felt great love for her friend.

A memory came to her one morning as she woke, just dropped into her head unwilled. When she was twenty years old and in nurse's training, she was asked to prepare the body of a man who had just died. "A fresh one," the head nurse had said. Hope climbed to the fifth floor and entered the room of the dead man and found him completely naked on his bed. It was not his nakedness that had disturbed her but the blood trickling from his eyes, which were closed. Upon closer inspection, she realized that the man had donated his eyes, and that they had just been plucked from their sockets. She looked away, and then looked closer, and for a moment she had the urge to lift one of the man's eyelids to see the hole that would have been left. She did not do this. She tagged the man's toe and wrapped the body, rolling it first to one side and then back the other way. Bizarrely, she was pleased that the man had been blinded, so that he did not have to suffer the shame of her gaze, even though he was dead.

That afternoon, she told Emily about the dead man. "I've been having the strangest thoughts. Memories just arrive. For instance, the other day I remembered sitting on my mother's lap. I was three. My father was driving the car.

The windshield wiper was slapping, and my mother was singing. I find myself talking to her these days, as if she were sitting right beside me. When I was a young woman and suffering some anxiety or generally overreaching, as she would call it, she told me, 'Just imagine you've arrived at the end of the road and there isn't anywhere else to go. Then you make do with what you have.'"

"I've thought of Paul lately," Emily said. "In a good way. I can't remember anymore why I left him. It's very disconcerting."

"Don't second-guess yourself, Em. Too late for that."

Too late.

In the evenings, when the ward was quiet and she was alone, she read her Bible by the light of the small lamp that Penny had delivered one day. She read Revelation, perhaps because she had drawn so near to death, or death itself had knocked at her door and then been sent away. She was not afraid of death, especially when she read chapter 21, verse 4: "He shall wipe away every tear from their eyes; and there shall no longer be *any* death; there shall no longer be *any* mourning, or crying, or pain; the first things have passed away." Well, that sounded impossibly perfect. It pleased her to imagine God's hand wiping away her tears, even though she had not had the capacity to cry for years. Still, after she turned off the light and lay in her hospital bed, aware of the whispers of the nurses in the corridor, or of some man sniffling in the next room, she suffered doubt. "Who knows?" she thought. And just before she slept, slipping sideways into the vivid dreams that arrived as the result of her medication, she said in a dry whisper, "It is all a darkness."

Conner had not come to see her in the hospital and this did not surprise her. Half a year ago he had lost his job at Mr. Lube, and after that he'd disappeared, resurfacing every six weeks or so, knocking on her door and coming in for a meal and a twenty-dollar bill that she pressed into his palm. Last she knew he was living in a bachelor suite and had traded in his car for a bicycle. He had become one of those men you see in the back lanes, digging through garbage cans and auto bins, smashing old computers, salvaging the innards, crushing tin cans, storing the flotsam in a backpack and delivering everything to a salvage yard in exchange for a few dollars. Conner wasn't embarrassed by any of this. He felt much freer. "Don't have to answer to the man," he said. Because Conner was content, Hope was also content. Who was she to judge her son's life?

The girls, when they heard about Conner's misfortune, were astounded and mystified, except for Melanie, who had always seen Conner as the protective older brother. What had she said? "Let him be. He's probably happier."

A few weeks after Hope had been discharged from the hospital, Conner finally appeared at her door, and with him he had Rudi. Rudi had moved to the city and was living with Conner, calling him Dad, in fact. And now here he was, saying, "Hi, Grandma."

Hope lifted a hand. Let it drop. "Oh, Rudi, is it you? Oh my. Look at you."

Rudi stepped closer and she kissed his cheek. She held

him at arm's length and studied him. "You're such a man," she said. "Goodness, I've left my lipstick on you."

"How are you, Grandma?"

"I'm . . . Oh, Rudi, I'm so pleased." She wanted to say that she was overflowing, but she didn't want to frighten the boy. She held his hand as they sat on her couch. She had so many questions. Why are you here? How did you come to get that beautiful face? When did you grow up? Are you dragging through dumpsters with your father? Where is your sister? Who do you love? But she asked none of these. She turned to Conner and asked him to fetch some ice water, please. Rudi should be thirsty. She believed that this was the beginning of something. All good things come to those who wait.

And yet, on any given day, she was mostly alone and still waiting, as if her name might be on someone's calendar out there, and certainly a phone call was on the agenda. To quash the feeling that waiting produced, she set out on various journeys. One hot day in June, she took a taxi to Zellers to buy some annuals to plant in the window boxes that sat on her balcony. She realized that her age might be marked by the number of times she had restored her small garden. Year after year after year. She grew tired as she tottered among the picked-over geraniums and creepers. In the end she returned home empty-handed. It was not a disaster. Come August, when annuals typically began to wilt and the leaves and petals dropped to the ground, the season would be over and not one person would be the wiser about Hope Koop's decision to forgo flowers.

She had come to believe that much of the sadness in the world resulted from the failure of love. Quite simple, really.

And her job in the end was to love her children well. Had she? Her thoughts gathered and then flew away like the sparrows that sometimes visited her balcony, a coming-together and a dispersal, and it was in the dispersal that she saw the end, because all was flying away: Roy, Arthur, her children. That night she dreamed of her mother, who was standing at a bus stop, a small leather carrying case at her feet. The bus arrived and her mother climbed on, forgetting the case. She woke and sat up and then climbed from the bed and went to fetch a glass of water. She stood in the darkness of the kitchen and looked out at the night sky. Her mother had been very young in the dream, dressed in a mauve coat and black high-heeled shoes. She had looked content and smiled, and Hope had understood then that there was nothing to be frightened of.

A NOTE ON THE TYPE

The Age of Hope is set in Fournier. In 1924, Monotype based this face on original types cut by Pierre Simon Fournier circa 1742. These were some of the earliest and most influential of the eighteenth century's "transitional" typefaces, and they .were a stepping stone to the more severe "modern" style made popular by Bodoni. Fournier's faces had more vertical stress than the old style types, greater contrast between thick and thin strokes, and disparate proportioning between the roman and italic. Fournier has a light, clean, even-coloured look on the page and provides good economy in text.